THE SLAVE OF LIDIR

'Her ladyship is now nothing but a bitch in heat.' Anya's neck was burning, in her shame. 'A common wench whose flesh,' he placed the back of his hand against her openness, and drew it sharply away, as if it had hurt him, 'whose flesh is boiling up with lust. A wench who pleads for satisfaction.' Anya was mortified. Her heat was there – she could not deny it – but she had been forced into this cruel state of degradation by what he had done, and now the guard was blaming her. It seemed so wickedly unfair. 'Do not look away from me. We soldiers like a simmering pot of flesh like this. In fact, we must not let its heat escape before we serve you up.'

A NEXUS CLASSIC

THE SLAVE OF LIDIR

Aran Ashe

This book is a work of fiction.
In real life, make sure you practise safe sex.

First published in 1991 by
Nexus
Thames Wharf Studios
Rainville Road
London W6 9HA

Reprinted 1994

This Nexus Classic edition 2000

Typeset by TW Typesetting, Plymouth, Devon

Printed and bound by
Cox & Wyman Ltd, Reading, Berks

ISBN 0 352 33504 1

1

The Eye of the Jackdaw

Picture this: a castle, set in dream-time, the Castle of Lidir. A jackdaw, balanced on a turret, his feathers cut and ruffled by a fitful, skittish wind, cocks his head in rapt attention at two faint yet clearly moving dots, two shadow-figures in the bleak November landscape and the darkly failing light. He watches as the figures slow, then fuse together, then stretch apart again; as if connected invisibly and elastically, the two progress, the resolve of the one drawing the other onward, for the other is reluctant. And the ultimate quest, the greater tide in which these humble creatures drift, directs them ever eastwards, against the buckling wind, to the great gate of the castle.

The jackdaw topples, and spirals downwards in a vortex, then beating back, he claws a purchase on a ledge above the gateway where the leading figure stands now, forearm raised as if in threat against the massive slabs of timberwork. The arm falls three times; three deadened blows are swallowed by the wind. The leader looks to his companion, whose hooded form remains detached and downcast, set back from the door, yet seems somehow even more remote from him. He turns to raise his arm once more, whereupon an inset door swings magically open, and torchlight spills out to freeze him and to illuminate the hooded but now lifted face in its warm and flickering glow.

The bird watches, mesmerised, as a single snowflake, drifting downwards, is netted on her eyelash. She does not move to brush it off; perhaps she does not notice, for the perfect oval of her face, her eyes of limpid blackness, are fixed intently on the doorway. Another flake now slides across the freckles on her cheeks, then catches, and cascading down her copper coloured ringlets, it alights at last upon her softly swollen lower lip and hesitates, then melts. The pilgrims are admitted; the arm that raised itself to strike the door now sweeps around behind her, not daring to touch, yet a symbolic fence that bars escape, a token of enclosure, reinforced now by the profound finality as the door at their backs booms shut. The jackdaw drops and hops and chases random snowflakes as they prance upon the ground, then baffled, he wipes away the fluff of ice now glued around his beak and battles back up to his turret.

2

A Purse of Gold

Anya had watched the bedraggled, quirky bird while she waited at the gateway. She wondered what he was about, strutting up and down the ledge and eyeing them, when all the other birds had long since disappeared to their roosts, and indeed, no other living creature was to be seen in this desolate winter landscape. And now the first snow was falling, large soft downy flakes which caught in her eyelashes and tumbled down her hair and kissed her on the lips. She liked the snow; she liked its gentleness when, as now, in the shelter of the massive castle wall, it floated down and tickled her skin like the tender kisses of a secret lover. She looked across to where her husband was being challenged by the sentry. She was indifferent to the outcome – either they would be admitted and her fate would be sealed, or they would be turned away and she would have to face once more the bitter windswept coldness and the night. Her choice, had she been offered it, would indeed have been a grim one, but of course the offer was not available. She glanced once more up at the jackdaw and secretly wished him luck in his quest, whatsoever it might be, then stepped through the portal and into the castle, and the door was bolted shut behind her.

'You are expected. Follow me.' The speaker, a hefty woman in a large leather apron, had appeared from the shadows to address the husband, and for one brief moment Anya had allowed herself the fancy that it might be him and not her who would be the object of the evening's barter. A wistful smile half-formed upon her lips and then faded as the sound of merriment drifted down, caught on the wind, from the Great Hall across the courtyard. She was weary – tired to the bone from the journey, a journey of despair. And as she crossed the yard and turned to the right to mount the cold stone steps, her body wedged between the wheezing woman in front and her stone cold husband behind her, she felt her throat tighten and her cheeks puff up and the tears began to well.

'Shh . . . Hush, my dear,' the woman said and threw an arm heavily around her shoulders. 'There's really nothing to be afraid of. Come now, dry your eyes.' And she produced a large clean rag and began dabbing Anya round the eyes as softly as she could. They were standing on the threshold of a largely empty, oak panelled room in which a fire was burning brightly. The wooden floor was bare; in the corner were a table and chair. 'Stand over here, by the fire, and let me look at you.' Her face was kindly, Anya decided, and her manner seemed protective. '. . . There, you see, the tears are gone.' And turning to the husband, the woman asked:

'I take it she has been your wife?'

He nodded. 'No, I *am* his wife!' Anya wanted to shout, but she knew that would be pointless.

'For how long was that?' the woman asked, looking at Anya but speaking still to the man.

'Three months, almost four . . .'

'Three months!' she cried. 'Why, you must scarcely have known each other . . .'

The man hung his head. That much was true, thought Anya.

Then the woman stroked Anya's cheek softly, with the backs of her pudgy fingers. 'Never mind my dear, for Marella will take care of you,' she said and she drew her to her breast. Though her ears were rubbed against the roughness of Marella's apron, still Anya felt secure like that.

The husband's head hung lower, in his shame.

Marella patted Anya's head and kissed her gently on the forehead, then took her face tenderly in the large warm cushions of her hands and looked into her eyes:

4

'What is your name, my child?'

'Anya.' Someone had spoken to her at last, asked her a direct question, and now she was elated.

'You are very beautiful,' Marella said simply, then watched as Anya's pupils expanded, their olive base consumed in liquid blackness. 'How old are you, Anya?'

Anya did not know. This question always made her so ashamed, no matter how often she'd told herself there was no reason for it to do so, that no guilt could possibly attach itself to her. But now her eyes were downcast; she could not look Marella in the face.

The husband interrupted. 'We do not know her age. She . . .'

But Marella cut him short, and turned again to Anya. 'So then, tell me, when do you celebrate your birthday, Anya?' Anya frowned so deeply that her eyebrows met, which made Marella smile, and yet her smile was tinged with sadness. 'I see,' she said, then took Anya by the waist. Shaking her, like she might have shaken a baby to make it giggle, she said: 'Well, we'll make you . . .' and she pretended to scrutinise her intently. 'We'll make you twenty-one. Yes, twenty-one years of age! And today shall be your coming of age, Anya; today shall be your birthday!' She laughed. 'So remember that, this twelfth day of November . . . from this day forth you shall always know your age, and you shall always have a birthday!'

Anya was smiling now, and her eyes were shining in a film of tears. But Marella hadn't finished. She winked.

'On your birthday, you must have a gift,' and she extracted, though not without some difficulty, a ring so tight it barely reached the second joint of her little finger. Then she held it to the light. Anya had never seen anything so beautiful before: it was gold, inlaid with plates of turquoise and tiny rubies which caught the torchlight. Marella slipped it on Anya's middle finger, and pressed the hand to Anya's cheek. 'There! It fits!' she declared, and then more softly, 'Blue for your mood and red to match your hair – and your fire . . .' and she pinched her playfully on the cheek, and Anya smiled, enough to show her teeth at last.

5

'But now, my dear,' the woman said, and pressed her palms together. 'To business. I have to prepare you . . .' Then she spread her hands in a half apologetic gesture, and raised her eyebrows. 'I'm afraid you must disrobe.'

Anya felt hunted now; she didn't know which way to turn. Although she'd expected something, at some stage, the thought of what might actually befall her, here at the castle, had remained as a formless spectre at the back of her mind. She'd deliberately pushed it aside rather than dwell upon it, because she'd hoped against despair that she would never be brought here, that *something* would happen to save her so that the spectre need never take definite shape. She knew now of course that it wasn't going to happen – nobody would rescue her, least of all him. This mellow thick-bodied woman had shown her more affection and consideration, even in this short time, than *he* had shown since the day they met – their wedding day. Perhaps Marella would turn out at last to be the one to save her, or at least to protect her. Perhaps she could learn something from the strength and softness of this portly matron, and who knows, even learn to trust her.

'But . . .?' Anya threw a meaningful glance in the direction of her husband, and then looked back at Marella. She did not want to have to undress in this man's presence.

Marella was patient. 'Anya, my sweet cherry,' she began, and then appeared almost to recite: 'In the Castle of Lidir, there will be much in store for you that you will find strange and difficult to bear, things which, if laid out now with you as witness, would make you shrink away in your innocence. Yes, there will be many greater trials than this, for this is but the beginning.' And she stroked Anya's cheek, very tenderly, like a mother caressing a child who is about to depart on a long yet very necessary journey, fraught with dangers unseen by the child, yet well known to the mother, a journey from which the child will not return until she is a woman.

'Be not afraid for now, my honeycomb, for Marella has attended many, many such disrobings – men as well as woman, I might add,' and she threw a sidelong look at the husband who flinched visibly then stared down at his nervously shuffling feet, before she added softly, 'but none, and this I'll warrant, *none* so beautiful as you ...' Anya lowered her eyes in bashfulness, but secretly she was pleased, and grateful for the unfamiliar compliment. 'And besides, you must surely have often done this, before your husband ...?'

Now Anya's lips were set, as the memories flashed back, acute visions of events so joyless and distressful, which she didn't want recalled.

'Come now, do it for me ...?'

Very slowly, Anya raised her eyes and examined once more that rotund face, searching for reassurance in the puffy pink complexion, with its cheek pouches, and those long red floppy earlobes, and the tiny, bright expectant eyes, and she thought: *This is the one friend I have in the world.* And she complied.

Marella stood beside her, watching but not saying anything, just accepting the garments one by one as they were offered, and placing them over the solid thickness of her forearm. First she took the great hooded hessian rough coat, so large and heavy it had almost buried Anya; it now lay supported effortlessly across Marella's arm, as if it were nothing but the lightest and flimsiest gauze, while Anya's curls had meanwhile tumbled out across her shoulders, in broad swaths of gold and red and copper against the tight, creamy ringlets of her sheepskin jacket. Marella waited patiently as Anya carefully unlaced it; her fingers were long and smooth, not cracked and dry as might have been expected. They worked deftly, but Marella noticed, with some pleasure, that they would stop at intervals and spread or turn and that Anya would regard the ring lovingly, from a variety of angles. It was evident that she'd never worn anything like it before, Marella realised, and this puzzled her a little, for surely it was the custom in these parts for women, regardless of their station, to delight in the wearing of trinkets such as this? And it was certain that a married woman always wore a ring. Perhaps Anya had never had one, she speculated, or worse still, perhaps her husband had taken it back, forcing her to give it up. Whatever the truth might have been, she did not propose to question Anya about it, for some hurts, she knew, were best left undisturbed, to rest and heal and mayhaps fade away completely.

The sheepskin, once removed, revealed a thick linen undergarment with sleeves, and a heavy moleskin skirt, fastened with a leather belt and extending down over Anya's boots and almost to her ankles. Anya undid the belt and then unwrapped the skirt, which was a single piece turned twice around her middle; the undercoat went right down to her calves – she had to bunch it round her waist to be able to pull it over her head. Then even Marella gasped at what she saw before her, and she nearly dropped the clothes down on the floor.

In all her time, she had never seen a girl or woman more beautiful than this. Anya wore nothing but a sleeveless deerskin top, shaped and laced up tightly to the curve of her bosom, and a pair of knee-length canvas boots with thick woollen stockings, reaching up her thighs. The deerskin stopped just above the navel – its small deep well looked black against the smoothness of her belly; the curls below bushed bright, like whirling filaments of fire. That narrow waist – its gentle downswell to the fullness of her hips – it made Marella want to touch her, to smooth her hands across, to trace that perfect curve down her back to where it joined invisibly with her thighs. And now Marella would have liked it to have been her fingers that hesitatingly unlaced the top which, with each freed-off loop, continued to swell against the constriction of the deerskin, until at last the lace was left dangling down below the final eyelet and the leaves of softened leather hung pendant, supported by those breasts. Then Anya paused, and looked directly at Marella. Her heart was racing, and with each breath she took, the lace was lifting, gently swinging, brushing to and fro across her belly. Her fingers hesitated, then lowered, and she spoke:

'You . . .' she faltered, 'you do it, Marella.' Marella's heart leapt, and much as she tried to hide her feelings, she could feel her face flushing red.

8

Anya did not know what had made her say this – something in Marella's face, perhaps – but at that moment, it was what she wanted. She wanted this woman to open out the deerskin and, not just to look at her, but to take her breasts and mould them in each of her soft, warm hands and caress them tenderly. It was what she wanted more than anything. But Marella did not understand, or perhaps she was just too afraid. This enormous woman was rooted to the spot, but she was also shaking. Her lips had opened to say something, but then closed again.

So Anya had to do it herself – to spread apart and then carefully remove the deerskin. Instead of handing it to the woman, she merely dropped it on the floor, which seemed at least to wake Marella from her reverie. Anya pressed her shoulders back. The freckles dappled downwards ever lighter from her neck, to fade at last to the pale smoothness of her bosom. Her shoulders seemed so slight to support such breasts, which projected outwards, full and heavy, almost as if Anya might be with child. Her nipples looked swollen, the shape and size of acorns, but deeper coloured. They were a very dark velvet brown, set starkly against the paleness of her breasts and, with no surrounding circle to shade them in, they looked almost as if they had been painted to blacken them.

Marella wanted to touch those teats, to wet them and rub them to see if the colour would come out and infuse into her fingertips, but something prevented her. Though Anya had closed her eyes, and her arms were hanging submissively by her sides, just waiting for the touch, still Marella could not bring herself to do it. She bent and picked the deerskin halter up and she waited for the boots and stockings; then, brushing Anya very gently on her pouted lips, she turned and deposited her clothing neatly on the table in the corner. She brought back a blanket to place around Anya's shoulders, and to wrap around her waist.

Anya closed her eyes again, imagining that tender touch, the touch that had not come, her bosom lifted up in those strong soft hands and her nipples stroked upwards very

9

softly with the thumbpads, then pulled, oh so gently, with a large plush finger curlicued around them, squeezing them compassionately, subduing her with their sigh-soft sucking traction. She wanted to give herself like this – completely – to someone who would drown in her eyes, to someone who would love her.

'Now you stay here, by the fire, while I'm gone, for I must bring the Taskmistress.' Then Marella frowned. 'She will want to examine you, Anya. You must do exactly as she asks of you. Promise me that?'

Anya nodded, though her heart was beating faster. The Taskmistress, she wondered anxiously, what will she want of me? In what way will she examine me?

'Do not speak unless she asks a direct question, and keep your eyes averted. Address her as "Ma'am", but only if she asks you something. You must not speak first. She may appear very . . .' Marella was searching for the word, '. . . stern, but that is her duty . . . You have nothing to fear if you do precisely as she asks of you. And she will be asking nothing that is beyond your capability. Now I must go.' And Marella disappeared through the door.

Anya was feeling really quite frightened by now. She did not like the sound of this person at all, and she was very worried about what might be done to her; Marella's reassurance had been too guarded to give her any comfort in that respect. She felt so vulnerable like this, with nothing but a blanket around her. And that man – he was no protection for her – it was he who had brought her to this. She wanted to cry, but the tears would not come.

When the Taskmistress arrived, Marella crept in quietly behind her. Anya, still stationed by the fire, felt a wave of cold; an icy plume enveloped her and she began to shake. The Taskmistress seemed tall and thin, and older than Anya but not so old as Marella; she wore a long red flowing robe; her hair was dark – it could have been black – and it was tied up at the back. Anya had been able to make out no more in the instant the woman walked in, for she had remembered Marella's words and kept very still, with her eyes cast down towards the floor. Her husband was still behind her; he had hardly moved since they arrived, and hadn't spoken since Marella had left the room. He was probably standing by the table, Anya thought. Marella remained over by the door.

The woman in red strode across to Anya and, turning her sharply, she looked her in the face. Anya very wisely did not look up. The woman's fingers were digging through the blanket into her arms.

'I am Ildren, your Taskmistress,' she announced ominously. Her voice had a hard edge to it, as if she had spoken through her teeth, as if, thought Anya, she were full to overflowing with hatred. 'You shall address me only as "Ma'am", or "Taskmistress".' The grip on Anya's arms tightened. 'Only if I speak to you shall you address me,' she said. 'And you shall not look me in the face unless I so require you. Is that clear to you?'

Anya nodded weakly. Marella had warned her, but it still seemed frightening to hear it said, and in so cruel a tone.

'Now – what is my name, child?' the woman asked more softly.

'Ildren.' Too late, Anya realised she'd been trapped.

Smack! 'Taskmistress!' the woman screamed. The blow across Anya's cheek nearly knocked her to the floor. She heard her husband jump and, at the same time, Marella's strangled cry, as if it were she, and not Anya, who had been struck. 'In future, pay attention to what your Taskmistress tells you,' the woman glowered, taking Anya's other cheek between her thumb and finger and pinching it cruelly. Anya could feel the tears beginning to well, but she fought them back again. She was determined not to give in and cry in front of this evil-hearted woman; she would deny her that satisfaction for as long as she was able.

'Let this be the first and last time I am forced to chastise you in this way,' Ildren warned, then she suddenly changed her tone: 'Anya . . .' she said slowly, 'yours is a very lovely name.' Marella must have told her my name, thought Anya, but she did not know what to make of this statement. Was it just another trick, to make her look at the

11

Taskmistress, or smile perhaps and then be struck down again for such a display of emotion? Her cheeks were burning now from her ill-treatment. She decided to say nothing, and to keep looking at the floor.

'And now we shall see if you are really as lovely as your name suggests,' the woman said very slyly. 'For now I must examine you . . . Open your mouth.'

Anya was terrified; she did as she was told, but she was shaking uncontrollably – she did not know what to expect of this woman.

'Keep still,' the Taskmistress ordered. Then she looked in Anya's mouth, examining her teeth it seemed, lifting up her tongue, then holding her mouth open with two hands, as if she were examining a horse to see how old it was, to see if it were a bargain. Her fingers tasted strange and spicy, not unpleasant really, but the way she pushed them deep into Anya's mouth made her want to retch.

'Now close your mouth. – Don't look at me,' Ildren warned. She had dark brown eyes, Anya had noticed, and full and luscious lips. She hadn't expected that. 'Fold the blanket down, around your waist,' the woman called; she was now behind Anya.

And what she saw made Ildren catch her breath, then bite her lip, and slowly lift up Anya's curls to expose a neck so white it turned the hair to fiery red against it. Anya's shoulders and her upper back were drenched in red-brown freckles; she looked as if she had walked nude underneath a cascade of freckle-tincture; the droplets coalesced to powder shades of bay and burnt sienna, then dusted down her back to pearly white, flecked here and there with nut-brown. Ildren ran her fingertip right across the shoulder, from one side to the other, then absent-mindedly turned over her hand and examined the finger end, as if perhaps subconsciously she had been expecting it to have changed colour. She took hold of Anya's arm and turned her round, so she faced away from the fire, then saw her nipples, which in this light looked black against the white swell of her breasts.

Ildren's breathing had changed. Anya noticed – it

12

sounded slower, yet heavier, and she was reaching now to touch her. Anya shivered as her breasts were lifted on the backs of Ildren's hands, and the hands next slid away to the sides, so her breasts fell and gently bounced; the feeling was delicious. Then Ildren cupped and pressed the breasts together firmly, until she made the nipples touch, and she rubbed them slowly up against each other, until they stiffened up to points, then pushed them wide apart again, so they brushed against the fine downy hair which covered Anya's arms. The Taskmistress was watching her face intently all the while, Anya knew, though she did not dare look up.

'Lift your breasts,' Ildren said quite simply, and Anya did as she was bid, though with difficulty, since she had to use both elbows to hold the blanket at her waist to prevent it falling away altogether.

'She is not with child . . .?' Ildren had addressed the man; once again, Anya had been ignored. How would *he* know, she wanted to say, this is *my* body. Anya knew very well that she was not pregnant, so why did the woman not ask her opinion? How could a man, especially a man such as this, who had scarcely ever . . .

'No . . . no,' the man replied after a pause, though he did not sound at all certain.

The Taskmistress brushed Anya's nipples very gently with her thumbs, then squeezed them harder, as if she were in some way expressing dissatisfaction with his answer, as if perhaps she expected milk to seep out from them. His response only made her probe more deeply:

'She is not then . . . a virgin?' It was clear from her tone that she now thought it a distinct possibility. Anya shifted uneasily; what if she would want to check for herself? A cold chill ran down between her legs. She hoped her husband would be more convincing this time.

'No! She is not!' he cried, as if he had been accused of some terrible crime. Anya relaxed a little, and allowed herself an inner smile, at the ardour of his words on this subject.

'Lift your breasts up higher.' The blanket almost slipped,

and Ildren's lip curled in a half smile. Anya kept stealing glances when Ildren was engrossed in other things, and she as certain the woman could not see her. She wanted to try to fathom this person, who seemed so calculating and cruel. The Taskmistress was now fingering Anya's nipples again, rolling them alternately between her fingers, sending little quivers through them, making it feel as if they were joined together by a thread which was drawn taut between them and looped around her backbone. She closed her eyes. Each stroke of the Taskmistress's fingers tightened the thread, until it thrummed inside her, making her want to . . .

'Black cherries . . .' Ildren said softly, 'with a stone.' Now she was tapping each nipple very gently. Anya felt her knees begin to sag. 'I wonder . . .' Ildren's voice was deeper now. Anya could hear her breathing; it sounded fast, as if she were out of breath but trying to control it. 'I wonder . . . Your rashers, your fleshy fin-tails, will they be shaded like your berries? Will they be a match for them in hue?'

The shock of what she'd said made Anya freeze. It was as if a long-embedded stone had been overturned, and slimy, crawling creatures were worming out in every direction – Anya's shame, long bottled up inside her, was spilling out again. She opened her eyes, to a second shock – the Taskmistress staring straight at her. Immediately, Anya dropped her gaze, but her heart was in her throat.

'No . . . look at me, my child. I am right, am I not?' Anya slowly raised her eyes, but kept her lips sealed tight against her shame. 'It does not matter; I can see your answer in your eyes,' the woman said, then suddenly she bent her head and pressed her ear to Anya's breast, and Anya could smell the faintly spicy aroma in her hair. 'I can hear it in your heartbeat, child. You can have no secrets from your Taskmistress – your body is my domain. I shall acquaint myself with every little thing about you; every detail of your make-up I will come to know, so I can understand your feelings and your needs . . . until I know you better than you know yourself.' And with that, Ildren placed her palms against Anya's breasts and then rotated

14

them very slowly against the nipples, barely touching her, until Anya wanted to close her eyes again. 'Now tell me,' Ildren persisted. 'For I shall see them soon enough: are your lips around your fleshpot black?'

Anya's heart was thumping and her head was buzzing. Her lips quivered; she hesitated, then coughed, then furrowed her brow, then finally took a very deep breath.

'Yes,' she said at last, then bent her head and closed her eyes. Her head was bursting and her cheeks were burning now with shame. It is true, she thought, I can surely have no secrets here, not from this woman.

She heard the Taskmistress sigh, then go very quiet. Anya waited. When the Taskmistress spoke, it was in a very subdued voice indeed, as if she were speaking to herself. 'Then it is true,' she whispered. 'She is indeed a rare beauty . . .' and she sighed again.

What could she mean by that, Anya puzzled? This stain upon her tenderness, this blackened rust burned into her flesh had been her bane ever since she could remember. How often had she scrubbed this blemish, rubbed it till the flesh was raw and bleeding, yet without subduing it one shade? And it had darkened with the years, as the affliction had ripened like some living evil imbued into her skin. She was branded; her stigma marked her out as different from other women – that much she knew, and the Taskmistress had now confirmed it – but *rare beauty*, she had said. Was her black shame, which had brought nothing but ridicule and degradation ever since she was a child, which she had even tried and failed to keep a secret from her husband, only to be made to witness his revulsion, giving way eventually to a grudging, complaining tolerance of her disfigurement – was this besmirchment of her womanhood then in some way *prized* in this castle? She could not believe it could be so.

'Turn round, my dear,' Ildren said, and Anya could hear the tremble in the Taskmistress's voice. She turned back to face the fire again. 'Re . . . remove the blanket.' The voice had faltered this time. Anya let the blanket drop to the floor. There were butterflies in her stomach. Her hearing

15

seemed heightened – it was as if she could sense everything in the room – Marella shifting by the door; the crackle of the firewood; its billowing warmth which licked about her belly and her breasts; her husband's heavy breathing; Ildren's breath upon her neck, tickling underneath her earlobes; the spicy scent which welled around Anya, threatening to envelop her; and in her mouth a salt-sweet taste of apprehension, mingled with suppressed desire. Anya swallowed. Her tongue felt swollen. She licked the fine-dewed salt-sweat from her upper lip.

'Now spread your legs.'

Those words sent crawling shivers up Anya's thighs; a wave of gooseflesh descended in a curtain down behind her, from her middle to her heels; icy shivers cascaded down her buttocks and the back of her thighs, and fingers of coldness slid around the front and out between her legs.

'Do as I say!' the Taskmistress commanded, and her hand came round and pinched Anya cruelly on the underbelly of her breast. 'Take that as a warning. In future, I shall not expect to tell you twice. Now proceed . . .' Anya was terrified as she slowly moved her legs apart, expecting those wicked fingers at any moment to intrude between her legs and pinch her there, in her intimacy. She stiffened, waiting for the touch to come, then jumped when the woman spoke again.

'Spread wider . . . Now bend over. Place your hands about your ankles . . .' Ildren caught her breath as Anya spread before her; those pure white globes were shaded-in too deeply at their parting, and the secret of Anya's staining stood revealed. The velvet darkness of the skin within her groove looked so unreal. It was as if Anya had been made to double over, in the pose she now assumed, while brown-black ink was poured precisely into the well within her cleft until it had filled the well, then had overflowed down around her flesh lips and dripped away at last exactly from their node.

Ildren inhaled deeply. 'Good,' she said, 'now your Taskmistress shall explore you . . . in your blackness.'

Anya started shaking. The involuntary movements of

her legs and hips were magnified by the way her body was held like this, in tension. She had never had to expose herself in this lewd way – not to her husband, not to anyone. And now *he* was witnessing her degradations; if it had been only the Taskmistress, then perhaps she might have been able to bear the shame, but with *him* here, and Marella . . . Marella, who was supposed to be her friend. Even Marella was doing nothing to intervene.

The finger touched her in the split between her buttocks. It traced a line downwards, from the small of her back, but working very slowly, in slow brush-like strokes, very softly, backbrushing the skin-hairs after each forward caress, so it advanced along the groove of Anya's bottom very gradually indeed. Anya had never experienced a sensation like it; every nerve within her split was a-tingle now, as if a spider was working up and down in there, strumming the fine hairlets of her skin between its legs, attaching them together with its sticky filaments, until each touch, each nervous spider stride across the drumskin tautness of her flesh, set every hair aquiver. The searching fingertip found the point of Anya's spine, then tickled in a circle till the trickles of pleasure ran up and down her backbone, on the side towards her belly, making Anya gasp out loud in her delight.

'So, you like to be explored, my lickerish beauty?' the Taskmistress murmured seductively. Anya did not reply; the fingertip was touching that secret, private spot, that place where Anya's outer self became instead her inside, in a tightened fleshy swirling pool of darkness. It was pressing lightly up against the mouth, then it whispered back and forth, then lapped across her tenderness as if it were a tongue-tip, caressing her unashamedly, and tasting her black desire. The stroking tickles resonated up inside her core and out between her thighs.

'Enjoy, my gentle honeybee,' the woman crooned. 'And you shall find that all inside these walls is not as you have feared; for within the Castle of Lidir reside many pleasures and desires, the like of which you, in your inexperience, have scarcely dreamt, not even in the most carnal of your fancies.' Anya blushed to hear such thoughts spoken out loud, even by a woman such as this. Then Ildren spread her cheeks and twirled her fingertip round and round against Anya's fleshy rim, and Anya's blush was crimson.

The finger then retreated, and Anya waited; she knew it would move lower, for she knew the Taskmistress would want to test that other very private place, to peel apart the burning leaves, and to delve within her fleshpot. And if she were to touch her *there*, if she were to touch her secret, her tiny tongue of hidden pleasure and desire, that point of flesh unexplored by anyone but Anya, that nub now swollen with a throbbing aching need, then she knew that she could never bear the shame of it.

'Marella, bring me a chair,' the woman commanded. Anya felt a sinking wave ripple deep inside her, and her belly contracted into a knot. She heard the Taskmistress adjust the chair behind her, then sit down upon it. When she opened her eyes again, she could see the hem of the woman's dress upon the floor. The Taskmistress was making herself comfortable, Anya knew, the better to examine her. She closed her eyes tightly when the hands brushed between her legs, and tickling amongst the curls, closed around her fleshpot.

'So hot . . . My child, your flesh is burning . . .' A finger curled around her fleshy leaves and gently pulled, making the sinking pleasure weigh into that very spot which lay nestled uneasily in between them. The finger now was joined by a second; the two were laid carefully to either side of Anya's leaves, which were slowly eased apart. 'Mmmm . . .' the woman murmured, making Anya's heart and belly sink. 'A rose bud, so pink and firm and swollen . . . and glistening with your dew.' The fingertip touched it once, exactly at the tip, sending strands of burning pleasure up through Anya's belly, making her gasp for breath and making her want that touch again; she wanted to press her bud more firmly to the finger, to wet it with her drops of liquid fire. The leaves were softly pressed together and worked around her flesh bud, in a gentle rolling pull which made Anya's heart begin to well in liquid, heavy waves.

'My black-lipped wild and wanton beauty . . . your pip of lust is growing. It bulges hard and brazenly against my fingertips.' She was squeezing now in rhythmic pulses which made Anya's legs begin to shake with shame and pleasure. '. . . Oh how I shall love to work you, my sweet, to steer you onwards to the limit of your pleasure and desire, and beyond, to test your boldness and your fleshliness.' Anya's cheeks and neck were burning as her belly quaked in delicious, honeyed ripples. 'What labour could more benefit your Taskmistress, what charge so sweet could be?' Then suddenly, the squeezing stopped. Anya was left suspended; her need was unfulfilled. '. . . But not now, I fear, for other duties vie for my attention.' And with that, Ildren brushed her hands up Anya's burning thighs and patted her on the buttocks.

'Arise, my dear. Hold up your head, for you have stood the test, and Lidir finds you worthy. Marella, bring me the chains.'

No! Anya thought, and pleaded with her eyes, but the Taskmistress only smiled.

'Fear not my child – for you see I read you in your face – these chains are but a symbol, a wedding ring . . .' Anya's eyes fell. 'A mark of your betrothal to Lidir.' Now she felt drained, to hear it made so clear.

The chains were three in number, and each was solid gold. The largest one was looped about Anya's waist, and the Taskmistress took time to angle it very carefully about her hips. The links felt cool at first and pressed heavily against Anya's belly; each movement of her hips made her aware of their presence, as the links adjusted and caressed or rolled or trailed against her skin, or their weight shifted with a deadened clink from hips to back to belly. The second and third chains were lighter, and looped around her left wrist and right ankle – but why this way round, Anya could not guess. She looked at them and tested the effect of moving her arm and her foot. The gold glistened in the light and tickled against her ankle; the wristband seemed to set off the ring that Marella had given her. To Anya, who had never worn such things, these golden

19

chains appeared an adornment, and not at all the shackles they were intended to be – and in reality were. The Taskmistress then explained:

'These chains you shall at all times wear, unless they be removed on the express direction of myself, or of your lord masters, and then only within the time they choose to use you for their pleasure. Their lordships may, from time to time, specify additional adornments or adjustments to your body, of a more lasting nature ...' This made Anya's blood run cold. '... But the chains shall remain, as a mark of your identity and your station. Is this clear?' The woman glowered. Anya nodded slowly, but the hopelessness of her situation made her very much afraid.

The Taskmistress now took something from the pocket of her robe, and strode across the room to address the husband, who had remained silent throughout the proceedings; he now cringed before her while she admonished him:

'You have brought to us a treasure, against which *this*,' and she flung down the pouch of coins contemptuously upon the table, as if it contained nothing more than dust, 'this is but a grain of sand, a candle flame dwarfed by the midday sun, had you but eyes to see – yes, and a heart wise enough to know it.' Then she stretched herself to her full height, and though she was barely taller even than Anya, she seemed to tower over the poor creature cowering now before her. 'This woman now belongs to Lidir,' she declared solemnly, as if she were passing sentence on him, and not on Anya. 'Now take your sop and go. Your claim on her is revoked.' The Taskmistress glared at him as if daring him to answer. He did not.

He collected his bag and skulked out past Marella, without a backward glance at the woman he had delivered into bondage, without one final look at Anya.

What manner of man would do this thing? What reason could absolve him from his blame? What heartless cause could justify it? What compulsion had driven him to do it – to sell this precious treasure to a fate he could not know, with no last word of tenderness or encouragement, no parting glance of love – and for nothing but a purse of gold?

3

At the Door to the Great Hall

'Take her down to the kitchens – have her fed and then
bathed, and then bring her to me,' the Taskmistress first
instructed Marella, who merely lowered her head in ac-
knowledgement. Then Ildren turned to Anya and added
coldly: 'I shall assign to you your duties for the remainder
of the evening, and perhaps the night, for when the banquet is done, my dear, then one of the lords may wish to
bed you.' Anya's blood ran cold when she heard these
words. Then Ildren left, and Marella closed the door behind her. How could anyone be so hardhearted, Anya
wondered, so indifferent to her feelings?

Marella hesitated for a moment and then walked slowly
over to where Anya was standing, still beside the fire. She
wrapped each of Anya's hands inside her own, and Anya
felt Marella's warmth infusing slowly up her arm.

'There now, that wasn't so bad, was it? She likes you,
Anya,' said Marella.

'But she hit me!' And yet that was the least of Anya's
hurts. She felt as if she had been torn apart emotionally,
and left in tatters by that cruel woman. Could Marella not
see that for herself? Then Anya felt the tears, the ones she
had suppressed so effectively in Ildren's presence, well inside her until she saw the firelight's flickers turn to
starbursts in her eyes, and Marella took her in those great
big arms and hugged her. 'There, there, my soft sweet doe,'
she crooned, while Anya's teardrops soaked warmly down
Marella's neck, then damply underneath her collar.

Marella waited till the sobs had died away before she
lifted Anya's chin and kissed her very tenderly on each

21

cheek and on her lips, then held her to her bosom. She stroked her locks and curled them round her finger.

'You must have strength, my gentle one, to bear your present sadness – for it will pass. This place – its ways – they are new to you and unfamiliar, but in time you will adjust, and tasks that now seem harsh and difficult, and mayhaps base and shameful, will yet become as second nature to you. You will take delight and pleasure in your servitude.'

Though Anya could not believe Marella's words, still she did not choose to answer back, but preferred instead to press her face against this woman's warmth and softness, taking comfort from her tender-hearted touch. 'Never fear my doe, for Marella will watch over you,' the woman said, and Anya, glancing down, could see the turquoise ring upon her finger, her birthday gift, the token of love so freely given, and she trusted in Marella.

'Marella – I'm hungry now,' she said, and looked up into the woman's smiling eyes.

'Well then,' Marella chuckled, and pinched Anya playfully about the waist, 'we'd better feed you up my dear, for you're surely thin enough to blow away altogether on a night such as this, without your clothes, and only a golden chain to hold you down! Now let me fetch your cloak.'

It was a simple cape without a hood, in heavy purple velvet, embroidered with gold thread round the hem in a bold zig-zag pattern. It fastened with a hook and eyelet only at the neck, and the cloak extended down to Anya's calves.

'Here, put these on, Anya . . .' said Marella. They were boots in softest deerskin. Anya reached to ease the chain from round her ankle. '. . . No, don't remove it, for you must keep your chains – the boot will fit around your anklet.' Marella laced them for her just below the knee. 'Now turn around; let me look at you. Right around . . . Good . . . No, you must not stand like that.' Anya was holding the cloak together where it parted down her front.

'But there are no fastenings on it,' Anya protested. 'It will . . .'

'No. It spoils the line,' Marella insisted. 'You must hold your head up, with pride, and keep your shoulders back – like this . . .' She straightened Anya's back and made her place her hands behind her. 'There, now let me see you walking. Walk around the room.' Anya tried it. She was sure the cloak kept falling open with each step she took. 'Hold your head up, Anya. That's better – you look wonderful.' Was Marella just deceiving her, Anya wondered, simply trying to flatter her? But it was true that she felt different like this – it was partly the fact that she was constantly made conscious of the caress of the chains as she moved, and then the boots and cloak felt so clean and fresh and luxurious, not used and careworn like her own things. How she wished there were a mirror here, so she could judge for herself . . .

'A princess, almost,' said Marella, and Anya felt her heart overflowing, now with pride, and her neck and cheeks flushing with embarrassment at being made to suffer such praise from the one person who loved her.

Anya was led away from that room and along the corridor, past many doorways and minor passageways branching from their route, until they reached the foot of a wide staircase. The walls were now no longer bare but were decorated with a series of large paintings, much larger than life size, of men and women dressed in fine clothes and rich jewellery. The pictures were arranged all the way up the staircase. They must surely be the images of the lords and ladies of the castle, Anya decided, although there seemed to be so many of them. She stopped to look at the first painting, which showed a beautiful woman dressed in white, who had long red hair and carried a sword, and seemed to stare fearlessly out of the picture. This woman appeared to have such strength; Anya very much admired her.

'The Princess of Lidir,' Marella whispered.

'Is she here, in the castle? Shall I get to see her?' asked Anya in a tone of awe. She would have loved to meet this person in the flesh, to see if she was indeed as beautiful and self-assured as this pose suggested.

'Why no, my dear,' Marella shook her head, looking first at Anya, then at the picture. 'The Princess is gone – long, long gone,' she added rather enigmatically. Anya took it to mean that she was dead. It made her a little sad.

Then Marella turned, threw her head back and sniffed the air. Anya realised that she too could smell the delicious aroma of roasting meat. It was wafting up a narrower set of steps which descended to the right of the main staircase. Marella nodded and smiled at the look of delectation on Anya's face. 'The kitchens are down there,' she said, then raised her finger and instead looked up the staircase. 'But I want to show you something first.'

The sound of music and ribald laughter rolled down the steps which the two women now ascended. The louder it became, the more vulnerable it made Anya feel; Marella had made her lead the way. 'I'm not so nimble as you young things,' she'd said, but Anya wondered whether Marella just wanted to keep an eye on her. But then, she thought, where would she go, even if she were to try to escape? There was no future for her now beyond the castle walls, and perhaps there never had been. And now the music sounded very near. She was on tenterhooks at the possibility that they might meet someone coming down the stairs, since at each step, her cloak fell open to reveal the chain about her hips, and a gap extending from her neckline to her thighs.

Then Anya saw someone move at the top of the steps; it stopped her in her tracks. 'What on earth?' Marella had cried when she'd walked into her and almost knocked her over. Anya could only point. At first she'd thought the figure was part of the stonework, since it had been stationary and the drab grey uniform had merged with the colour of the wall. 'That's one of the castle guards, that's all,' Marella laughed. 'And drunk, at that, I'll warrant.' And as if to prove her point, there came a sudden metallic ringing, then an indistinct sound rather like a muttered curse, and a goblet rolled over the top step and began clanking, step by step, down towards the women, followed at a distance by the guard, still swearing and looking very much the worse for wear and almost overbalancing in his haste. Anya tried to press her back against the wall; she meant to let the jumping goblet pass, trusting she would not be noticed, but Marella trapped it underneath her foot and stopped the flying guardsman by slamming a decisive hand flat against his chest.

'What's this, my man? Do I detect wine upon your breath?' she berated him. The smell of liquor mixed with sour cheese and stale sweat rolled across and almost suffocated Anya. His beady, bloodshot eyes were on her now, making her flatten herself to the wall and grip the rough-hewn stonework tightly with her fingers, as if she expected him at any second to try to prize her off it. His hair looked oily and matted; she doubted if he had ever washed it in his life, and his hands were filthy, with the blackness grained into the creases and underneath the thick, encrusted snailshells of his nails. He was standing very unsteadily with one leg balanced above the other, on the next step. Then his teeth showed brown and yellow in a twisted grin as he reached shakily towards the gap in Anya's cloak. She could not run, for she was frozen now with fear, her mouth had opened to her last defence, that rising scream that fought against each sharply indrawn gasp of frightened breath. But before that sound had even formed, the man simply grunted very loudly and collapsed onto his knees, with his hands pressed inexplicably about his tender parts. Then he slowly doubled over until his head was almost touching Anya's feet.

'And so you should apologise – and most humbly too,' said Marella. 'This woman is not a plaything, to be mauled about by a drunken sot like you. Now let that be a lesson. And if I catch you ogling her again, I'll have your ballocks as mincemeat for the chickens.' With that, Marella took Anya by the hand and hauled her up the stairs.

Anya had never heard such coarseness from a woman such as this, who appeared otherwise so tender and so kind. 'You have to keep them in their place, you know,' Marella explained. 'They're not allowed to touch you . . .' That was a relief, thought Anya, for she knew she could never bear it. The memory was enough to make her flesh go cold and creepy. 'That is, not unless . . .' Marella fell silent.

'Unless what, Marella?' Now Anya was perturbed.

'No, my dear, you need not concern yourself with that.' Marella's comment only made things worse. Anya stopped, and held Marella by the arm.

'With what? You must tell me.'

Marella finally relented. 'It could happen only . . . only if a girl was very bad. The Taskmistress, or their lordships, could then decide . . .'

'. . . To hand me over to one of these creatures?' Anya was horrified by the thought of being touched by someone like that.

'To assign you to the guardroom.' Marella's eyes were downcast now; it was clear she found it painful to discuss. Yet Anya still persisted:

'The guardroom? How . . . how many of them?' she asked, but did not want to know, and Marella did not want to answer. 'Marella – how many?' she repeated.

'There could be . . .' Marella took a breath, 'six or eight, depending . . .' then she bit her lip, and held Anya tightly by the hand. 'But that couldn't happen to you, Anya – I know that you're a good girl . . .' Yet even Marella did not sound completely sure, which made Anya even more apprehensive, so that now she wished she had never asked at all.

The passage widened and grew higher, and now the wall to the left was covered by a great plasterwork frieze depicting female figures in white upon a pale red background. Each figurine was placed within an arch and each of them was nude apart from her chains, picked out in gold paint, about her waist, her wrist and ankle, exactly like the chains which Anya wore. Above the arches, looking down upon the slaves, were faces so grotesque they made Anya want to shudder.

Anya pointed to the faces. 'Are those the souls of the guards?' she asked, for these creatures still loomed large within her mind. Marella laughed out loud.

'No, my darling,' she said, and threw her arm around Anya. 'Do not fret; the guards are not all so bad as that one was.'

A short way along this corridor, and to their right, they came upon the doors of the Great Hall, crowned at their apex by a painted carving of an eagle perched upon the hilt of a blue-white sword which pierced a crimson heart. The doors stood unguarded now, and narrowly ajar. The light and sounds of merriment spilled through the gap. 'The banquet,' Marella whispered, and she peeped between the doors. 'Anya – come and look!'

Anya had never seen anything on this scale before. The room seemed thronged with people laughing, shouting, eating, dancing, and playing music; it was alive with colour and excitement. Lords and ladies garbed in exotic finery were waited on by busily rushing servants clad in simple brightly coloured tunics, while the sound of pipes and lutes and drums made Anya want to throw open the door and join the dance. The great table, extending around three sides of the room, was laden with cakes and pies and carcasses, strangely coloured fruits and jugs of wine and beer. At the centre of the table sat a young man, slightly taller than the rest; from his position and his bearing, and the deferential way in which the lords and ladies seemed to treat him, Anya took him to be some lord of great importance.

'That is the Prince,' Marella said.

'He sits alone,' said Anya. 'He has no princess, then?' She was recalling the image of the woman in white, with hair as red as Anya's.

Marella shook her head, but Anya was staring intently through the gap, with a distant, wistful look which only made Marella shake her head again.

'Spies! In the Castle of Lidir!' The voice behind them made Anya jump, and Marella cried out with shock.

'Oh, your lordship,' she bowed, 'you frightened us, Lord Aldrid! I was just showing –'

'Aha! So the bond-girls are brought in early tonight?' He leered at Anya. Anya did not like him, not one bit. Not

27

because he was old, with grey whiskers and wispy hair, and an angular bony face, but because, to Anya, he seemed arrogant and hard. His eyes were a cold grey-blue, like the winter lake up in the mountains. He stood over her like a hawk about to jab and tear her flesh with his vicious cutting beak.

'No, no, my lord,' Marella said, but rather shakily, as if she were afraid. 'I was just taking Anya down to the kitchen . . . on the Taskmistress's instruction,' she added more loudly, as if mention of that woman's name might ward off this unwelcome interference.

'Anya – such a pretty name,' he said, making Anya shrink back against the door. 'So, she has misbehaved?'

'No, most certainly she has not, my lord! I'm taking her to have her fed.' Marella sounded affronted at the suggestion, and Anya was thankful for her support and her protection from this person.

'I see . . .' he said, deep in thought, yet with a sinister expression.

His long thin bony fingers reached and lifted Anya's chin. 'Very nice,' he said, and traced her fingers lightly underneath until he touched her burning earlobe, which he took between his finger and his thumb and massaged very slowly. 'Yes . . . very nice indeed.' Cold ripples ran up her back and round across her belly; her breath came short; she felt as if her body was being lowered slowly into a deep pool of ice-cold water. His other hand was at her cloak, just below the neckline, toying with the fastening. Why did not Marella do something to stop him? She must have known what he was doing. 'And beautiful red hair, do you not think so?'

Marella answered. 'Yes, my lord,' was all she said, and Anya knew then that she was lost.

The finger moved across her lips. 'Why are you trembling, my dear?' he asked. 'You must be cold. Let me feel your skin.' The other hand had slipped beneath her cloak. She tensed, and wanted desperately to close her eyes, for she could not bear to look him in the face a moment longer. She wanted to run, but she was too terrified to move – his eyes snared her so she dared not even blink. The hawk was poised to strike and tear her heart out.

His finger touched her in the hollow of her neck; it felt like the point of an icicle was pressed against her, and at any moment it would pierce her skin and slide to block her throat with its icy coldness. The finger started moving downwards, tracing out the line of her breastbone. His face moved closer, and in that brief movement, his gaze had faltered, the spell was lifted, and Anya closed her eyes.

'Open your eyes and look at me,' his voice came, soft and crisp, like winter footfalls on frosted drifts of leaves. Anya could hear Marella behind her, wheezing and shifting her feet. 'Now keep your eyes firmly fixed on mine,' he whispered. 'And do not move.' He laid his icy finger down along the line between her breasts, causing shivers down her belly, and making her pull back. His eyes then widened threateningly and his jaw, already angular, now set firmly to a point. 'Keep still, I said,' he hissed, and it echoed round the passageway. 'Now do not try my patience any further . . .'

'Sir,' Marella tried to interrupt, 'she is . . .'

'Keep quiet, woman.' But he never took his eyes from Anya's while he shut Marella up, and his voice was never raised above a whisper.

His fingertip was tickling the underside of Anya's breast, moving slowly up, then down the tender skin just below the nipple, barely touching, just teasing very gently, until she could feel her flesh begin to gather against her will. But he just kept up the stroking till his finger ran smoothly against the tightness of the underbelly, and her nipples reached to brush against the velvet of her cloak, which undulated softly with the shaking of her shoulders. And now it seemed that, locked as she was in the gaze of those cold blue eyes, her body did not belong to her – it reacted as it chose, so she was compelled by it to welcome each unwanted ripple of illicit delight that the brushing tickles gave to her. The hand next moved lower, searching back and forth until at last it stroked into her navel. Then his thumb was fitted in the well while the finger stretched on downwards. 'Keep

29

your hands behind you. Arch your back and push your belly outwards. I want you to present yourself correctly for my touching.' Her skin felt drum-tight, sensitised, and the thumbpad sank in deeper, until it felt as if his thumb was pushed inside her belly. The reaching finger touched her just above her fleshy lips, then pulling back the skin, it pressed slowly from side to side, making her want to close her eyes and push her hips out further against the pleasure of the pulling. She felt her desire begin to drip, warmly and heavily, deep inside her belly.

'Don't move – not yet, sweet child of lust.' His voice was barely audible. 'For it seems your lord has found your measure, and now we must take our time, to pleasure you yet more fully.'

Now Anya hated herself more than she hated him; she hated her body for reacting in this way, but still she could not help herself, for she was burning up with shame and hate and so much fear and wanting.

The fingertip was kissing her, right against her flesh bud. It kept pressing it then releasing, pushing it back inside her body then waiting till it pushed itself out again more stiffly than before; it was palpitating her gently, tapping, turning, flicking, sweetly probing, making her fleshpot swell hot and soft and liquid, and yearning with desire.

Anya began to feel that she was drifting, her body almost floating in a pool of oily lust. She wanted to press against the hand, to let it take her last remaining weight and lift her feet right off the floor, to concentrate the pressure and the pleasure in that spot. She began to sway, gently in the tide of her desire; she heard murmurings, like some distant calling creature in a strange and far off land. Then suddenly the hand was gone; Anya dropped to earth and nearly overbalanced. As she was turned around to face the door, she caught a glimpse of Marella, who was standing back from Anya with a very strange expression, as if perhaps she no longer recognised this woman.

'Spread yourself against the door,' the man had said quite simply, and Anya did it freely. She welcomed the firmness of the wood – she extended her palms against it, until she felt the metal chain links trapped and pressing sweetly in her belly. She minded not that her cloak fell open from the neck, in fact she wanted that to happen, so she could press her belly and thighs more closely to the fabric of the door. She wanted to be urged against it, from behind, from her shoulders to her buttocks, until her nipples were forced out to the sides and her flesh nub touched the woodwork. She wanted to be held like that, just rocking gently, until the reverberations of the music and the dancing soaked through the wood into her nub and set her smouldering lust alight.

'Stretch your hands up; mould yourself more intimately to the grain.' He lifted her cloak away from her body and gathered it around the back. He must be looking at her, Anya thought. 'Now spread your legs and lift up on your toes. I want you more accessible. Hold yourself in that position . . .' He knelt behind her; Anya heard a soft, deep sigh. His finger stroked down inside her thigh at one side, then the other, then he sighed once more and released the cloak so it brushed against her bottom. He stood up again behind her, yet although she wanted him to, he did not press against her. His hands moved lightly up her sides and tickled her armpits.

'Press your cheek against the wood,' he said. Turning, Anya's edge of passion was tempered now with guilt as she faced Marella, whose eyes were downcast, as if she could not bring herself to watch her charge being subjected to such debasement. The hands moved round to Anya's front and up, to ease her breasts apart, so they pointed to each side. Then Anya heard him catch his breath. 'My luscious, black-tipped beauties . . . let me watch you in your swell-age,' he sighed, then he was flattening her against the door; the bellies of her breasts were distended underneath her armpits. He leaned his weight against his palm, which pressed between her shoulders and prevented her from moving. He pushed the fingers of his other hand into Anya's mouth and underneath her tongue, saying: 'Wet them with your spittle.' She could smell herself and even taste her saltiness upon them. He took them out and wiped

31

them round the fullness of her teat until it went slick and shiny with her own saliva, then he worked and pulled the nipple wetly till the pleasure made her tongue slide out and stroke her bottom lip. He kept alternating from breast to breast, changing hands and pausing only when his fingers dried, to wet them once again, or when he wanted to slap the nipples with the pad of his middle finger, or sometimes just to roll them in-between his finger and his thumb, while keeping them at all times wet, until Anya was beside herself with the pulling tickling pleasure. 'I want your nipples soft; I like to shape them . . . I'm going to shape that other flesh tip now – I want to sharpen up your nub,' he whispered up against her ear, and Anya felt a sinking shiver down between her legs.

'Now stay like that, and keep up on your toes.' She almost overbalanced when the hand was taken from her back She had to fight to hold herself against the woodwork. She willed her skin into the grain; it felt as if she was balanced on a narrow ledge, out above a chasm: she was terrified of falling, and yet in that fear it seemed she fell a thousand times, until at last she wanted so desperately to fling herself out and back to let the abyss swallow her up; her muscles ached; her body yearned to take its sweet release.

Then from behind, and underneath, his hand pressed up against her, at the joining of her thighs, and moulded to her body like a saddle. 'Lower yourself and spread your fillets out upon my palm,' he said. 'I want to feel you in the heat of your desire.' He worked her flesh lips open with his fingers and held them with a finger flat against each one, so Anya's nub stood out, defenceless and burning hot, against the cool caress of the air. She wanted him to touch her there with his long and delicate middle finger, to brush just the ridges of his fingerprint against her taut and polished nubskin, back and forth and side to side until her nubbin thrummed gently with desire. Then he could shape or draw it as he wished, or turn her round and close his lips around its base and suck it till it burst . . .

'My dear, your flesh is dripping wet upon my fingers. Hold still and I shall try to stem your flow.' His middle finger entered her, sending shivers up her core; her body tensed away at first, then her slickness gloved around his finger. 'Now rock your hips, and you may milk my finger with your flesh.' Anya squeezed and tried to draw her legs together. 'No, no my sweet – you have much to learn,' he reproved her very gently. 'You must keep your legs apart. Do your milking with your fleshpot. Now try once more, only this time you shall grunt . . .'

His lordship then addressed Marella, who had remained, unspeaking, rooted to the spot: 'It seems your training is remiss, matron, in this respect at least.' His remark seemed to shake Marella from her private thoughts.

'But she is new, my lord,' she explained in mitigation. 'Her training is not yet begun.'

'Hmmm, new, you say?' He sounded doubtful. 'Not new to this, I'll warrant. Not new to lustful ways . . .' Anya's cheeks were flaming now; his thumb was in her bottom groove and was striking at her rim. 'Not new to lickerishness, I'd say.' Anya shut her eyes in shame, and she wished she could have closed her ears off too. How *could* he say it? It was not true! 'Not new to lewd desires – your drippings tell me that, my dear. Your nectar is too copious.'

Now Anya was mortified to have him say such things out loud, and in Marella's presence. Yet he would not stop: 'Now tighten – squeeze your flesh around me; use my finger for your pleasure. Your training in the avenues of lust shall start right now, with my finger as your tutor.' She was burning up with disgrace and heat to hear him speak so plainly, to have such private needs and cravings displayed for all to see. Her breasts and belly felt full and heavy, as if hot oil was running in and slowly weighing down inside them. Her sex felt swollen with desire; the leaves were filling up with blood which pulsed against the pressure of his fingers held against them in a pleasure-ache that throbbed up to her throat. She felt she could not breathe; she had to arch her neck and open her mouth so she could gulp the air more freely. Anya squeezed until her sex could feel the knuckles of his joints, and then she contracted tighter, to a knot, which forced her pip out from her body and locked

33

his finger rigidly. Then she relaxed again, and panted very deeply.

'Good,' he said. 'But I did not hear you grunt ... For, you see, my lascivious one, you *shall* express your pleasure. Now this time, keep your legs spread wide, and remember – I'll be listening.' Anya felt so ashamed at what she was being made to do, and with Marella here as witness; it seemed this lord was taking pleasure from her degradation, as if he wanted her to behave, not only wantonly and lewdly, but like some animal braying in the byre. She wanted it to be over as quickly now as possible, but she could never bring herself to make such debased sounds as a sign of inner pleasure. Such things were private, intimate, to be taken with a bitten lip, a catch of breath, or a gentle muffled sigh, and a face pressed in a pillow perhaps. Or sweetest yet, she guessed, a lover's palm pressed to her mouth at her moment of deliverance, so she could show her strength of pleasure silently, in the way she sucked and bit him ...

So Anya squeezed again and held him, trying to crush his bone, and then she heard the groan, a wrenching sound from deep within her – an animal in her throat. 'Good, now grunt again, each time I oil your nubbin.' The finger then slipped out and joined the others to oil her flesh and squeeze it till she grunted; it dipped again into her pot, then worked her wetness over and around the pip and underneath the hood, until she became too slippery to hold, though he kept trying while she squelched between his fingers, and she grunted now without having to be told, until her body balanced on that peculiar edge of pleasure which made her grunting change to a continuous pleading moan, causing finely misted sprays of heated droplets to bead her upper lip, her neck, and back, and then behind her knees. The fingers withdrew, so he could savour her ecstasy and keep her teetering on the brink, while he held her thighs apart and very gently rocked her, until she wanted to plead with him, to beg him to finish her there, with his fingers or his knuckles pressed against her.

'Throb, my sweet,' he murmured softly, 'and relish now

34

that salt dry taste of lust, which thicks your saliva and swells your tongue, and soon shall block your throat . . . Reach up, my child, push your belly to the woodwork and take your pleasure now . . .' And with that he slowly slid two stiffly curving fingers into the warm liquidity of Anya's fleshpot and tried to hold her open; yet her body closed around them, sucking them and drawing them to herself, in that first tightening honeyed half-contraction which took her breath away and made her stretch her limbs and squeeze, and even rise up on her toes that she might press her mound against the door to assuage that delicious burning.

His other hand pressed flat against her, at the tip of Anya's backbone, so her weight was taken; she was pinned against the door. And now she reached instead and stretched her arms out backwards so that her back was arched and she was floating, out above her chasm of desire. Her breasts felt heavy and rolled out, weighted, to each side, making her nipples pulse and tingle as if soft slow lips were sucking them in rhythm with her breathing. She wanted the hand that pressed her back to turn her to one side, then the other, so that in its turning it would rotate her body back and forth about that one most intimate of points, her tiny fleshy rod of lust, would make it twist against the wood grain in its gripping until her cry was drowned in giant gasps of pure delight.

The fingers pushed more deeply up inside her. 'Now stir your fire, my darling, push and roll; charm out your pleasure very gently, so I may feel the swelling of your desire and then again its waning, each tiny ripple you suppress to let it draw again more deeply; each tightening of your thighs, each nervous breath which quivers your breast; your flesh glove moulded to my finger; your stiffening as at last you lose control and can no longer bear it, and you cry out loud for all to know your ache of wanton pleasure . . .' Then his fingers, curving inside, up and forwards, found the core of her delight, and pressed, to force her nubbin outwards from her body.

Anya hung defencelessly. The fingers reached and stroked her flesh bud wetly on the woodwork, once, then

35

waited till her pulsing ebbed, then stroked once more its oily slick, then paused until she'd stopped contracting, then pushed it till it scarcely touched the surface, and held it without moving. Her pulsebeat now took charge; it brushed her pleasure out in a long persistent tickle, until she felt her breathing shallow and her belly tighten to a slowly splitting drum. Her nectar, dripping hot around his fingers, splashed upon her thighs; she did not move; she waited for her lust to take her in its own good time; the fingers tapped her slowly, very gently from behind, until the palpitations merged and formed into a bolt of bittersweet surrender. She thrust and wrenched and cried and pushed until she felt her pleasure burst, its burning tendrils licking up inside her, to root and draw at first behind her nipples and then deep within her womb. A wave of warmth rolled up from Anya's toes and enveloped her in its softness; she sank slowly to the floor.

Then Anya heard a very distant voice amid the gentle humming in her ears.

'. . . Anya, you say her name is, matron? Hmmm . . . this girl is full of untapped passion. Yet we must temper it, I feel, and teach her more control, for she is too impetuous by far. I shall speak on it to Ildren. You may continue now about your business, and I thank you for your efforts, matron. An interesting diversion . . .'

'Thank you, Lord Aldrid,' Marella said. She weaited till he had disappeared down the stairway, before turning round to Anya, whose head was buried in her hands, from shame and degradation. What would Marella think of her for allowing her body to be used this way, without a single word of protest, for taking her pleasure wantonly, and at the hands of a perfect stranger?

'There, there my doe,' Marela said and put her arms around her. 'Lord Aldrid has been very cruel to force his will upon you. The Taskmistress shall hear of this . . .' She placed her palm to Anya's face; Anya's eyes were pools of loving blackness. 'Oh, your forehead and your cheeks feel hot – my darling, you're fevered with starvation. Let Marella help you up again; we'll get you to the kitchen.'

Marella reached out to take her hand as Anya, pushing herself up, leaned back against the door. And at that moment, with Anya's weight against it, the great door suddenly moved, and she felt her fingers slipping through Marella's, as she overbalanced backwards. She saw the look of horror on the woman's face as Anya's other arm swung up and back to save herself, only to smack that innocently emerging servant very squarely under the chin and send his tray of plates and chicken bones flying through the air. And she heard the terrible crash, the groan, the exclamations of surprise, and then the silence as the music stopped – all of this she took in, even as she toppled backwards and broke her fall against the soft and tender cushion of the servant's sprawled out body. Marella, standing above her, looked distraught.

Anya wanted to crawl away, out through the circle of noble faces that was gathering around.

'Bring her here,' a voice boomed down the hall. 'The Prince would look upon this woman that breaks down doors to gain entry to his banquet – and floors his servants in the process.' The laughter echoed round the hall. Anya's cheeks were burning. Marella merely stood there, biting at her fingernails, as Anya was lifted to her feet. The circle opened and she was led through the lline of grinning faces until she faced the Prince across the centre table. She kept her head down, from embarrassment at being made the object of everyone's attention, feeling isolated now that Marella was no longer by her side. She knew that if she were subjected to any further ridicule, she would never be able to control her tears.

'Lift her head.' The voice was very brusque. Anya's chin was forced up. The speaker, dressed in emerald green, sat to the Prince's right. His eyes looked hard and calculating and filled Anya with dread; she did not want to be made to look at him. 'Now, slave – explain. Why have you taken it upon yourself to disrupt the entertainment?'

Anya tried to summon up the courage to speak. She was very close to tears, and she hardly knew how to reply to so sarcastic a question.

'I . . . it was an accident,' she answered very meekly.

'Carelessness, more likely.' He was very stern. She did not know how to take him. 'And do you know how a careless slave is dealt with?' Anya could well imagine. 'Answer!' But she could not reply. The tears slowly welled to overflowing. 'Stop whining. Speak!'

'Wait, my lord.' A gentle hand had passed before this lord to stem his cruel attack. The voice was very soft, yet very determined. 'Do not upset her.'

For the first time, Anya turned to look fully on that face, at that man who had spoken on her behalf – who had intervened to save her – and it seemed that, in that spellbound instant, something inside her melted, and she could see nothing but those eyes, those very soft and gentle, melting, deep green eyes, which widened until they almost seemed to look inside her soul. And in that moment, those delicious, beautiful eyes seemed to kiss her. Before the assembled host of the banquet, the Prince had kissed *her* with his eyes, and she had kissed him back, and no one else had noticed.

Anya was uplifted by that thought, and now she was not afraid.

'Anya, Sire,' she whispered, in a soft and sultry voice, for the Prince had asked her name.

'Then go about your duties, Anya, for this transgression,' and he glanced at the lord in green, 'be it deliberate or accidental, is forgiven.' He raised his voice, so all could hear. 'It is forgotten.' And then he said more softly, 'but you are not . . .' Again, he kissed her with his eyes.

As Marella led her out, Anya felt drugged by the Prince's words; she tried to form a picture of him in her mind, but all she could see were those soft, sweet eyes, and all she could hear was that gentle voice and – there was something else – she was sure there was something out of place, something odd about his ear . . .

And Marella looked upon that lovestruck slave, and shook her head again, and put it down to lack of proper food, for she knew the girl was starving.

4

The Taskmistress of Lidir

Ildren's apartments were situated high up in the east wing
of the castle, well away from the Bondslaves' House, which
was located beyond the Great Hall, the kitchens and the
servants quarters, in the vast and sprawling west wing. The
Taskmistress, had she so desired, could certainly have re-
sided much closer to her slaves, but she preferred things
this way. Why? It was no accident that Ildren's rooms lay
directly above the Council Chamber, the political heart of
the castle, so that, although she was not a formal member
of the Council of Lidir, Ildren was still readily to hand, to
advise, or perhaps to lobby their lordships, or on rare occasions – although this was Ildren's secret – to overhear the
confidences of the Council through a gap in Ildren's floor-
boards, which Ildren had by accident enlarged – for use
strictly in cases which Ildren judged it to be of dire necessity or national need. And yet, even if political expedience
had not dictated Ildren's choice, she would still have selected these rooms, for their early-morning quality,
whereby Ildren's bedroom would fill with that special lu-
minosity of fresh daydawn, and the beautiful creature
within her bed would stir and gently waken to pleasures
undreamt of by the slave, games devised by Ildren in those
early hours before the dawn, as Ildren planned and rum-
maged through her storeroom of delights.

For Ildren loved to play with her slaves – and they were
her slaves, whatever anybody said. After all, it was she
who chose them, then examined them and set them to their
duties. And was it not she who saw to their training, en-
couraging them and certainly – when necessary –

disciplining them, and bringing out the very best in them? Did not their lordships rely on her to take these raw untutored souls and mould them to the intricacies of love, to match them to each lorship's whispered need, each secret vice, each nuance of delight? And Ildren oftentimes would devote long hours, or if needs be, days and nights, or sometimes even weeks, to the tutoring of a single slave to some particular end for which there existed a requirement.

Frequently, the Prince would chide her, saying: 'Taskmistress – why do you waste so much time and precious effort on so difficult a slave?'

And Ildren would reply: 'Sire – I see a slave with *promise*, that is why.'

The Prince would merely shake his head, yet time would prove her right. For Ildren knew, although she would never say it to the Prince's face, that in truth, there was no such creature as a difficult slave; there were only difficult requirements which, however rigorous they might seem could, with patience, certainly be met. To Ildren, no challenge was impossible, no nervous and half-expressed request which their lordships might hesitatingly and apologetically proffer for consideration was too extreme, and Ildren would take time to reassure their lordships in their illicit cravings:

'Mm . . . interesting . . .' she would say, for where slaves were concerned, she took pleasure in making even the impossible come true, in bending those exquisite creatures – very gently – to her will. For she loved them.

But most of all she loved to play with them. Not to toy with their emotions necessarily, though sometimes this might prove to be a crucial facet of their learning, but to toy with their bodies – physically to touch them, especially the girls. Those other calls, the direction and chastisement and supervision, were part of Ildren's duties, and she enjoyed them, that was definitely true, but her greatest pleasure was rooted deeper, in those quiet tender loving searching moments – or on occasion, hours – which she would spend with a girl, particularly a new girl, touching her.

She liked first to let a girl acclimatise to her nudity, and to the constant presence of her chains, so that when at last she had the girl secure within the confies of her apartments, Ildren could instruct her thus:

'Remove your chains – drop them to the floor. I want you totally nude,' then watch with carefully suppressed delight as the trembling girl – who had come to feel the chains to be, if not exactly clothing, at least a symbol of protection from her nudity – would achieve that higher plane of nakedness and utter vulnerability which Ildren now intended.

And Ildren would previously have instructed that a good strong fire should fill the grate, and her couch be drawn up close, so that the girl would be kept warm and comfortable in her nudity, for like as not the evening would be long as pleasures swelled then ebbed again under Ildren's close direction. Besides which, she loved to watch the play of firelight across a nubile body.

She liked to have the slave on her lap, so she could cradle her very lovingly, and normally Ildren would wear her velvet robe, because she knew that this would serve a double purpose – it would maintain the girl's awareness of her own nudity, by way of its contrast with her state, and at the same time, would bring her pleasure, by brushing delicately against the girl's skin in a thousand places, with every little movement covering her with soft velvet kisses which would then be counterpointed by Ildren's own more intimate and precise caresses. She loved to stroke the woman's body with her eyes before she even touched her, to absorb each smoothly swollen curve, each flutter of an eyelid, the soft inviting bush of hair between her thighs or underneath an armpit. She would have the woman raise an arm to place it behind her head, so she could watch the way in which her bosom moved, and exactly how the nipple lifted. Sometimes, at this early stage, Ildren would turn the bond-girl on her side, to test the way her breasts would fill in weighted, soft resilience. At this point, a little shiver might run up through Ildren, for she would be imagining the girl lain like this, on her side upon the couch, with Ildren on the floor, her lips pressing by turn around each fully swollen nipple. But she would deny herself this tactile pleasure for the present, preferring simply that the anticipation sharpen up the pangs of her desire and thereby render the realisation, when it came, sweeter yet by virtue of her wanting.

Then, having made the slave turn back again, she would stare into her eyes until the girl's pupils dilated blackly in reflection of Ildren's loving look, and the Taskmistress would then say:

'Spread your thighs, my dark-eyed beauty; open yourself to me ...' And every time, without exception, the slave would glance downwards and away, in sweetness and in innocence, sending another shiver through the Task-mistress, this time to her core. It would make her want to take that beautiful face in her palms and cover it with kisses, to press her lips softly upon those eyelids which were closed in gentle bashfulness and were weighted with desire. And always, the girl at last would look again at Ildren, with eyes more liquid than before, and then she would comply with the Taskmistress's very clear directive.

Ildren's head would swim in waves of pure intoxication each time a girl would spread herself this way, and do it of her own accord, without ropes or chains or even other hands to bend and mould her form to such a luscious purpose. And, she found, the girls never would refuse – or rather, would do so only very rarely, and even an unlikely eventuality such as that, she knew, could have its compensations – albeit of a rather different kind.

When a girl was spread before her – opened across her lap – then Ildren would suffer a nervous moment of indecisiveness, so totally out of character, but delicious yet for that, in which she could not make up her mind exactly where to touch her first. The slave would wait, and frequently her eyes would close, and Ildren would watch that bosom quickly rise and fall in short and frightened breaths of taut anticipation, and she would hold back until her own excitement welled so strong that Ildren's breathing now outpaced the girl's. And then she would say, provided she could haul those heavy-weighted sentiments of lust successfully from so deep within her breast.

'Open your eyes, my darling . . . Look lovingly on your Taskmistress while she plays with you.'

And if Ildren managed to deliver that, her vision of desire, without a single catch of breath or falter, then it was a very rare happenstance indeed. And if, upon the opening of her eyes, the girl's pupils did not expand to utter blackness – well, such intransigence was totally unknown.

Ildren might now insist that the girl spread wider, and for two very significant reasons. The girl, whilst looking fixedly into Ildren's limpid eyes, would by this action make a gesture of submission so profound that Ildren would go queasy in her belly and below, as if a large strong hand had slowly closed around about her sex and squeezed it. The second reason, whilst certainly more practical, was no less stirring where Ildren's belly was concerned. It was this: the tender skin which stretched across the crease where thigh joined body in the girl was now so taut that it was ripe for tickling with Ildren's little finger – for her finger to touch, very, very lightly and move down the crease as slowly as she could. And when at last the girl's leg would lift, in involuntary reaction, as Ildren was well aware it would do, then Ildren would smile and remind the girl:

'Do not lift your knee, my sweet – you must keep very open to my caresses. Now this time, open your mouth, and push out your tongue, but very slowly, while your Taskmistress continues to brush you in your crease.' For Ildren had discovered long, long ago, that this simple sign of rudeness would help the girl in her abandon, which would in due course constitute a very necessary adjunct to desire.

The Taskmistress preferred that a girl have very prominent lips, as part and parcel of her sex, and she would justify this on the simple grounds that there was thereby more for her to play with. The slave-girls varied in their make-up and each was structured differently; their individual strengths and weaknesses made each of them unique and Ildren loved them in their diversity – she took great pleasure in seeking out and coming to know their secret features, both physical and emotional. And she would never – or would hardly ever – abuse a slave or cut one with her tongue on account of some particular desired characteristic in which that slave was wanting; that is, unless she lost her temper, which was very rare indeed. No, either the deficiency was one of emotion or natural inclination, in which case, with Ildren's careful training, success was sure; alternatively, if the physical make-up was flawed, then nothing could, or need be done – unless success was possible with some very minor bodily readjustment. So Ildren would always try to help the slaves to make the very most of their existing physical assets; and yet, secretly, she could not escape the fact that she loved those prominent lips.

If, therefore, a girl was in her lap and was appropriately endowed, the Taskmistress would be in seventh heaven at this particular juncture. She would temporarily permit the girl to retract her tongue, while Ildren spent some time developing her:

'I want to play with your lips – to make them very full and swollen,' she would say. 'Now – ask me to do it to you.' She loved to play this little game, to show her domination.

'Pl ... Please, ma'am,' the girl would at length request, though in a very nervous voice.

The Taskmistress would sigh, in pride and pleasure at that sweet entreaty, and a shiver would run through her. 'Yes, my dear? What is that you want?' And Ildren's eyes would widen and she'd pout her lip.

'Please ... dd ... do it to me,' the slave would then add very meekly.

'Do what, my dear?' Ildren's voice would now sound very husky.

'Please ... please pl ... play with me,' the girl would manage to say. Then she would avert her eyes, and Ildren's heart would leap. But she would want to press things further:

'Tell me what I should play with, darling; do not be ashamed.'

44

'My . . . my . . .' The Taskmistress would be delighted that the girl was too embarrassed to say it:

'Mmm? Your what? Do not be afraid to tell.'

'My . . . my love lips, ma'am.' Ildren would be elated if the girl should remember to match the term correctly to the occasion, which currently was, of course, a loving one.

'And for how long should your Taskmistress play with your sweet and succulent love lips, my precious?'

'For . . . for as long as it should please you, ma'am.'

And playing with a woman's lips of love usually would please the Taskmistress for a very long time indeed, particularly when those lips with which she dealt were, by their nature, already very well developed.

As a rule, she would begin with a very gentle touch designed to test the lips' resilience. Three fingertips of one hand would be placed to one side of the lips and then would nuzzle very softly up against them. This action might elicit from the girl a slight catch of breath, as the cool smoothness of Ildren's fingers was laid against her heat. Ildren would wait – perhaps the girl's flesh would involuntarily wrinkle against her fingertips, although sometimes it would expand. Ildren had found, by experience, that she never could be sure exactly how a pair of flesh lips would react; it didn't depend necessarily on the girl's physical constitution. More probably it related to her mood. It was this kind of thing that made these explorations so fascinating to Ildren – not knowing precisely what might happen, or quite how a girl would take to being fondled in this way. Sometimes, the excitement might be so intense that Ildren would feel her heart was in her throat, especially when she closed her thumb across those lips to trap them while she pulled them, very slowly, then relaxed her hold and watched the lips retract again, under their natural elasticity.

She would, in due course, test that elasticity, if not quite to its limits, then certainly very thoroughly, but by that time the girl might find such intensive treatment really quite acceptable, assuming that by then she even cared at all. Ildren liked to steer a woman's lips through two states, the first of which was *rigid*. By this she meant that the lips should stand hard and proud, and rather like a cockscomb. In fact she would often use this very term to a girl whose state particularly pleased her, saying, 'My dear, your mound has such a pretty cockscomb,' which might make the girl flush crimson in her shame. If this should happen, then she would have the girl hold a looking-glass between her legs and watch herself in reflection, as Ildren's fingers flicked her cockscomb from side to side to demonstrate her point.

'See,' she would declare with satisfaction. 'Your cockscomb flips from side to side, just like the real thing – when the cock gets quite excited . . .' Usually the girl would shut her eyes from embarrassment, and Ildren might tolerate this for a while, since she was by now full to bursting point with love and genuine affection. 'I wonder if *your* little cock is equally excited . . .?' she would add very rudely, just to make the girl's eyes shut even tighter. In truth, Ildren really would not want to investigate that point yet, at so premature a stage, for of course the lips would still be in their first state; although by now, in some girls, they might look as if they were polished.

The second state – what was that and how was it achieved? In part it puzzled Ildren. She did not know quite how it was effected: for example, she might have been playing with a girl for a very long time, or sometimes merely briefly, and then quite suddenly the change would strike; the girl's breathing would seem shallow, and tiny straining movements would ripple her belly and curl her toes. Her eyelids might appear heavy; her lips would then feel warm and damp and very, very floppy, so much so that Ildren would have no difficulty in curling them round her finger.

She would know then that the time was ripe to have the girl turn over.

The massaging of the lips was in fact a very useful preliminary; it would help a girl accustom herself to things like this, which to some girls might prove, if not offensive, then certainly unfamiliar, although Ildren had found that the boys had little difficulty with what she now proposed to do.

46

And it was true that some of them really got to like it, so much so that Ildren, when dealing with the boys, would routinely don an apron to cope with the emissions. The girls, in her experience, were generally far less enthusiastic, which to Ildren seemed a pity, since she preferred, by far, to do it to the girls because it gave her so much greater pleasure.

When a girl was esconced on Ildren's lap and in this bottom-up position, Ildren would find it necessary to make some preliminary adjustments which, in Ildren's view, might help the girl enjoy it. The most important thing would be for the girl to spread apart her legs as far as was convenient, so her mound would press against Ildren's thigh, and Ildren, reaching underneath, could ease apart those flaccid lips and thus expose the cockstem, which she had yet to see; holding her breath, she might allow herself one tiny touch, which in its turn might make the girl briefly lift her hips and gasp in promise of great delectations which her Taskmistress might yet choose to license. For the present, Ildren would secure for her some gentle stimulation by keeping apart the girl's soft lips whilst her fleshcock brushed against the velvet.

'You may move your hips and brush your cock against me – but only when my finger strokes around and in your bottom,' was how she liked to put it, because she knew that would embarrass the girl.

However, before the Taskmistress would begin to touch the girl in that very private place, she would first of all place a cushion underneath the girl's head – not, as some girls seemed to think, so that they might bury their faces and hide themselves from their disgrace, but rather – so that they might layone cheek against it and face towards Ildren, who could thereby watch the girl as she proceeded to touch her. Possibly Ildren might catch the girl's eye in the midst of some very intimate procedure, or she might talk to her, or have the girl explain to Ildren exactly what it felt like, or alternatively she might make the girl express in words precisely what Ildren was doing to her. This de-lightful game could bring Ildren very great joy; if, in her

47

explanation, a girl should be forced to use a word which was especially rude, then Ildren would feel once more that invisible hand between her legs close strongly about her person.

The Taskmistress would be quite insistent about one more preparation for this venture, namely that the girl should spread her bottom cheeks with her very own hands. This was in point of fact a most necessary procedure, since not only did it present her bottom in the framework of subjection, but also it provided the tension in which the pleasure would be rooted, whilst leaving Ildren's hands quite free to administer the delight. A few girls, it was true, would refuse co-operation in this crucial matter, in which event the Taskmistress would not argue; but neither would she give in to an insubordinate slave. With very good grace, she would simply suspend the game and say:

'You are not to blame, my child. Your training is remiss,' and she would commence immediately a course of appropriate correction, in the first instance by means of the equipment that was kept within her apartments. In due course, however long it took, the slave would then be ready to resume the game at the precise point where a halt had first been called. But Ildren never would chastise such a slave by saying, for example: 'If you'd seen sense, we could have got this over days ago.' No – that would be quite inappropriate and very unfair. She would instead say: 'This time, my dear, I feel *sure* that you'll enjoy it,' which was a far more optimistic way of looking at things. And the Taskmistress was always very optimistic, where slaves were concerned.

She liked to match the finger used to the size of the woman's anus, so that after that first upward stroke within the groove, which commonly would make the woman close her eyes, she could hold the fingerpad against it, covering it precisely, while she made the woman open her eyes and she questioned her. Ildren would always try to keep her face expressionless during this dialogue of delight, so the slave could never tell in advance when the next stroke would come; frequently, the stroking bore very little relation to any spoken words, since Ildren would be using it simply to make the woman's face infuse with pink. The Taskmistress also liked to vary her technique, by scratching lightly across the tightened rim with her fingernail, or sometimes smacking her finger very sharply in the centre. This latter treatment gave Ildren almost as much pleasure as it did the slave. She would insist, furthermore, that a girl should keep her mouth wide open at any time when Ildren cared to push a finger into her; she could close again only when the finger was removed. It was Ildren's rule for this particular game; it meant the girl acknowledged that she was being penetrated in this very intimate way.

Ildren had devised many such rules for various occasions; some more formal, others mainly designed to enhance their lordships' pleasure. Their lordships would frequently allow the slaves to flout her rules, believing that they were perhaps unnecessary, or too restricting, but in fact almost every one of Ildren's rules was there for a very definite purpose. Only one or two existed solely for Ildren's private amusement. Their lordships did not seem to understand that, where rules were absent, then slaves could not exist; without Ildren there to keep Lidir strong, their lordships' weaknesses would in time secure their own demise. In that sense, the Taskmistress was Lidir's saviour – even the Prince relied on her support. She was his strength – alone, he was too weak-hearted, too readily influenced by those lords around him who were as soft as he was, too easily beguiled by beautiful slaves.

Sometimes, Ildren would require that a slave take a more active part, by squeezing with her anus. 'Squeeze my fingertip very tightly,' she would instruct the girl in such a case. 'And brush yourself against me.' Once more, Ildren would use one hand to hold the lips apart, so the woman's tiny nub of flesh could sink into the velvet, to be tickled by a thousand tiny hairs which would prick themselves against it. And when at length the girl would move her hips and simultaneously squeeze against her finger, then Ildren would feel drenched in luscious waves of pleasure; her joy would know no bounds at having made that girl display

49

herself so lewdly, and take her pleasure in so delectable a way. She would love to test that strength of gloving round about her finger, by pulling very firmly, until that tightened bottom mouth would grip her in its cup of flesh which, in its unsheathing, as she pulled again, would contract and send a quaking shock of pleasure up inside the girl, and indirectly, up through Ildren.

'Tell me,' she would ask the girl, whose eyes would be pools of liquid darkness, 'has anybody pleasured you in quite so sweet a way?' A girl could hardly ever bring herself to answer, and Ildren would not force her, preferring rather to repeat that pleasuring and take delight from the way the girl's open sex would move against her thigh. Ildren might then feel urged to stroke that sweet girl's belly; her hand would slip more deeply underneath the woman's mound, so her fingertips could tickle across the skin above her curly bush. While this tenderness continued, Ildren's other hand would spread once more those soft and fleshy lips, and hold them thus, apart, so Ildren's wrist could kiss repeatedly against the woman's burning openness, and Ildren's skin could, by this kissing, come to know that woman's heat. Ildren would withdraw her wrist, wet with female nectar, and ensuring that the girl was watching, would close her eyes and breathe that scent, then lick it from her skin. The woman's musk might drive her wild, and fill her with a desire so strong that she would lose control; she would penetrate the woman with her fingers and open out her sex, crying, 'Submit your body to your Taskmistress.' She would work her fingers deeper, as the slave would spread her thighs ever wider as a sign of self abasement. Ildren would take slow deep breaths and then regain composure, and stroke the woman gently on the cheeks as her fingertips withdrew.

What happened next depended not so much on Ildren's moods or sudden compulsive cravings, as on what she might have planned for this occasion. She was well aware that deep inside she was, by nature, gentle, though naturally her mask of duty might often seem quite stern; yet within the Taskmistress lay a certain quality of *mischief*,

50

which on occasion might be permitted to add some interest to the evening, provided it was kept more-or-less in bounds. For instance, if Ildren had decided that a girl should achieve that ultimate release of pleasurable satisfaction (which frequently, she withheld), she might set about it in the following way. The girl, assuming she was on Ildren's lap, might be made to stand and face the Taskmistress, whilst Ildren, still seated on the couch, would carefully instruct her:

'Place your feet apart and push your belly outwards. Now, use a finger of each hand to hold apart your love lips.' The girl would next feel even more embarrassed.

'Use your thumbs to pull back the hood; make your fleshy tongue peep out.' The girl might now be shaking.

'Ask me now to milk you with my fingers, till you die of shame or pleasure.' And Ildren would be most insistent that the girl repeat every critical word.

'Now, do not take your eyes from mine, that in them I may gauge the swelling of your pleasure, so I may prolong it, thereby making your coming sweeter.'

Ildren would milk the girl very, very slowly, and she at times would pause as she had promised, when the girl had reached the brink, to make the pleasure wane, and then gently coax her back again in the direction of delight. She might make the girl behave with more abandon, by having her open her mouth and push her tongue out very far and roll her hips about the point where Ildren's fingers pressed around her nubbin. And Ildren might have the girl squeeze her other lips repeatedly about that stiffly poking tongue, saying:

'Pretend it is a man's part. Show your Taskmistress how you would work your lips around that fleshy stem.' Each squeeze the girl would press about her tongue would then be mirrored in another squeeze that Ildren gave her flesh nub.

The Taskmistress's purpose in all these games was really very simple – she wanted to train the slaves to ways of wanton lewdness, with which the slaves, in turn, could bring delight upon their lordships, and thereby their lordships' pleasuring would be enhanced. It was also true that Ildren really quite enjoyed it. She took pleasure in her work. And her pleasure was most acute when Ildren felt a woman deliver herself to long-awaited wantonness upon Ildren's fingers, or sweeter yet, upon the tip of Ildren's tongue.

The Taskmistress would love the girl to tell her stories throughout this prolonged and dripping pleasuring, tales of fleshy acts or intimate games, exotic ways of love or lust of which the girl had of late partaken. She would ask her how the lords, or ladies, liked to have her pleasure them, and what they liked to do to her in turn – in what stance, with other slaves, or by herself and using what equipment? Ildren would require a very detailed account of every one of these procedures, for she might hear of one which might captivate her fancy. In this case, she would question the girl with even greater intimacy, having her clarify certain aspects which might have been ill-defined, or if such were feasible, Ildren might instruct the girl to demonstrate, perhaps on her person, precisely what it was she meant. She would determine from the girl which games or methods had given her most delight; the girl would be required to explain exactly what she'd felt and why she had enjoyed that particular delectation. And all the time, Ildren would be squeezing at her nubbin, or merely tickling at the end. If a girl should find a topic perhaps too embarrassing to discuss, Ildren would have a way of dealing with such an unfortunate eventuality. She would make the woman bow her legs and rub herself against Ildren's finger, whilst she justified to Ildren why it was she found this fascinating subject so very, very shameful.

The value of this exercise was twofold – the girl would get to know that pleasure was associated with lasciviousness of tongue, and Ildren would get to know many of their lordshipss' little secrets.

Some girls, Ildren had found, could be made to bring about their pleasurable release by their own contractions, accompanied by the repetition of key words or phrases which Ildren might previously have elicited, while Ildren merely held their swollen flesh bud very still between her fingers. She would encourage such a girl to make quite lewd ejaculations, saying:

'How your nubbin loves that shameful word! Now say it very rudely!' or perhaps, 'Tell me what she did to you – keep saying where she pushed it . . .' or some such turn of phrase as that. At times, the Taskmistress might feel faint before the girl did.

Alternatively, it might happen at some critical point, when Ildren's hand was playing with that sweet and oily pinkened nub of sensual gratification, that a knock might come at Ildren's door, and some lord or lady enter; in fact, it would be planned that way as part of Ildren's little game. The girl probably would gasp and try to hide her shame in simple reflex action, which, however understandable, would of course be quite wrong, and would reflect some fundamental defect in her training. In turn, this would re-quire corrective action, to condition the slave to total lack of inhibition, where her (and Ildren's) pleasure was con-cerned.

Ildren would enquire of the lord or lady where he or she would prefer the slave positioned. His lordship might well defer to Ildren, on so technical a matter. The Taskmistress, commonly, would have the slave lie back upon the table in order to afford his lordship a more comfortable view. The slave would then be required to pleasure herself and with the very minimum of direction, but such pleasuring would necessarily incorporate certain features pre-ordained by Il-dren.

The slave would have to keep her legs quite straight at first, and pointed up and outwards; she should open out her sex using the two middle fingers of each hand, so his lordship, if he so cared, might look inside her body, and then, pulling back the hooding of her flesh by means of her thumbs, she should thus expose her nubbin; she should stay in that position until his lordship, who might on im-pulse delve a tentative finger through the entrance to her sex, might then instruct her to proceed.

Her pleasuring should be administered by her forefingers,

which should cross and stroke her nubbin from each side. At all times, her middle fingers should keep her body open; her sex should never be allowed to close. During her working, she should move her hips very slowly and breathe only through her mouth; she should work herself to the very edge of pleasurable excitement, then beg her lord to allow her release, which would certainly be denied, whereupon the slave would have to work her pleasure button that much harder, not stopping until by her lord's explicit request, during this working, the slave must under no circumstances suffer accidental release. If a slave should find her pleasure very difficult to control, so that, clearly she was gasping at a very early stage, then Ildren might temporarily intercede and pinch the slave's nubbin very sharply with her fingers, which would allow her sufficient respite for pleasuring to continue until her lord at last felt able to allow the slave her satisfaction.

As a rule, her lord would wish to execute her pleasure with his own finger. The slave would be required to develop her flush nub very fully while her lord would slowly stroke her, at a constant pace, until she came. Ildren would hold the slave's head, but this time she would not be looking directly into the slave's eyes, for Ildren would be checking; the girl must take her pleasure silently, and with the minimum of fuss; certainly no contraction should tighten her belly, and no quiver should disturb her breasts; her legs should stay unmoving, her toes quite straight; her breathing should remain at all times fully under her control; no flicker should tremble in her eyelids; her nostils must not flare. That woman's deliverance to the altar of desire should be marked, at most, by the merest whisper, a faint, delicious, yet barely perceptible shimmer of her person, as Ildren's tongue, after drawing slowly back and forth across the woman's fully opened lips, was pushed inside to fill the woman's mouth and thereby form the trigger of her desire.

When this was done, then Ildren would be filled with love; his lordship would be, of course, redundant. The Taskmistress would be rid of him as quickly as she could. She would stroke the woman's forehead very gently, and then address the lord.

'This poor girl is exhausted now,' she would say. 'She has given her all, to bring pleasure to your lordship.'

Upon that point, his lordship would certainly agree.

'Her training has been long and hard this night; we hope that in some way, our simple efforts pleased you.'

His lordship would then heap thanks upon the women, especially upon Ildren, for taking so much trouble just to satisfy his wants.

'I thank your lordship, most humbly, for your kind remarks and gentle consideration. The slave shall, in due course, show her gratitude in kind . . .'

His eyes would light, and Ildren, with a deferential arm, would lead his lordship in the direction of the door, then whisper in a tone of confidentiality: 'Perhaps her training could be extended in ... er ... some particular ...' She would not need to find the word; her meaning was quite lucid; his lordship's eyes would widen in delighted anticipation. 'We would discuss the details, perhaps, in private ... possibly tomorrow ...' she would add as she closed the door behind him, leaving his lordship to his idle dreaming and, as chance would have it, leaving Ildren to the girl.

And whilst the girl slept peacefully, in Ildren's bed or upon her couch, with Ildren's furs to keep her warm, the Taskmistress would plan the means whereby, close upon her awakening, the girl should be delighted further. However, Ildren never would disturb the slave in slumber, even if she slept till dawn, for Ildren's joy would be the greater for her waiting, her plan of action would be that much more precise, and Ildren loved to hear those heartfelt cries of girlish pleasure rise to greet the dawn – that is, if Ildren did not decide to gag her.

The Taskmistress had many little devices garnered about her apartments – aids to pleasuring for the slaves and masters, and, it was certainly true, for Ildren also, who, despite so many of their lordships' fond beliefs, was herself by no means averse to the delights of physical pleasure. It was merely that Ildren preferred to take it slowly, with due consideration, not like their lordships, whose cry was always, 'Instant satisfaction!' In truth, Ildren held these silly creatures far lower in esteem than she held the slaves, who supposedly were beneath everyone. She knew that the slaves, unlike their masters, could always learn new ways and that their lowliness of station was not of their own choosing; she could respect the slaves even as she was bound by duty to tame them to her will. She loved the slaves. She loved to bend them to her pleasure, even more than she loved simply to play with them.

Ildren would spend long hours, well into the night, in sifting through her storehouse. She loved to touch those things, those harnesses and chains, those masks and gags, those moulded, polished lengths of wood and intricately carved bone, those tiny tongues of softened leather, feathers, rabbit's tails, and metal clamps, those knotted cords, and little balls-and-chains, those phials of strangely smelling oils and salves, with mysterious sensual properties, those angled mirrors, spoons and brushes, and very tiny scissors.

One of Ildren's favourite toys was carved, from pure white marble, into an arching curve like a man's erect appendage, though simplified in form and possibly marginally smaller. She liked to heft it in her hand, her palm curved round the tight-curved double bag, to feel the way in which the polished stem expanded smoothly upwards to a plum, then tapered to a rounded point, so that when Ildren closed her fingers round the stem, it felt tight – and when she pulled against the bag, the stem would not slide out. She loved to slip into bed beside the slave and introduce this tapered stem into the woman's body, as a precursor to their early morning lovemaking.

But Ildren's favourite toy of all was one which Ildren liked to use upon herself. It came in two parts, the first of which was a golden chain, secured round Ildren's waistline. The critical part, however, was a polished pear-shaped pendulum of gold which dangled from a second chain. This golden fruit was for insertion into Ildren's sex, or sometimes, depending on her mood, Ildren's anus. This insertion would normally be performed by Ildren herself in the night, while she was in the midst of sorting through her things, as a preliminary to any lovemaking which might involve equipment. She preferred to use a mirror, so she could watch the way her body spread to take the golden pear. Its shape was quite important. It meant that Ildren could contract repeatedly against it without it slipping out. If in time, she chose to have it taken out, then this could certainly be done with comparative ease, by means of the integral chain. Ildren might care to leave the latter dangling, so its coolness would brush against her inner thighs and constantly remind her of its presence; alternatively, items could be attached to it, or Ildren could, in rare instances, allow her body to be chained to stationary objects in this peculiarly intimate way whilst a favourite slave was permitted to pleasure her. Quite commonly, however, the chain would simply be looped upwards, with Ildren's fleshy lips around it, and fastened to the chain round Ildren's waist, so that each contraction of Ildren's sex would draw the chain up tight against her nubbin.

She would try to wear the golden pear at all times when she worked a woman with the aid of her equipment. It gave her so much greater pleasure to feel it move within herself at some critical juncture – at the height of a woman's pleasure, perhaps, or possibly when Ildren, having worked the woman to the precipice of delight, would at the very last second decide instead to turn the woman back. Ildren loved to have a woman enjoy herself repeatedly, in this way – especially a woman who, to some misguided eyes, might be considered more beautiful than Ildren. The Taskmistress had two *special* devices on which she preferred such a woman to be disported. She loved to bend a particularly beautiful body to the Horse, or more exquisite still, she loved to have that body mould its inner self about the Rod, so she could simultaneously love and work that body in its secret moulding – that the slave's training thereby be advanced, as her duty so required of Ildren.

5

A Punishment Ladled Out

Anya had to help Marella down the steep flight of steps, through the overburdened suicidal servants who kept rushing up and down between the kitchens and the banquet. The smell of fresh-baked bread greeted the women as they passed the bakehouse; then they were enveloped by the mouth-watering aromas which drifted through the entrance to the kitchen.

'Marella! – What have you brought me? Not another wench with thoughts above her station?' The short and fiery woman frowned and prodded Anya's ribs with the handle of her ladle, making her jerk away in fright.

Marella laughed. 'Cook – don't be so rude! Anya is a guest tonight; she isn't here on duty. So feed her well and be very kind to her, for she is feeling very lonely.' And she looked at Anya and then at the cook. 'This is her first night at the castle,' she added.

'Ah – fresh and tender,' said the cook. 'But not for long, I'll be bound. You'll soon be sporting airs and graces, like the rest ... Yes,' the cook went on, though Anya shook her head, 'you will – and then you'll get sent to me. And when that happens ...' she puffed her chest out, 'mark my words, my girl – I'll knock you down to size.' The woman shook the ladle in front of Anya's face, and by now seemed quite excited. Anya could not understand what was making her so irate. 'That's the trouble with them upstairs – their *lordships* ...' She jerked her head back contemptuously, which made Marella frown. '... No, it's true Marella, they let the bondslaves get away with it, and then Cook must sort them out. I'm here to run these kitchens, you know, not to chastise wayward hussies!'

'Calm down, calm down,' Marella said. 'You only need to feed her. And anyhow, the slaves are sent to help you, as their duty. Their punishment . . .' and then she lowered her voice as if she'd said too much in front of Anya, 'lies in our domain. . . . But Anya shall not need it,' she added, as reassurance.

'Ha! So you tell me *now*, Marella.' The cook moved very close to Anya and stared up into her face, as if trying to read the future in that innocent expression. 'But take this as a warning now – if you, my girl, should present yourself in my kitchen, for correction or chastisement, then it's *that* for you – before you start your duties,' and she pointed to the corner. From the tone of the woman's voice, Anya knew it had to be bad, whatever it was.

It seemed to be a trestle, a support from below a large table perhaps, just a single thick oak bar attached at each end to a triangular arrangement of poles. The bar was padded. Anya wondered why. 'The Horse,' the cook said ominously, and Anya then knew. It made her shrink back, but Marella put her arm protectively around her.

'Stop frightening the girl,' she said. 'She's done nothing wrong, have you Anya?' Anya felt like crying now. 'And when are you going to feed her? This girl has had nothing to eat since she set foot here in the castle – and probably nothing to eat all day.'

That seemed to be the magic spell, the key to the woman's heart. The cook was suddenly transformed into a completely different person.

'Why, they've been starving you, my dear. How could you do it, Marella? You should have brought her to me straight away, and never mind the banquet! Those greedy gluttons there upstairs, they don't know when to stop, why they . . .'

'Yes, all right Cook, I know,' said Marella. 'You've told me . . . many times before. So I'll leave Anya with you for now.' Oh no, Anya thought, and she was very apprehensive; this woman seemed unbalanced. 'You'll take good care of her?'

'Of course I will, won't I dear?' Cook said, yet Anya was not reassured.

* * *

Anya sat alone to eat, away from the steam and clamour of the cooking, and the heat of the five great fires, at the far end of a very long table. A steaming bowl of soup was brought by a kitchen boy, who eyed her shyly and did not speak at first; he waited beside her and nervously fingered his apron, until Anya relented and tasted the soup.

'Mmm – good,' she said. It was; it tasted rich and aromatic, though she could not decide what was in it. The boy perked up and smiled.

'Would you like some bread?' he asked. He was admiring Anya's breasts, she knew, for her cloak had fallen open, and yet his glance was innocent and frank, not evil like the guard's had been. For once, she did not feel vulnerable; she found she could relax and smile back.

'Mmm – yes please.'

The bread was hot and crisp outside and soft and warm within; it tasted yeasty, just fresh-baked, not hard and sandy like the bread to which she was accustomed.

'I made the bread myself,' he said and intertwined his fingers.

'It's very good; I'd even say it's the best I've ever tasted.' Her compliment turned him red, and now he wouldn't look at her.

'Oh, I forgot your beer,' he said and suddenly was gone. Anya smiled because she knew he was only escaping from his embarrassment.

Though most of the banquet fare had been prepared and shipped up from the kitchens, there was still much activity, with servants bringing trays or plates of left-overs, and re-filling jugs of wine, and others cleaning out the pots and stoking up the fires. Anya noticed that everyone allowed the cook a very wide berth, as if they did not trust her. She had started shouting now, at the far end of the kitchen, and was trying to club a servant with her ladle, though whether he had been guilty of any wrongdoing, Anya could not tell. She felt sure the cook was demented. So when the woman finally approached her, Anya felt like hiding underneath the table.

'Is everything to your satisfaction?' the cook asked very

60

quietly, surprising Anya, who had been expecting her to shout.

'Yes – I really liked your soup,' she said, which was true, although Anya might well have said it anyway, for the cook still clutched the ladle.

The woman smiled, then just as quickly frowned ar.d shouted, 'Didn't he bring you beer? The little – I'll box his ears!'

'No – he asked – I didn't want it,' Anya interrupted. 'Unless you had brewed it, that is ...' she risked, very diplomatically.

'You know what you like,' the cook said. 'I like a girl with spirit. Perhaps I misjudged you earlier.' She turned her head to one side to look at Anya. 'You're not the same, you know – not selfish, like the others.' The compliment surprised and flattered Anya, coming as it did from a woman she had thought demented.

Loud scuffling sounds and muffled sobs made Anya turn her head to see a grey guard dragging two bondslaves down the steps into the kitchen. They were a male, and a female; each was nude and wore golden chains like Anya's; they looked a very sorry pair. Anya's heart reached out to them; it seemed she saw in them her own innocence and her helplessness personified, as if they were a mirror of her inner self, as if the hopelessness of her situation were now made clear to her for the very first time by the state of their dejection.

'Aha!' The cook looked gleeful now. 'See what I mean – two jumped-up friends of yours.'

'But –' Anya tried to protest. Yet in her soul she knew the woman was correct; for she would gladly draw these poor defenceless creatures to her bosom if she could, though she had never even met them; she loved them in their simple fragile state; she neither knew nor cared about the nature of their transgression.

The cook was quite oblivious to anything but the two bondslaves; her eyes seemed set to fiery points and she was slapping the ladle against her palm as if she meant to use it. 'What's this, guard? More idleness for Cook to deal with? And one of each, I see . . . Good! We'll have the one chastise the other. They shall earn their punishment for a change,' she said with satisfaction, '. . . instead of sitting back and letting others do the work, you idle good-for-nothing wasters.' The bondslaves prostrated themselves upon the floor while she heaped abuse upon them, until at last her cheeks had turned a very deep shade of purple.

'They've misbehaved – they disobeyed an order,' the guard explained. 'They would not entertain their lordships by –' he changed his mind, 'in the way that was requested.' At this the bond-girl burst into tears and the young man hung his head. 'So the Prince instructs that they be assigned to yourself for a period of one week.' He seemed to hesitate as if trying to remember his directives. 'To help you with the kitchen tasks, howsoever menial they may be . . .' his brow furrowed in concentration, '. . . and that thereby they may learn their lesson – not to disobey.' The guard seemed relieved that he had managed this speech.

'A *week*?' the cook screamed. 'Am I then to have these layabouts under my feet for a *week*?' Anya thought Cook might now explode.

'Those are my orders ma'am,' the guard announced quite curtly.

'Right! You two – you'll learn a lesson which you won't forget in a hurry!' Then suddenly she stopped, took two deep breaths and closed her eyes and swayed. When she opened her eyes again, her voice was very much quieter. 'Guard – you'll have a mug of beer with us, for your trouble?' she smiled. How could anyone change mood so quickly, Anya wondered? This woman surely could not be normal.

The guard had noticed Anya; he was eyeing her with a sidelong look.

'Why, thank you ma'am,' he said, and pulling a chair up, sat by Anya.

Anya now felt very uncomfortable indeed, with the guard sitting very close beside her, and Cook still on the loose. True, this guard did not smell like the one on the stairs had, yet he still seemed coarse and lecherous. She hoped Marella would come to collect her soon, for if she were forced to stay much longer, then she feared that Cook might turn on her, regardless of her promise.

'Bring the Horse over here,' the cook instructed the servants, 'so our guest may witness their chastening.' The bondslaves flinched in unison at the mention of that contraption; it was clear to Anya that they must be well acquainted with it as a punishment; either they had been sent here for discipline on previous occasions, or such devices were to be found elsewhere in the castle. Whatever the reason, it gave Anya cause for great concern, for it indicated that such punishment was not in truth the rarity that Marella had implied.

'Now' the Cook pointed at the man, then at the woman, both of whom still crouched upon the floor. 'Which of you shall take your measure first?' The two looked down, and the girl began to sob very quietly, which only made Cook even more determined. 'Well – who is it to be?' And she prodded each of them in turn with the handle of her ladle, until at last the girl started shaking, sending ripples through the long blonde curls that spread about her shoulders, and tender shivers through the underbelly of her breasts. Anya wanted to reach to stroke her hair, to reassure her, to take the poor girl's hand in hers, as Marella had done with Anya, to calm her fears, to show her that she had a friend who really cared. And yet she was too afraid to make any move which might incur the cook's displeasure.

The man then rose without a word and stood before the cook; his head was bowed and his wrists were crossed before him, in what Anya took to be a formal gesture of submission. How brave, she thought, to sacrifice himself to save the girl, if only for a while; to shield her from her inner fears, when perhaps he did not even know her, when probably they had been thrown together by the vagaries of fate and forced against their will to engage in the most intimate of couplings, as entertainment for the entire assembly of banqueters. And if Anya were made to do such

63

things, she knew that she would die first, of shame and degradation. Yes, even with a young man such as this, whose body seemed so firm and muscular, with smooth bronzed skin which looked like it was polished, whose dark brown hair was matched in darkness by his eyes, whose gentle chest curls thinned down to his belly, then thickened again to blackness down below his folden chain towards his ... No, not that way, even with this man, who was beautiful in soul, a man who gave *himself* to save a woman, a man so utterly different from the one that Anya had known, and come to hate, her erstwhile husband – if indeed he could be termed a man at all. But in private – yes, that might be admissible; she could if needs be give herself to a real man like this one, whose strength was tempered with inner beauty and gentleness of nature ...

'Good!' Cook said. 'I like a man with spirit.' This turn of phrase, heard once again, but in this very different context, made Anya wonder how she could be safe at all beneath this woman's fickle wings.

The guard now made a move; his hand stretched out across the table top to try to open Anya's cloak, which she had held tight closed against just such an unwelcome advance. Cook spotted him and rapped him sharply on the knuckles with the spoon end of her ladle. 'Finish your drink now, and be off with you, or the Captain shall hear of this. This girl is under my protection.'

Anya was thankful for this timely intercession; perhaps she might have misjudged Cook after all. The guard grunted some complaint and then left quietly, after one long withering look at Anya. It made her hope that she would never have the misfortune to cross his path again.

Cook turned to the man. 'Now, would you care to mount the Horse, so we may see what you are made of?' she asked in a very police voice. The man still had not spoken when he stepped astride the beam. He had to use his hands to steady himself, for the height was such that his feet would not reach the floor. Although the beam was well padded, Anya knew it could not be comfortable with all his weight concentrated in that single spot at the joining

64

of his thighs. She imagined herself spread like this astride the Horse; it made her belly sink at first with fear and then with a tiny wave of excitement. She opened her thighs very slightly, to focus her weight more clearly in that self-same spot and let the plank on which she sat press more firmly up against her saddle.

His roll of flesh was visible; it looked full and heavy, lolling to the side. It had a strange effect on Anya – she had never before thought of *that* part of a man as in any way desirable; yet somehow on *this* man, it seemed so very different. She could not understand her feelings – why her heart was in her throat; was it fear she felt for him, or was it something else? She wanted to protect him – that was it – to gather his lolling vulnerability in her palms, to cup it and to stroke it, like she would a nervous crippled bird. And though she was fearful of what might happen to this gentle bird, this dove of her desire, yet she could not move to help him, and now she dared not even blink, as if convinced her gaze was his sole protection.

'Here girl – tie his hands back; you might as well begin.' The bond-girl was still shaking as she took the thongs, though her sobbing had died down. The young man helped her by placing his hands behind him; his wrists stretched back beyond the end of the beam to where an iron ring was fastened to its underside. Anya had not noticed this before, but now she saw that rings were anchored to the Horse in several strategic places, both below the beam and on its supports. The girl secured him quickly to the ring, and Anya's heart sank at that, for then she knew that to these slaves the Horse was indeed a quite familiar instrument of discipline.

His back was arched now; his muscles were placed in tension. The flickering torchlight played upon his skin, which seemed to ripple with his breathing; his gold chain caught the light and, once more, Anya experienced that peculiar feeling. In a sudden flash of wanting, she saw herself stretched out along the Horse, its padded beam pressed firmly to her back and hips, while he, poised above her lowered himself very gently, kissing her with his deep brown eyes, until at last she felt his dangling gold chain brushing first against her skin then sinking into her belly in that precious moment of sweet anticipation before his weighted rod of flesh would touch and push and split her, and her burning oil would spill to drown him in the heat of her desire . . .

Yes, she felt that she could willingly open her heart and body to a man like this one.

Then Anya experienced a very great surprise, which shattered the illusion of her dreaming. The girl, of late so cowed and mindful of her fate, now stretched up to her full height. She seemed suddenly ennobled, as if the simple act of tying bonds around the man had freed her from the thrall of fear and steeled her in her purpose. Her hair hung down to bridge, almost, her curving arch of back; the heavy locks reached down and swayed above, yet did not touch, the outcurve of her bottom; fine downy hair, soft and blonde, coated her back and outer thighs and the taut skin of her buttocks, like a hazy mist upon which a lover's tongue might browse in sensual delectation. Her belly curve was smooth and round and her nipples pointed upwards; no freckles broke the flawlessness of this perfect girl's complexion. And Anya knew, although she could not see, that this woman's secret self was tight-lipped, pink and tender, and projected from her mound. She knew this from the way the woman said so – with her posture – as she stood before the man and watched him stiffen, while she pouted.

Anya suddenly wanted to test that length of hair, to pull and stretch it down until she made it bridge the gap, if it needed all her weight to force it, and even if that forcing made that perfect neck curve backwards until Anya's hand could close around that tender throat and choke it . . . for she was jealous; it seemed to her this bondslave was a rival – albeit for a man that Anya had not even met.

She bit her lip – she wondered what was happening; how could she harbour cruel thoughts like this? The girl was innocent after all, and forced to do these things against her will, and at the cook's direction. It could just as well have been Anya there before the Horse, had the circumstances differed, and then what would she think – and do, if placed in that position? Would she hate herself for looking wantonly upon his manly stirrings?

The room was quiet now, even Cook stood quite unmoving. The bondslave raised her chin and kept looking into the man's eyes, while she very slowly felt her way and climbed astride the beam. The two sat facing – the woman free, the man's hands tied behind his back, his stem erect. Her hair was hanging down in front; her nipples peeped between the strands, as if inviting him to kiss them, in their impudence, through the springing tickling wetness of her hair. She fixed her gaze upon him while he watched, seeing only in her mind's eye his slow insistent burgeoning of desire, as carefully, and with progressive readjustments, she spread her moist and tender clinging pinkness more closely to the beam. Anya was beside herself to witness that a woman's pleasure could be take thus – from the reflection of her own desire within her lover's eyes.

The woman gripped her thighs tightly around the beam, and placed her hands behind her, clasped together, in a mirror of his restraint, then bent forwards till her outstretched tongue could touch and lick around his nipples. The tongue next traced a line precisely down his middle, to the point at which her chin was almost resting on his thickness. She lifted briefly, wet her lips and closed them round the end, and sucked him very slowly, making prickles in the back of Anya's neck run up into her hairline, for she was imagining what it might be like if she were doing this. His taste – would it be the same upon her tongue as her own fingers, salt–savoured with her seepage at her height of silent pleasure, as she slaked her body's burning need beside the dead log of her husband?

Anya glanced round, beheld the cook, and suddenly was frightened.

Cook's face had changed from one of silent contemplation of the two; it now seemed set and grim, as if this gentle scene was not as she'd intended. Anya wanted to make some sign to warn the lovers, but their eyes were closed, their bodies touching, searching out delight – her gripping thighs, her neck outstretched, his hips pushed strongly forwards – loving lips on rigid flesh in sucking, suckling pleasure.

Cook's hand descended in a cracking slap across the woman's upturned bottom; the shocking sound of it brought everyone to their senses.

'You slaves are all the same,' she cried, 'forever bent on pleasure. But I'll soon bring you down to earth. I'll pop your bubble.' She tapped the man's upstanding sex with the handle of her ladle, while she continued to lash him with her tongue. The girl sat upright, very still. Her eyes were darting from side to side, as if searching for escape. 'That's why they send you here – to me – because they can't control you. But Cook has her ways, as you'll find out. I'll have you counting the hours until your week is up. You shan't be back *here* in such a hurry, that much I'll warrant.' And she whacked him even harder. 'Now you,' she hooked him in the crook of the ladle and tugged him without mercy, 'since you take such pleasure from your idle impudence, shall stay like this for the time you're here, only I'll see to it you're bigger. Your flesh shall never feel respite, or loll or angle idly, for you shall remain always at attention.' Then she slid the crook down his length and pressed the skin back to the root, until the end looked tight and polished. 'And you shall be drawn off thrice per day – at morning, noon and evening – and also at such other times as my servant girls direct; except, that is, for tonight, when the drawings shall continue by the hour until such time as your well flows drily three times in succession.'

The cook seemed calmer now. The man was shaking visibly, although Anya noticed, his stiffness stood undaunted by the woman's threats; in fact it now seemed thicker. 'And should your flesh unsinew . . .' Cook tugged his stem again. 'Well . . . we'll leave that much unsaid for now. But there are many ways to charm a snake against his will, as I'm sure you can imagine.'

Now Anya was very concerned indeed at what she'd heard; her mind was racing. For if the man was treated thus, how might they use the woman? How would they ensure that she was kept always *at attention*? And on those occasions, thrice per day, how might they *draw her off*? What cruel and public display of lust would she be made to suffer in subjection? And at whose hands? The servants', women's or worse yet, the men's – or worst of all, her own while all were gathered round to watch her? And where might this abasement happen – at the Horse or on the table? So many fearful questions, so much potential for shame; no wonder that the girl upon the Horse now looked really very worried. Anya hoped that Marella would come very soon to save her from the chance of any such kitchen duties.

But the cook still had not finished. 'This girl now shall work your cock until it swells to bursting, but be warned, do not let it burst until I so permit it.' She turned to the girl and shook the ladle until the girl shrank back in fear of being hit. 'Now work him till I call a halt, and do not stop before that – but first, restrain his ankles.' She made the bond-girl tie back each ankle to the ring which held his wrists, so his body bowed forwards and rotated to focus his weight more firmly through his root zone, as doubtless the cook intended that it should. The pressure in that tender area made the veins in his stem stand out. The girl checked his bonds for tightness, then resumed her place astride the Horse, and once more readjusted her position; she spread her flesh upon it with her fingers, then closed her eyes and slowly rocked into position. And with each rock, her pleasure nub must surely have pressed against the padding. Anya wondered if the cook had let this pass, or perhaps she had not understood the significance of the bondslave's gentle swaying movement. The girl opened her eyes and reached for him, but the rocking still continued – her fingertips pushed beneath his stem to tease his bag from underneath, and spread it to the sides. Then she worked him, with her fingers, as instructed.

She did not kiss his lips or lick around his nipples, or stroke his belly with her tongue-tip; neither did she close her lips around his end nor suck his ballocks gently. No tenderness, no loving touch, was shown on this occasion.

Instead, she used her finger and her thumb to pinch him shut and stretch him while she flicked him with a fingernail, working slowly upwards from the base, and only on the underside, until at last her snapping finger reached his plum. She kept flicking him in that single spot, until his skin had stretched so tight his plum turned livid purple, and the only sounds within the room were his laboured breaths and the rhythmic snaps which echoed from the ceiling. The finger flicked back down towards the bottom of the stem and hesitated, then flicked again, continuously in his root zone. Her other hand released its squeeze then pushed his cock tip back until it touched against his belly. The cockstem now seemed longer in its arching, as if the bond-girl had in some way drawn that extra length from deep within his body, perchance for her inspection and further ministration.

The flicking then resumed, again precisely at the root, though on that part that formerly had lain inside him, or at least, well out of reach beneath the joining of his thighs. Cook seemed pleased so far at the way the punishment was progressing.

Anya wondered why the bond-girl had chosen this particular way to work him, why her finger snapped only against the underside of his flesh – which now, of course, lay uppermost, by virtue of his curving – and why she should have concentrated only on those spots, the root zone and the plum. She wondered also what it might be like if someone were to do this thing to her, to press and stretch her up and flick her – but softly – with a finger. It made her want to close her eyes, like the man had done, and ease apart her thighs and then to test the flicking on herself, whilst – and this was quite important – imagining the fingers were a stranger's. But she dared not close her eyes, for she was mindful of the cook, and she was interested, despite her fears, to know exactly what would happen next. Very gently, Anya pressed a finger to her mound, which stretched her flesh leaves upwards, under cover of her cloak, for she wanted to know how the man might feel, in his tension and his wanting, although she could not bring her self to touch her flesh directly, to stimulate her nubbin wantonly as the bond-girl was still doing.

The woman spread her leaves and rocked herself more vigorously against the padded beam, then clasped her hand around the man's flesh and moved it very quickly, sliding him about his inner stem; his end appeared to swell and tighten at each and every downstroke. She kept doing this until she had elicited a moan, whereupon she pressed a single collared finger round his base until his skin was stretched back tight enough to split him. His cock swayed heavily in its moorings; the tip moved very slowly in a circle. His breathing could be heard – it came in long slow indrawn breaths and rapid exhalations.

'Slap him – smack his pleasure, work his flesh more roughly,' the cook demanded, now the pace had slowed.

The woman smacked two fingers once upon its undersurface; it jerked; he groaned, and so she smacked again; then carefully she timed her smacking until she'd found his rhythm. Each jerk he made set off another smack until it almost seemed his cock was bouncing off her fingers of its own accord. Then she closed her hand around it, as if it were a bird, and as Anya had wished to do under rather different circumstances. This woman, it seemed, would kill the bird by squeezing out its life, then rolling it between her hands to stretch and shape its body. The man was gasping and straining against the rubbing of her hands, as she kept pushing his swelling tightly through her fingers. His bag was lifted by his force of thickness; his fleshy bumps gripped firmly up to the stem.

'Stop!' Cook cried. 'I shall test him.'

The bond-girl sat back away from him at a safe distance, while Cook examined him. 'Hmm . . . He's very swollen,' she said and trapped his flesh against the beam with the handle of her ladle, then pressed until a bead of fluid issued from the end. 'Tut-tut,' she said and shook her head, 'it seems your flesh is leaking . . .' and she squeezed the end again. He held his breath, and Cook was almost smiling now. Quite clearly she enjoyed taking him to task like this.

71

'You must learn to hold your saltings better yet than this – however full your bag may be.' She released her hold. His stem sprang stiffly up again.

'Good,' she said. 'Your cock is now much thicker ... though not thick enough, I fear. Now squeeze yourself; let your pumping swell your cock and draw very deep inside you – but do not spill one drop, I warn you. And do it now and do not stop until I so require you.'

Anya watched in puzzlement as his flesh stem moved unaided. The man was fastened, hand and foot, his eyes shut tight; his muscles seemed hard and knotted; the tendons in his neck stood out; his mouth was open in a silent cry. He looked as if he were harnessed to an ox-cart, the strain seemed so intense; the sweat was beaded on his face and chest and down across his belly, which tightened so the gold chain shifted. The cockstem moved again; it pulsed as if an invisible hand were squeezing it.

'Strain, my slave, and let your blood pump through it. Keep squeezing ... There, that's much better ... perhaps after all, you can respond to training. Now keep like that – very stiff and tight, and Cook shall prove your thickness.'

She held the ladle by the spoon and crooked him in the handle. His cockstem now seemed almost too large to fit, which meant she nearly had to force it. Then she worked it slowly up his length, as far as it would go before his swollen plum prevented further progress, whereupon she pushed it down again until it snuggled up against his bumps and threatened to strip them from his stem. She made him squeeze again, in rhythm with her working, only slowing when she heard him moan, but even then, not stopping.

'Hush now; enjoy it very quietly, but do not take your pleasure yet – just squeeze it very nicely.' His cock looked fit to burst now, and it suddenly started twitching; his head went back; he gulped the air, but Cook reacted very quickly. She pulled the handle off his stem and used it once again to trap his tip hard against the beam, and held it till the pulsing slowed and he gave a long deep sigh.

'Another leak!' the cook declared. 'You're very slow to

learn.' She turned to face the girl, who had remained very quiet throughout. 'I think we'll need to train him further. Would you care to baste him now, and put him to the plug?'

Anya was horrified at what she thought she'd heard. How could Cook be so cruel? After having taunted him almost to distraction, and in such a tender part, she now would have him beaten; not only that, but she would force the bond-girl to execute this very evil deed. This made Anya very angry; it seemed so wickedly unfair.

'Release his wrists, girl, and lie him down – so his buttocks are to hand. No . . . his ankles must be left secure to hold him steady for the basting.'

The man was stretched along the beam, with his cheek pressed to the padding; his wrists were retied underneath the beam, as also were his knees and elbows. It kept his body firm against the Horse and his buttocks spread apart; his fleshy stem was pointed downwards, curved against the padded end of the beam. He was exposed in a very intimate way, Anya thought; he was totally defenceless. It made Anya very sad for him, and also rather frightened, for she knew in her heart that Cook would never hesitate to do this even to a woman.

A tray was brought, upon which several items lay. The servant held it apprehensively, as if he wanted to be rid of it as quickly as possible, as if perhaps he were nervous of the contents.

'Don't give it to me, you stupid dullard,' the cook cried angrily, then looking round, she spotted Anya, who held her breath and closed her eyes, for she knew well what was coming. 'Here girl, you can earn your supper, and see him take his medicine into the bargain. Take this tray and stand just there. You can learn how idle meat is basted.'

Anya! was forced to stand behind the slave and witness his abasement. His buttocks seemed spread wide enough to split him; his stem looked heavy, thick and livid from his recent punishment. His fleshy bumps were still shrunk tightly up against him, as if held thus by his fear, which was trying to retract them. And Anya could see his secret tender tightness contract at intervals, as if the man could scarce contain himself against his inner tension. It made Anya almost want to touch him in that deep dark cleft, so she could thereby feel his strength of wanting. A strange feeling then came in Anya's belly; it made her look away, in shame for having allowed herself to dwell on such thoughts.

Her gaze fell on the contents of the tray – no whip was present – she was relieved, at least, at that. A silver jug sat on the tray and several short wooden rods of differing length and girth. These devices must be the 'plugs' to which Cook had referred. Each was carved after a similar fashion – a stem of polished wood, thick at the end and tapering downwards then flaring out again into a flattened base. Anya guessed what was in the jug; she could smell the aromatic fragrance of the oil. Her heart was beating fast in her anticipation of what she would now be compelled to witness. She looked once more at the poor slave, so open in his spreading. Even the smallest plug of wood looked large – too large for the place for which it surely was intended.

The bond-girl took the jug of oil and spread his cheeks more widely, then poured it in a long thin stream directed against the high point of his furrow. It trickled quickly down, and Anya heard him moan, then it ran on, welling down the stem and running round the rim. The woman caught the spillage as it dribbled from the end, and swept it smoothly up his length and back inside his groove, while the pouring continued unabated from the jug. Her fingers opened him and worked the oil into his body, making him moan once more, this time a long-drawn moan of deepest wanting. 'Good,' said the cook. The bond-girl held him open next while she poured the stream inside him, till at last he tightened shut against her persistent ministrations. 'No,' the cook said firmly, 'he must not be allowed to refuse your fingers access to his person. For that he shall be punished. Now, smack his cock, and work him till your fingers slip in and out quite freely.'

And then to emphasize her point, she took the woman's

hand and held it before the man's upturned face. Stretching out the first two fingers she said, 'Your body shall accept these to their full extent and without question – but first, they shall chastise you without mercy. Yet, I warn you once again, do not let your swelling flag or suffer an emission. Now kiss the hand that shall administer your correction.' The poor slave was forced against his shame to press his lips to the bond-girl's well-oiled fingers. 'Now proceed.'

The bond-girl dipped her fingers in the jug of oil and then began to slap his very rigid cock, working up and down the exposed undersurface of his length, then concentrating on the plum, using only the tips of her fingers in a rapid smacking which caused his body to jerk against his bonds, until his moan came very softly. It was clear to Anya that the girl very much enjoyed what she was doing, for she took her time. Each tiny blow upon his flesh was precisely placed for maximum effect; her other hand was used to brush a dangling fingertip very slowly down his spine. How his anguished body must be suffering, Anya thought, under such contradictory feelings; that all-pervasive delicious tickling; his pleasure drawing deep inside; those tiny intermittent bursts of pain below the cocktip of his swelling; and in the background, all the time, that aching pressure-ball of tight delight which was threatening to burst him. The smacking stopped; the woman dipped her fingers in the oil again, then placed their tips upon the spot which she had only just been slapping. She slid the fingers very slowly along his curve, up past the root, and then into his groove. The fingers caught, then hesitated; the pressure was increased until at last they slowly slid inside him, making him moan once more. The girl kept pressing until they had slipped in to the knuckle. The man's breathing seemed to come in short quick gasps; Anya wondered if the woman's fingertips were perhaps moving deep inside him. The bond-girl withdrew them very smoothly, though not smoothly enough, it seemed, for his muscle seemed reluctant to release them. The smacking had to be repeated. This time her fingers, moving up his length and past his

bumps, slid into him more easily; it appeared he was learning to control the reflex of his more intimate contractions.

Yet Cook still was not satisfied; she insisted that he
needed more correction, to the point where his maleness
next began to spasm, though somehow he managed to prevent a direct spillage. The cook seemed pleased at this.
'Now, keep very open this time, while her fingers test your
tightness.' And this time – though Anya could not guess
how he could possibly have managed it – the fingers slid
quite uninterruptedly back and forth, through his fleshy
rim. The cook was quite delighted. 'A lesson learnt well at
last – I'd say he's ready now for plugging.'

Anya waatched with mounting apprehension as the girl
checked each device in turn, then finally selected the largest
one of all. This bond-girl must be very cruel, she thought,
for any reasonable person would know that a plug so wide
as this would surely split him. The girl lifted it and
squeezed it and slowly ran her fingers down it, then tested
it for girth by trying to close her finger and thumb around
it at its widest part; she failed to make the closure, as Anya
had predicted that she would. Then Anya realised with
horror that this failure, far from making the girl reject the
plug, had instead caused a smile of satisfaction to spread
across her face – she meant to use it anyway. The bond-girl
tried to dip it in the jug; it would not fit. Instead, she had
to smear the oil upon it with her fingers. She placed the
head precisely to his rim. Holding it there, she very slowly
turned it whilst the jug was held above him, dripping oil
upon his point of contact. The pressure then increased. The
oiling continued, accompanied by the slow insistent turning, back and forth until, with a groan, he opened just
sufficiently for the plug to gain a purchase on his inner self.
The girl moved the jug downwards, and used the lip to
lever his sex away from the padded beam and into the
mouth of the jug; then she very firmly pushed the plug, by
leaning all her weight against it. His gasp came very deeply.
The plug slid slowly into him; the jug was made to swallow
his length and filled to overflowing. When the woman's
palm was lifted from his buttocks, the base of the plug was

all that could be seen, held tight against him by his strength of gripping.

Throughout this spectacle, Anya could not help but wonder whether this cruel degradation was reserved purely for the male slaves; she feared it likely that people such as this might also want to use it on the girls. If this was true, would the devices be scaled accordingly, to take account of a woman's differing dimensions, and if so, where might they be introduced – at the back, like this, or towards the front inside her sex, or – her belly quivered at the possibility – surely not in both?

'You have done well,' the cook complimented the girl. 'Now, massage his flesh quite slowly, and take him to the brink of pleasure; I shall do the rest.'

The woman gripped his well-oiled stem and worked him in slow motion; her other fingers probed about in several different places, oiling his bumps and squeezing them, then pressing at the root, tracing out his lines of tubing up towards the plug, then tapping it repeatedly in precise time with the working of his sex, until his body tightened and his stem began to jerk. The girl released him and waited till the pulsings ebbed away. She lifted his length away from him, until it lay almost horizontally backwards, then held her hand out towards Anya. Anya frowned; she had no idea what the girl could possibly mean. The girl frowned back, and pointed to the tray. Anya still did not understand what it was she wanted. At last the woman helped herself – to a second plug, which, although much narrower than the first, was certainly longer. She took it by the base, between her thumb and finger, and holding it directly over his stem she swung it down and tapped him very firmly underneath his root zone, exactly where his curving flesh and stiffened tubes reached up into his groove. Her other hand kept him stretched out horizontally, while she tapped him once more, in that self-same spot. And then, she stretched his cockskin back and held it tight against the root, while she tapped him slightly harder. His sex pulsed; she tapped him and he pulsed again; she stretched his skin back tighter; a droplet was forming at the end of his stem and slowly stretching downwards.

The bond-girl kept the male slave in this attitude of tension; his muscles were tight and shining with perspiration as he tried to fight back his burgeoning pleasure, against that persistent stretching of his skin about his stem, and the slow insistent tapping in that single spot underneath his sex. His salted liquid slowly welled; the tapping still continued; like the pumping of an extra heart it was drawing deep inside him, pulling slowly at his bursting bag of pleasure. The cook watched and waited, until at last a swaying length of glass-like liquid broke away and fell across the floor.

'It seems his idleness is ready to deliver. Quick! Sit him up, so he may feel the full benefit of the plug.'

The slave groaned as he was untied, lifted upright and his weight was concentrated in that tight-filled space. Yet the cook was still unsatisfied with this; she insisted that a length of wood be passed beneath the Horse and shackled to his ankles, to keep his legs apart and so prevent his thighs from gripping the beam and thereby relieving some of his weight, which was now entirely taken by the plug. His stem rose rigidly and the veins stood out; it looked like it might burst. His hands were fastened once again behind his back.

'You see,' the cook said cruelly, 'it will help to keep you firm by pressing from inside.' She tapped his stem, which Anya noticed was now so hard it scarcely moved at all. 'Now deliver up, my boy,' she said. 'And do not stint, for Cook requires good measure.' With that, she levered quickly underneath him with the spoon end of her ladle, so his sex was cupped inside it at the base and still projected stiffly upwards. When Cook tilted the handle of the ladle away from him in a very slow pumping action, it made him murmur very softly. Anya knew that the lip of the spoon must be pressing underneath his sex, and up against his pipework.

'Now pump and squeeze – keep pumping till you burst. Your essence must fill my ladle good and full.'

And at these words, the bondslave bit his lip and gasped and pushed his belly forwards, then cried out loud –

whether from pain or pleasure, Anya could not tell. Cook began quickly levering the ladle back and forth. His cock-stem convulsed repeatedly, as if trying to shake off the continuously bubbling stream of fluid which issued from the tip and, running down his length, at last collected in the ladle. Cook waited until the twitching died away and she was sure that all his spurts and dribblings had welled into the spoon. Then very quickly, before the man even had time to realise what was happening, she tilted back his head and pinched his nose, then tipped the ladleful down the poor man's throat; she held him until he'd swallowed every choking drop of his emissions.

Anya felt the blood draining from her face and neck. She was really very frightened. She could not understand how anyone could be so cruel as to subject a slave to that.

'Good,' Cook said. 'Your medicine is well taken – which is fortunate, for you shall need your strength again within the hour.' Then Anya was certain that this woman was a very evil one indeed.

'Right! Who's next?' Cook said grimly.

Anya had realised with shock and horror that Cook was looking directly at her now, her face set in that very pur-poseful expression.

6

A Preparation for Pleasure

Anya started trembling as the cook advanced towards her.

'And what did you think of our little display?' Cook asked her. 'Our brand of kitchen humour?'

Anya did not know what to say; she assumed it was a trick – regardless of whether she said she approved or whether she told the truth, she was certain that the cook was so deranged that she would force Anya to try it for herself. So she chose instead to keep her eyes downcast, and not to speak at all, while she waited for the cook to make a move. Her neck felt warm and clammy where her cloak was fastened round it, and the tray suddenly felt very heavy under the weight of that woman's gaze.

'Speak up! Cook has ways of dealing with a wench that's very sullen.'

Anya felt very frightened now; there was nothing she could say, or do, to get herself off the hook. And even worse, she did not dare look up, for she was fighting back the tears that welled inside her.

'Do you like Cook's Horse?' the cook persisted. 'Perhaps you'd care to . . .'

The woman was interrupted by the sound of footsteps running down the steps behind her. Anya now looked up. A bondswoman, dressed exactly like herself in a purple cloak and leather boots, walked confidently up to Cook and bending, whispered something in her ear. Anya's heart leapt to her throat – she hoped and prayed that this woman was her saviour, sent by Marella to rescue her from the cook's cruel clutches.

Cook looked at Anya while the woman spoke, and then finally she frowned.

'Well, my tongue-tied hussy; now you really are in trouble. You're wanted upstairs straight away, and you're already late for duty. So be off with you at once. Do not clutter up my kitchen a moment longer with your worthless self.'

But Anya was already on her way; she didn't need telling twice. 'And remember what's in store for you, if you show your face again – be warned!' the cook shouted angrily after them, as the woman disappeared up the stairs with Anya very close in tow. Anya certainly had no intention of ever coming here again.

The bondswoman ran at breakneck pace, so Anya's cloak flew open. 'This way,' gasped her rescuer, and led her, not the way she'd come, but to the right and through a maze of passageways, then up some winding stairs, until Anya was totally disorientated. They finally emerged onto a wide and brightly lit hallway which overlooked the darkened courtyard, and only then did they pause for breath. Anya could make out, through the swirling snow, the light spilling from the Great Hall to her left, and then in the distance, almost straight ahead, the dimly lit towers of the gatehouse where she had entered the castle. To her right, as far as the eye could see, the dark shapes of the castle buildings stretched until they merged into the vastness of the night.

'We can relax now, Anya,' the woman smiled. She had very short black hair. 'I'm Axine.' She kissed Anya on the cheek. 'Come on. I'll show you where we live.' And she took Anya by the hand again and led her down the hallway until they reached an entrance, almost like a gatehouse in scale, with two huge panelled rectangular doors covered in gold leaf. It was guarded by two enormous men who were nude apart from loincloths. Their heads were shaven and their arms were folded across their chests. They stood as still as statues. Anya was very wary of them, but Axine just ignored them; only their eyes moved to follow the woman as they entered the Bondslaves' House.

Anya was standing in the centre of a very large room – the lounge. Axine had called it – which stood on several levels, linked by marble steps and separated by intricately carved balustrades and columns, and was carpeted throughout in soft, deep red. The walls were decorated with a mural extending right round the room, showing female nudes dancing and playing in a leafy summer landscape. The room was so large and was partitioned in such a way that it did not appear crowded yet many slaves were present, some dressed in purple cloaks, like Anya's, though most were nude, and all of them wore the golden chains of bondage. They stood in laughing, chatting groups, or lay on couches, sat around tables, playing cards or sewing, or simply lay upon the floor. Anya was surprised to see that several girls were looking at books of ciphers, almost as if they might understand their meaning.

'There are no male slaves here?' Anya asked.

'Not here – the males have separate quarters. They are many fewer in number. We are not permitted to mix, except by our masters' choosing . . .' Axine trailed off. Anya could imagine.

Axine next showed her the sleeping quarters, which comprised a large dormitory with rows of single beds, and one huge one in the middle. There were also a number of doors to smaller rooms adjacent to this main one. 'A slave much in demand with the masters will sleep here only rarely,' Axine told her. 'I doubt if we need reserve a bed for you,' she laughed, then realised that her compliment had only served to make Anya very anxious. 'There's nothing to fear,' Axine said, and took her by the hand. 'We're all friends here. You'll feel better after a bath.'

And Anya did. The bathhouse was centred on a large pool, floored with deep red tiles, with a white marble surround. The walls and colonnades were soft blue and the pool was filled with bond-girls, laughing, splashing, sitting on the side, washing each other's backs and brushing out their hair. They waved to the two women standing on the side, and Anya waved back shyly. She thought that she might get to like these women, though she doubted if she could ever feel so free and unabashed about her body as to display it in the unself-conscious way that they did. 'We have some private bathrooms, too,' Axine whispered, as if she had read her mind.

'How could anyone be so cruel?' repeated Anya, partly to herself, as she lay back, wreathed in steam, and soaked her tired body in this beautiful, peculiar bath which was sunk into the floor.

Axine began massaging Anya's shoulders. 'The cook is . . . very strange,' she said. 'And yet the masters seem to tolerate her. I think they use the cook to frighten us.'

'Yet you were not afraid of her when you came to collect me?' Anya ventured.

'I felt reasonably safe – I had orders from the Task-mistress. Well, from Marella, actually, but I didn't tell Cook that.' Anya was reassured that Marella had not forgotten her.

Axine's hands felt very soft about Anya's shoulders; they helped her to relax. Axine, like Marella, seemed genuinely kind, but unlike Marella, Axine was a slave. And yet it seemed she was a slave with dignity and self-assurance, unlike the slaves who had allowed themselves to be abused so mercilessly by the cook. Anya could not imagine this woman cowering down before the cook or doing anything that she did not want to do. But, as a bondslave, she must surely have had to do just that as part of her training, at the very least.

'Axine?' Anya said. 'May I ask you something?'

Axine laughed. 'Of course. That's what I'm here for. Ask anything you want.'

There were many things, of course, which Anya needed to know. 'Why do you wear your hair like that? Did the masters command it?'

'No – it suits me, don't you think?'

Anya had hardly ever seen a woman with hair so black, and certainly never so short. Cropped tight, almost to the scalp, it formed a soft black brush.

'What will happen to me?' Anya asked.

83

'In what way?'

'What will they have me do, here in the castle?'

'Your duties will be varied, as would any bondslave's. The Taskmistress will direct you. A slave need not concern herself with the precise nature of her duties, and should never try to guess.'

This seemed a very strange philosophy, thought Anya. 'Is the Taskmistress really so cruel as she seems?'

Axine looked shocked, and glanced around as if to see whether anyone could have heard. 'Never say such a thing out loud,' she warned Anya very gravely. 'The Taskmistress has her duty too, just as we do. She is responsible for our training. At times, she may be required to discipline the bondslaves. That does not make her –' Axine herself avoided the word, '*unfair*. In fact she is quite the reverse. She will want to help you to develop your talents to the full.'

Anya wondered what this could possibly mean in the context of her slavery.

'Axine – will she beat me?' Anya felt Axine was being very indirect, and should set things out more clearly.

'Anya, I can't answer that. You are very beautiful . . .' Anya bowed her head. Why did people keep saying that and making her embarrassed? 'The Taskmistress expects much from slaves as beautiful as you are. Your training shall certainly be exhaustive.' Axine had a far-away look, as if she were reliving some very vivid memory. Axine was very beautiful, Anya thought, with that short black hair, those deep blue eyes, and those delicately formed features which belied her strength of character. Her breasts were small and boyish, with very tiny nipples; her waist was slender and her hips, though small, were full and neatly rounded. Her bush was trimmed to a perfect triangle of blackness.

'Stand up now and let me dry you.' Axine helped Anya from the bath and, wrapping a large soft towel around her, proceeded to dab her very gently. Anya was quite unused to such pampering and secretly enjoyed it. Then Axine spent a long time brushing Anya's hair. 'I like to see it shine,' she said. But then she could not decide whether to tie it back, or to work it in a plait. 'I think we ought to keep it simple, for tonight; the Taskmistress will probably prefer it so.'

Axine's words made Anya apprehensive: 'Will I then be . . . I will have to spend the night with her?'

'No. Well, probably not. She will want to begin your training, though what form that might take depends . . .'

'On what?'

'That which she judges is required.'

Anya was remembering what the Taskmistress had threatened. 'She said . . . that she might put me . . . with one of the masters.' Anya hoped that threat had merely been to frighten her.

'That is certainly possible,' Axine said.

'What . . . what will they do to me?'

Axine looked surprised. 'Anya,' she sounded quite concerned. 'Are you . . . you are not a virgin? Have you been with men?'

Anya now felt very foolish for having asked in such a way, when that really wasn't what she'd meant to say at all. She had wanted to know if their lordships might ill-treat her, might take delight in forcing her to do things against her will, or would they be gentle? But now she was too embarrassed to discuss it any further, and still her fear was undiminished.

Axine next had Anya sit and then lie upon a low, back-less couch, rather like a padded bench, and place one foot to each side, so that they rested upon the floor, 'so that I may complete your preparation,' Axine explained. Anya naturally was very self-conscious about this; she did it with unease. Axine sat astride the bench, between Anya's legs, and looked at her, which made Anya look away in shame.

'There is nothing for you to worry about,' Axine reassured her. 'I have to brush you, that is all – to make you more presentable, to emphasize your beauty.' But that made Anya feel very much worse, for Axine would, by her grooming, only draw attention to Anya's deepest shame, which even now must be clearly visible to the bondslave.

Axine began to brush her very gently, the softened strokes directed always upwards and outwards, away from Anya's sex. It was as she'd feared – this preparation would only serve to emphasize her blackness.

'You must not shrink away from this, your secret beauty,' Axine said very softly, but Anya only closed her eyes. 'It should be your pride and joy. Few woman are so fortunately endowed as you have been. Such beauty is very rare, and known in Lidir only in legend . . .'

So *that* was what the Taskmistress must have meant, thought Anya, by those strange comments which she had made when she had examined her.

'In legend . . .?' Anya asked, and looked at Axine now, intrigued.

Axine smiled. 'Mm . . . Legend has it that Lidir was once ruled by a very beautiful woman – a princess – who had your colouring of hair, and the markings which you now display . . .' Axine watched Anya very carefully.

'A princess?' Anya asked. Her eyes were very wide, for she was fairly sure who this must be; she had seen her picture on the staircase.

'Mm . . .' replied Axine.

'What manner of ruler was she?' Anya was sure that she was very good.

Axine began brushing Anya once again. 'It is said that she was kind and very just. Her people loved her, but . . .'

'But . . .?' Anya was entranced.

'One day, she just disappeared.' Marella had said only that she was 'gone'.

'Disappeared? Where?'

'That was the mystery. No one knew. It was as if she had vanished,' Axine opened her hand to emphasize the point, 'into the air. She could not have left the castle, for it was at that time sealed fast, under siege from a great army from the west. At dawn she could not be found. Her bed had not been slept in. Many of her subjects thought she had been spirited away by magic, but whatever the truth was, she was never seen again . . . Ever.' Axine was looking at Anya very intently again, as if expecting her to say something very significant. Then she continued in a voice so soft that Anya almost could not hear her: 'Yet all of that was so very, very long ago ... long before any living person's recollection ...'

So, the Princess must be dead, after all – and yet this mystery had captivated Anya. 'And was the castle then able to repel the attack, or did the army conquer?' she asked, because this seemed to her important.

Axine, however, seemed very deep in thought. 'The army then withdrew,' she answered vaguely. Anya had to press her futher. 'Legend has it,' she then went on, 'that the Princess, by her disappearance, somehow wove a magic spell which would protect Lidir and keep it strong until she could return. Many subjects give this legend credence still ...' Axine was still looking at her very strangely. Anya formed the opinion that Axine might be trying to test her with her words; she knew well what Axine was driving at.

'And what do you believe, Axine?'

Axine was silent for a very long while before she spoke: 'I see a very beautiful woman,' she said. Anya did not let Axine's flattery sway her.

'But do you see – a princess?' And now Anya was surprised by her own directness. The legend had charmed her.

It was now Axine's turn to be very bashful, and to cast her eyes away.

'Enter!'

Anya froze when she heard that woman's voice. Axine had to force her across the threshold of the Taskmistress's apartments.

'The bondslave is delivered ma'am, according to instruction,' Axine announced very gravely. Anya, surreptitiously glancing up, looked about the room. The walls were unadorned; bearskins were scattered here and there upon the floor; the only furniture seemed to be a table, some chairs, a cupboard and a large upholstered couch, upon which the Taskmistress sat. She was not alone; a slave-girl who looked very young was standing in front of her, facing away from the door and towards her.

'Thank you, Axine,' said the Taskmistress. Her tone was quite polite. 'That will be all for now. You may return to your duties.'

Anya waited by the door while the Taskmistress ignored her and whispered something to the girl. Anya could see, now that her face was half-turned, that she was very close to tears. Then the girl seemed to bow her legs very slightly outwards; the Taskmistress was smiling. Anya could not see the woman's hands, which were hidden behind the slave. The girl's hips began moving very slowly in a circle. Anya knew that the woman must be doing something to her. Then the girl lifted up on her toes, and Anya flushed with embarrassment and shame at what she had to watch, for she could see the Taskmistress's fingers moving between the girl's legs; her middle finger was stretching up between the cheeks of the bondslave's bottom. The Taskmistress disappeared from view – she was kneeling in front of the girl, who was making low, sobbing sounds in the Taskmistress's hand, reaching under, now spread her cheeks whilst the middle finger was pushed very deliberately and very slowly up the bondslave's bottom.

Anya did not want to witness this degrading scene a moment longer. She could hear soft kissing sounds, or gentle sucking noises, which she did not want to hear, and sudden catches of breath which, every so often would interrupt the slave-girl's sobs, as the finger then began working out and slowly in again, forcing the girl up higher on her toes.

The bond-girl started gasping. Suddenly the Taskmistress was visible again, standing beside the girl, not touching her at all, and yet the girl's legs and shoulders were shaking. She was still balanced on her toes.

'Stand down, my dear,' Anya heard the Taskmistress whisper. 'Save your pleasure for the present. The night, as yet, is very young.' The girl's heels returned to the floor and Anya could hear her sobbing very quietly. The Taskmistress's palm smoothed over the bondslave's bottom and for the first time, she addressed Anya, who immediately glanced down.

'So, you have arrived at last. You are tardy, beautiful one. I hope this will not become a vice of yours.' She said that word so viciously that she made it sound as if she really hoped the contrary. 'For then we shall have to seek appropriate correction for that unfortunate condition – to ensure that you are kept at all times on your toes.' Anya knew full well what the woman meant. It made the bond-girl sob again, and the Taskmistress deemed it necessary to whisper something sharply in her ear, which made the girl stand bolt upright and keep silent.

'Did you enjoy your sojourn in the kitchen?' The woman laughed. 'Did Cook lead you a merry dance?' Anya's teeth were clenched tight. She hated the Taskmistress for her calculating cruelty. 'Speak up, slave . . . I can have you sent back to help the cook if you'd prefer that. Hmmm?'

'No!' Anya could not stop herself from crying out. 'Ma'am, please . . .' she added very weakly.

The Taskmistress strode quickly over to her and lifted up her chin, then searched Anya's eyes minutely. Anya could not bear this woman's stare so close; it seemed to pierce right through her. 'Look at me,' said the Task-mistress. 'Beg me not to do it.'

'Please, ma'am,' Anya wanted to look away, but the Taskmistress's gaze paralysed her. 'Please, I . . .' she faltered. The Taskmistress's eyes widened as if to swallow her; that faint and spicy smell pervaded Anya's nostrils. 'I beg of you, do not send me to the kitchen.'

A very strange feeling came in Anya's belly as she heard these words spill out; she felt almost as if it was not she who had spoken them, and yet it seemed this standing out-side of herself served only to heighten her shame and nourish it now with forbidden excitement. The Task-mistress bent towards her and Anya froze. The woman closed her mouth about Anya's lips and, sucking them very slowly, she quelled them in their trembling. The feeling surged once more inside Anya. She could smell and taste the bond-girl's musky heat upon the Taskmistress's lips.

The Taskmistress gently pulled away, leaving Anya swaying unsteadily. 'My child, it seems you adjust well to

. . . training,' the woman said softly. 'Now, once again, but this time you shall beg your Taskmistress to do with you what she will . . .'

Anya was very frightened now; she felt very cold.

'Proceed,' said the Taskmistress in a very steady voice. 'Your Taskmistress is waiting.'

Anya could not bring herself to say it. For the second time, she felt outside herself; she was willing herself to comply with the Taskmistress's instruction, willing her tongue to say this thing to satisfy the woman, willing herself to save her body from Ildren's persecution. And yet she could not do it. Even if she died, she could not do it.

'Mmm . . .' The Taskmistress made a sound as if she had just tasted something delicious. 'Do not . . .' she began, and seemed almost to shudder, 'do not be fearful of your resistance. You still have very much to learn. Your spirit shall adapt in time. But now, we must advance your training . . . very gently. And teaching you will be so very great a pleasure . . .'

Ildren spun round on her heels and walked back to the bondslave, who was plainly very scared – her head was down and her shoulders were hunched around her, as if she were expecting to be beaten. She was taken over to the other side of the room and stood against the wall, at a point where Anya could see an iron ring set into the stonework above the bond-girl's head. The Taskmistress lifted the girl's hand, then unfastened the gold chain at her wrist and looped it through the ring before refastening it, so the girl's left hand was now suspended above her head. Although the bondslave had been chained, it seemed to Anya that this was a token gesture, for the girl could very easily have freed herself with her other hand. It was, of course, most unlikely that she would ever choose to do such a thing, or even try to move unless by the Taskmistress's explicit directive.

Then Anya realised that the Taskmistress had not finished. The girl was turned around to face the wall, and the chain around her middle was similarly secured, by a second ring at waist height, which Anya previously had not noticed. Somehow this seemed very much more sinister, since the girl not only had her back to the room, and therefore could see nothing which might be taking place behind her, but her chaining now appeared that much more intimate, her potential movements that much more restricted, making her appear to Anya very vulnerable indeed. The Taskmistress now bent down, and sure enough attached to the wall, very low down near the floor as might have been predicted, was a third ring; to this, the slave-girl's right ankle was finally chained. These restraints left the bondgirl very uneasily balanced with her body on a diagonal line, and by virtue of the small size of the middle ring, held very close up to the wall. The muscles of her legs and buttocks appeared to be in tension; her bottom formed two tight round curves, over which the Taskmistress carefully smoothed her fingers. Then suddenly, apparently on impulse, she squatted down and spread her palms behind the girl's knees and, pressing, slowly ran them up the bondslave's legs and on towards her bottom, kneading the tight-sculpted muscles until her palms were reaching up the slave-girl's back as if in supplication. Ildren threw back her head and closed her eyes in obvious delectation; the bondgirl merely whimpered.

The Taskmistress arose; her outstretched hands continued moving up the girl's back and at last, reached her shoulders and massaged them very gently, or so it appeared to Anya. The whimpering gradually subsided. Ildren bent and kissed the bond-girl long and fully on the neck, below her ear, and Anya felt her own face flushing at the thought of that, for she was imagining what the girl must be feeling at this moment, fastened as she was, tight against the wall, her breasts and belly pressed up to the roughness of the cold stonework, while Ildren's moist lips burned relentlessly into the tender skin below her ear, and Ildren's velvet dress stroked against her thighs and bottom, making her want to spread her cheeks to let the folds of velvet in to brush pleasurably to and fro across that tiny pulsing mouth within.

The Taskmistress's fingers were tickling underneath the

bond-girl's raised left arm, while the kissing still continued; now Ildren was kissing the girl's ear – her lips were sucking gently at the lobe – and Ildren was whispering to the girl. Saying what, Anya wondered? Not tender words of love or endearment? Anya was sure that Ildren was quite incapable of that, and yet the girl did not seem frightened now; Ildren's words and caresses seemed in some measure to have calmed her. But she must be very foolish indeed if this calmness were to extend to trust of the woman standing now behind her. Then Anya realised that the slave-girl's left foot, the one which had remained free, was moving very slowly up the wall. The girl's knee was bending and her weight was taken by her other leg; the foot moved as if it were levering itself upwards on the stonework until her leg, though bent, was flat against the wall and her foot was level with her waist, which left her very much exposed.

Ildren's hand had moved out to meet the foot, which twitched briefly as contact was made and Ildren's fingers ran tickling underneath it, then kept moving along, past the ankle, tracing the curvature of the bond-girl's calf and in behind her knee, then hesitated before moving down towards the joining of her thighs. Ildren kept kissing the girl's neck as she touched her in between the legs, and Anya felt herself turn almost inside out, for she knew exactly what the bond-girl must be feeling. The Taskmistress would certainly be opening her with her fingers, slipping them inside, and penetrating her bottom with her thumb, no doubt, and all the time that kiss was sucking upon her neck, filling her with desire. The girl's leg very slowly lowered, yet Ildren's hand remained in place. The girl's foot reached the floor; her thighs wrapped tight about the Taskmistress in her penetration. Then at last the Taskmistress edged away from her and, squatting once again, watched the bond-girl's bottom moving, cheek by rounded cheek, alternately, as her weight was shifted first to one leg, then the other as, by small readjustments, her body gradually accommodated and took to itself Ildren's ever reaching fingers.

'Dance, my sweet, in your desire,' Ildren whispered.

92

'Mould your body to me while I search your inner softness and your warmth.'

Now Anya was beside herself to think that the slave was doing this willingly, and taking pleasure from the way the Taskmistress was choosing to degrade her. Would Anya be made to do this next, or would the Taskmistress have planned something even worse for her?

The Taskmistress had finally withdrawn her hand from the girl and now was licking her fingers one by one; then she slowly sucked her thumb whilst looking directly at Anya, making her feel hot and at the same time, shivery. The girl had been left in that position, facing the wall; the Taskmistress had stopped before the girl had reached her pleasure, and seemed to have lost interest in her for the present. Had this display then been for Anya's benefit, she wondered? Had it been done to stir up her desire by having her witness the bond-girl's pleasuring by a woman otherwise so cruel? Was the Taskmistress trying to break Anya's will by keeping her in doubt about what to expect next – cruelty or pleasure?

And now the Taskmistress would deal with Anya. This was quite clear from the way in which she looked at her, as if she were waiting, like a she-wolf about to pounce upon her prey and devour it. Then Anya realised that she had been doing the forbidden – staring fully at the Taskmistress – and she was filled with fear at this transgression. And yet she was frozen, like the stricken doe, unable to move even the muscle of an eyelid against the fierce intensity of this woman's gaze. The Taskmistress made a very low noise, a deep-throated laugh or growl at Anya's discomfiture. Those deep brown eyes widened to imprison her and to take delight in her apprehension.

The Taskmistress approached, but never took her eyes from Anya; those eyes only got larger and more liquid until they filled Anya's vision. Invisible hands now lifted Anya's hands, hung very limply by her sides; long cool fingers intertwined with hers and raised those hands until her arms were stretched out horizontally; Anya could feel the coolness in her armpits as her moistness and her warmth took flight and filled the air around her. The Taskmistress inhaled very deeply and deliberately, opening her mouth, then said in a very clear whisper:

'Delicious heat . . . let me taste you, let me drink you in your burning . . .'

The woman closed her eyes and Anya burned with shame. Slowly, the Taskmistress lifted up her heavy eyelids; those eyes were black desire. 'We must . . . encourage you in your muskiness . . . distil and concentrate your essence. No – do not avert your eyes, my child. Your musk is my delight; I shall have you drip with desire upon my tongue, and I shall drink my fill . . . Yes, do not shake your head, however slightly, to your Taskmistress . . . I shall assuage my thirsts upon your salted nectar while you drip into my mouth. But first, your Taskmistress shall ask your permission, which you shall freely give without refusal.' The Taskmistress raised her voice. 'Is that not so?' The woman's fingers tightened very cruelly about Anya's, and kept squeezing very hard. Anya was so afraid and so very ashamed. Her throat was tight and dry. She opened her mouth to speak, and yet no sound came out. The Taskmistress merely raised her eyebrows, and she waited, her fingers tight about Anya's, squeezing to the bone.

'It – it is so, ma'am,' Anya croaked at last; she felt her heart beat very fast, and her belly tighten. Ildren's fingers then relaxed, and Ildren lifted Anya's hands above her head and had her link them, back to back, leaving her breasts uplifted and her underarms exposed. Ildren's lips and tongue grazed under each of Anya's arms, licking the salt-misted fronds in careful upward stroking tickles; next, Ildren's tongue transferred to Anya's black-tipped breasts, licking upwards underneath her acorns, and then to Anya's lips, in the same slow upward strokes – a cat's tongue lifting her upper lip and probing underneath, tracing round the tender inner skin in front of her teeth, depositing Anya's scent on Anya's lips and into Anya's mouth.

The Taskmistress took hold of Anya's hair and, after twisting it, curled it up onto her head, then had Anya rest her hands upon it. She led her to the corner of the table and, making her lift on tiptoes, edged her forwards, so the rounded corner of the table pushed between her legs and opened out her thighs, so that when at last the Taskmistress instructed her to lower, her weight was taken in that place at the joining of her thighs. Ildren now forced her to lift her legs and reach underneath to wrap them round the table leg as tightly as she could. Anya found it very difficult to keep her balance, with her hands upon her head, for Ildren insisted that she should not bend forwards, but should keep very straight throughout. Anya almost felt that she was falling over backwards, which perhaps was Ildren's intention – to keep her feeling very insecure. Then Anya stiffened, as the Taskmistress's hand was slipped around in front and down between her legs. Very gently, Ildren's fingertips eased Anya's fleshy leaves apart, allowing Anya's weight to spread them fully across the surface of the table. 'Your blackness must remain open,' Ildren said, quite calmly and detachedly, and then she pushed Anya's hips more firmly forwards, which forced her thighs to open even wider than before.

Anya jumped – a tightly coiled rope of very thin leather had been thrown onto the table. Her heart was beating wildly; the Taskmistress spread her hands on Anya's back and slowly moved them downwards, then did likewise down her front; the outspread hands swept firstly down across her breasts, which sprang back again, the nipples tightened by the squeezing pressure, then swept up again, across the hardened nipples; the hands moved upwards to her neck. The woman's lips were moistening Anya's shoulders, moving step by step across, planting warm soft kisses upon her skin, which cooled to gooseflesh as the lips moved on. 'So brown, so smooth and soft,' she heard the Taskmistress whisper. Ildren released her grip, then picked up the coil. Anya's heart stopped. What would the Taskmistress do?

The rope was carefully uncoiled in front of Anya's eyes. She wanted to cry out, to plead with this woman not to do it, and yet, terrified as she was of what might be done to her, still she did not dare speak out, not even to abase herself by begging of the Taskmistress. She bit her lip and felt like crying. The rope was lowered over her right shoulder and down her front; the leather strip felt cool. Eventually the end came to rest between her legs and, as the Taskmistress paid it out, it tickled against her thighs. Ildren then lifted the tip and fed it, from above, underneath the chain about Anya's waist, then drew out the rope across the table to a point about two feet in front of Anya. The leather now ran along the table, up between her legs, below the chain, between her breasts, then over Anya's shoulder. Anya was still very frightened, though less so than she'd been before the rope had touched her. And now the rope was passed around the back of her neck and down in front again, but on the left side; this time, after passing between her breasts, it was looped back below her left breast, tight against the underjoin, then wrapped once again and back up again behind her neck. The leather rope was pulled; she felt it press into her flesh; her breast was lifted up and outwards to the left. Ildren very gently touched it with her fingertips, as if to test its resilience. The process was repeated, with the leather now passing over her right shoulder, again between her breasts but underneath the right one, then once around and up again and pulled; the right breast pointed up away from Anya's body and outwards to the right. Ildren must have known exactly what the tension in the rope would do; she was trying to emphasize Anya's breasts, to keep them well apart, to make her more aware of them, to tenderise them and make them prominent.

Then Ildren worked methodically, looping the rope completely around each breast in turn, hard against the last loop, and up around the back of Anya's neck, at all times keeping the leather as taut as she possibly could, so Anya would feel each individual turn, each firmly gripping circle around her flesh, as the substance of her breast was squeezed ever forwards, towards the teat, until at last the rope ran out, whereupon Ildren secured the end behind Anya's neck, to maintain the rope in tension.

Anya felt her breasts were bursting, as if powerful hands

were wrapped around them, squeezing very tight and never letting go. Each breast stood stiffly up and outwards; the ends looked hard and swollen, their black nipples engorged and surrounded by a very deep purple halo. Anya was sure that this woman meant to bruise her with this treatment.

The Taskmistress had Anya turn around and face towards her while she admired her for what seemed a very long time. Ildren's eyebrows slowly furrowed in displeasure; it seemed that something was amiss.

'Your hands must be restrained,' she decided; she took a second, smaller rope and fastened Anya's hands high up behind her back, securing her wrists as closely as possible to the twine which passed around the back of Anya's neck. Anya bent forwards to try to ease the tension in her arms. 'No. Sit up. Your breasts are beautiful; they must be displayed, for my attentions . . .' Anya now felt very exposed; her arms, although they did not hurt as yet, still felt very uncomfortable. 'There, that is much better,' Ildren said. 'And now your feet.' She used the end of the rope which dangled down between Anya's thighs, though this was barely long enough for her purpose. In the end, Anya's feet had to be secured to the table leg very near its top, in such a way that her knees were bent quite tightly, which spread her thighs very wide indeed, and left her unable to move, and consequently totally defenceless.

'My sweet and ink-splashed beauty,' Ildren murmured in a very deep voice. 'Now I have you where I want you.' Ildren was almost shaking. 'Your training to the ways of tempered fleshliness and controlled delight is now begun, my precious. Your Taskmistress shall steer you ever onwards, to the very brink of pleasure.' Her voice was now unsteady. 'This night shall see your body burning with desire – for you shall, with my assistance, stave off your pleasure many times before the dawn is nigh . . .'

7

The Tautening Bowstring

Anya felt herself a prisoner of those deep brown eyes more
surely than she was a prisoner of her bonds; those black
and liquid centres expanded now to drown her. The Taskmistress touched her, high up on her inner thigh. Those
fingertips brushed her there and tickled very gently across
the downy hairs of Anya's tender skin, making her catch
her breath and want to close her legs against that touch,
although, fastened as she was in this widely spread position, she knew this to be quite impossible. Ildren smiled.
Her lips looked very full and soft, not cruel at all. This
woman was deceptive, Anya knew, for it seemed that Ildren walked the knife edge between loving desire and
cruelty. Which way would she fall? Anya had no way of
telling. Her own desires and needs were tempered constantly with anxiety in this woman's presence.

Ildren's fingers stroked very lightly in the groove at the
top of Anya's leg, sending tickles up inside her belly, making Anya twitch with pleasure. 'Keep very still, my darling.
Your pleasure must be reflected only in your eyes. It must
be taken gently.' Ildren's words seduced Anya; a warm
voluptuousness was suffusing through her veins. 'Your
Taskmistress shall kiss your breasts. Would you like that,
Anya?' Anya's heart leapt to hear the Taskmistress use her
name, and say it so tenderly.

'If . . . if it should please you, ma'am,' Anya said with
very wide eyes, and now perhaps, with love.

'Mmm . . .' The Taskmistress closed her eyes in obvious
delectation at the thought of doing this to Anya, and Anya
closed her eyes in loving anticipation.

Ildren licked by turn those hard and swollen burning nipples, encircled by the thongs. Her tongue was drawn around, wetly in a circle, then spreading flat, was drawn across in a broad brushing upstroke which first lifted up the nipple, then let it fall again; her tongue then formed into a soft wet tube which, in dabbing repeatedly at Anya's teat, kept swallowing and releasing the nipple in a gentle sucking pull. Ildren's finger meanwhile tickled in the groove of Anya's leg, making Anya want that tickling to move across, that sucking tongue-pull to progress in dabbing down across her belly, to give succour to the hot hard pip of flesh which pulsed between her legs. The Task-mistress now ran a finger down the leather strip that descended between Anya's breasts to the chain about her waist. The finger traced over the chain, then hooked itself around the leather and kept on sliding downwards to the point at which the tension held the leather tightly into the join of Anya's thigh, before the rope, on passing down across the table edge, was secured to Anya's ankles. The Taskmistress pulled gently at the rope, as if testing it. 'I want you more spread – more open to my caresses,' Ildren said, and placing her hands around Anya's hips and closing them on her buttocks, she pulled her forwards, towards her, so Anya's sex now projected out above the corner and the thong bit deeply in the groove between her thigh and mound. And Anya was thereby spread very wide indeed. The leather thong imparted a pressure line of pleasure down the side of Anya's sex; her fleshy leaves were slowly pumping up with blood.

'Your lips – so black and beautiful. They stand so proud,' Ildren said. 'Ask me to open them, to expose your fleshy bud.' Anya's face was burning at what the Taskmistress was asking her to say out loud. The bond-girl, fastened to the wall, had moved and made a sound. Had she overheard Anya's secret? Ildren glanced briefly over her shoulder to check the girl, then turned again to Anya. 'Well, my dearest? What is it that you want me to do?' And her finger barely touched the side of Anya's fleshy leaves. The feeling was delicious; Anya wanted more. She swallowed and then said as quietly as she could, for she did not want the bond-girl to overhear so shameful an expression:

'Please, ma'am ... open them ...' The Taskmistress frowned. 'My leaves,' Anya added.

'And?' said the Taskmistress very loudly. 'And do what in addition?'

'And ... and make my bud peep out.' Now Anya was mortified that she had said it in a way that Ildren had not even asked of her.

Ildren was delighted. 'You sweet and lustful thing,' she said. 'It shall be my pleasure now to split you very gently.'

The Taskmistress had Anya open her mouth, so that whilst she carefully, and by feel alone, teased apart Anya's burning leaves, she could stroke her tongue very lightly round Anya's lips, just tickling, in a mirror of that tickling sensation down there between Anya's legs, as the leaves of flesh at first clung to each other, sealed by Anya's sticky juices, and then very slowly and deliciously split, until she felt her bottom pushing strongly outwards from between them. But Ildren took great care not to touch that morsel of delight; instead she ran her fingertip round the very edge of Anya's leaves at a carefully controlled rate such that the tickling resonated up inside Anya, making her want to spread her sex, so the Taskmistress might freely push her long cool fingers up inside her body and thereby feel the strength of Anya's burning heat.

'Open your eyes, my dear,' the Taskmistress said softly. 'See what your Taskmistress has in store for one so delectable as you.' Anya's eyelids felt heavy with desire; Ildren's face appeared at first hazy and indistinct, but it was evident that she was holding something black. Then Anya's eyes widened in dismay – it seemed the Taskmistress had in her hand a kind of plug, that evil thing in which the cook had taken such delight by having it applied in so cruel a manner to the male slave.

'No, no ...' she began, for she was rather frightened, though it was true that this device was in certain ways quite different to the ones that Cook had ordered to be used.

'Shhh ...' Ildren tried to calm her, 'this is purely for a

woman's private pleasure. It can bring delight in many ways; I do assure you that you shall find this plaything interesting.' And Ildren held it horizontally, so that Anya might assess it. It was fashioned after the likeness of a man's flesh-stick, complete with fleshy bumps, but it was smoother than a man would be and certainly more polished, and perhaps a little smaller. It looked like it was made of wood; the curve was slightly upwards; the under-surface at the top was flattened, so the end seemed to form a smooth round-pointed triangle.

'I could push it very gently into you,' the Taskmistress suggested. 'Either this way round,' and she inverted it so the bumps were uppermost, 'or this way, if you would pre-fer it.' Then she twirled the rounded point against the pad of her finger. 'There are several ways of utilising an instru-ment such as this one. Here, let me demonstrate ... No, you will like it, I assure you, besides which, this shall be a tiny sample only of this pleasurable delight.' And Ildren very deftly fitted that flat triangular point of rounded pleas-ure underneath the hood of Anya's flesh-lips, so it pressed against her bud. Then she made Anya wet her lips and form her mouth into a very small 'o', and Ildren pushed her tongue in and out of that tightened fleshy circle while she very gently turned the point to and fro inside the hood, until Anya's sex was squirming with delight.

'You see – I'm sure your flesh nub likes it, don't you?' Ildren held the hood back and very lightly tapped that nubbin with the wooden point, three times in a row. 'Speak to me, my tiny fleshy darling, give Ildren some little sign of your delight and pleasure.' Anya was burning up with shame. The bond-girl moved once more in the background. Ildren tapped Anya several times in quick succession. She felt that she would burst at any second; the pleasure in that special spot was so exquisite. Ildren very carefully worked the point around the stiffly poking pip and back again, then tapped it once again, but this time much more rapidly. 'Speak to me, my pretty ...' Anya felt her pip pulsate. 'Ah ... that is so much better. Ildren loves to see a woman's nub enjoy its little self.'

She stood up again. 'Now let me demonstrate, by proxy as it were, a second application of this tool . . .' and then she raised her voice, '. . . with our nervous friend over there, whose constant shuffling seems to require the Taskmistress's corrective attention.' The bond-girl now went very still and silent. 'Excuse me just one moment.' After making sure her flesh lips were opened out quite fully, Ildren left Anya still in her state of burning while she went over to the girl and muttered something, whereupon the girl went very stiff. The Taskmistress then released the bondslave's ankle restraint and began edging her feet away from the wall, which turned out not to be effective with the slave's middle attached, as it was, quite firmly to the wall. Ildren edged the golden waistband up the slave as far as it was possible to do so, then again moved the girl's feet back, and also now, apart. The girl's body appeared to hang, since her left wrist was still attached to the ring above her head, and the chain about her middle was now pressing up and underneath her breasts, preventing further movement; her back was very strongly arched, and by this arrangement, her bottom was pushed out sharply, which quite possibly had been Ildren's intention all along. The Taskmistress now patted this tightly curving and slightly spread bottom, so invitingly presented, as if the bondslave were a beast which had performed well and pleased its rider. She left the girl in this position and returned to Anya, whose pleasure was now no longer quite so imminent, and whose arms were beginning to ache.

She made Anya hold back her head, so she faced up to the ceiling, and then push her tongue straight upwards, whilst Ildren dangled the device vertically above her and simultaneously tickled her between the legs. With her head in this position, the leather thong pressed more tightly into Anya's join; it made her flesh leaves throb as they engorged more fully.

'Reach up, my sweet, with your tongue, and touch it to the tip . . . Do it very nicely . . . There . . .' said Ildren, and Anya shivered with delight for Ildren had tickled her nubbin precisely at the moment that her tongue had touched the rod. 'Touch again, my darling – arch that naughty tongue into a point, and this time, touch it very lightly.' Ildren raised the wooden cockstem so Anya had to stretch to reach it. And once again, the tickling tip of Ildren's finger brushed very lightly up against her. 'Good. You do that very sweetly. Now, pretend it is a tongue that tickles you in between the legs ... my tongue. Would you like it if my tongue were to lick around your nubbin? Hmmm? To stroke it and make it very stiff? Now pretend. Close your eyes and reach ... there ...' Anya shivered once again. 'Was that very nice?' Anya was slowly liquifying inside. She felt her nectar start to drip. It seemed the Taskmistress could surely do with her exactly as she wished. At that moment Anya wanted to beg that woman to keep touching her, really to lick her, until her pleasure burst against that woman's tongue.

'Now, wet your lips and pout them. Good.' She pushed the cockstem in. 'Pretend it is the Prince's flesh now entering your mouth.' Those carefully chosen words of Ildren's caused a peculiar feeling deep in Anya's belly. 'Show me how you would welcome the Prince very fully in your mouth.' Ildren now released her hold upon the stem and held Anya's head back further with one hand while, with the other, she slowly opened Anya and pushed her fingers in. Anya wanted to open out so those fingers could push right up into her belly, and deep inside her womb. 'There – swallow him, my child.' The cockstem filled Anya's mouth and almost blocked her throat; she was gagging. And yet Ildren's words and slippery probing fingers had seduced her, for she was imagining it was indeed the Prince that filled her mouth and opened her with his hand. And now, she wanted the Prince's lips and tongue to close around her bursting pip of hard and polished pleasure, and to suck it till it split and released that sweet intoxication very softly into his mouth.

The stem and fingers were withdrawn, glistening. Ildren smiled. 'Your Prince is very pleased my love, with your well-controlled exertions.' She sucked her fingers. 'Your Prince delights in your honeydew, which you, in your love

for him, have secreted.' Anya was so ashamed, now that
she knew she had been tricked into this very lewd display
for Ildren's sole amusement; she hated Ildren for casting
herself in the Prince's role, for usurping his position, and
thereby cheapening Anya's secret admiration for his noble
self. It seemed the Taskmistress took evil delight in render-
ing heartfelt feelings worthless.

'Let your Taskmistress now demonstrate for you that
. . . other application.' Ildren's eyes half closed in wicked
pleasure before she turned and went over to where the
bond-girl was still tethered with her bottom angled outwards and her legs still spread apart. Ildren knelt. The
cockstem, wet with Anya's spittle, caught the light as Ildren, spreading the slave-girl's bottom cheeks, fitted the tip
precisely to that inner mouth and carefully twirled it as she
encouraged the girl to lickerishness, saying loudly enough
for Anya to hear:

'Spread, my darling, let your tight and tiny mouth kiss
and suck this stem, as if it were the Prince's. Show the
Prince how you would draw his swelling deep inside your
body. There . . . You do this very sweetly. The Prince loves
the way your soft warm flesh closes round him as he slips
inside you . . . There, you see, he likes to have his bag press
firmly up against your cheeks . . . Now, milk him very gently . . . The Prince would like to touch you now, between
the legs. He loves that special part of you. Ask him now to
do it, if it pleases him.' The bond-girl muttered something
indistinct. 'And shall you make your little cockstem stand
up for the Prince? Hmmm, my precious? So he can feel it
between his fingertips, to test your heartbeat in its pulsing?'

Anya wanted to close off her ears. She hated this woman
now for subjecting her to this second degradation, by forcing her to witness the bond-girl's seduction and delight,
while Ildren continued to take the Prince's name in vain.

'And will you promise now to take your pleasure with
the Prince moving deep inside you? You must cry out very
loudly when your pleasure comes. Is that clear?' Then Ildren whispered something to the girl, something which she
must not have wanted Anya to overhear. The Task-

mistress's fingers slipped between the bond-girl's legs; the bond-girl's hips began to move at first in a slow erratic circle, then back and forth, as Ildren's other hand, with very slight but deliberate movements, worked the wooden stem inside her until the bond-girl's legs went stiff, and she lifted on her toes, as if reaching up and outwards with her bottom. She stayed like that for quite some time, with tiny tremors rippling through her back and hips, after which, still balanced on her toes, she went completely rigid. The only sound was her very steady panting; the only movement was Ildren's, who very leisurely pulled the cockstem out of her and pushed it in again, while she worked that hand between those legs, until the girl suddenly caught her breath and pushed violently against the stem to take it fully in, screaming 'Take me ... my Prince,' and ground her hips as Ildren slowly turned around and smiled a smile of evil triumph at Anya, who felt completely drained of all emotion now, and was very pale indeed.

Ildren kissed the bond-girl very delicately in the small of her upturned lower back and left the cockstem in her.

Now she was back in front of Anya, and was smiling very sweetly. 'There, you see, a simple thing like this can provide many little comforts.' She lifted Anya's chin, for Anya did not wish to look upon so horrible a person. 'Would you like to try it in that special place yourself? Hmmm?' Ildren was standing very close to Anya, so her soft velvet robe was brushing Anya between the legs. 'Look into my eyes, my sweetness. Let me search your soul ...' The velvet kept brushing up against the tender openness of Anya's sex, still widely spread, as the Taskmistress had earlier left her. 'What secret needs lie buried deep, so deep you cannot know them ...? What precise and calculated ministrations shall your body yet require? Your Taskmistress has many ways of eliciting your pleasure, and prolonging your desire. Trust in me, and you shall know no shame, for I shall yet deliver you to pleasures so protracted and exquisite that you shall feel that you are dying of delight.'

Anya's cheeks were filled once more with colour, for she

felt that the Taskmistress could indeed in some way see inside her heart and soul, could glimpse that inner self, that private lust, that burning at her core. 'Now, push out your tongue, as a sign that you accept your fate as I have now decided,' crooned Ildren. Although Anya hated this woman, and was filling with fear, still her body felt a longing for that taste of pleasurable delectation, those forbidden transports of desire, which it seemed that Ildren now was offering. She pushed out her tongue – she ventured down that path of sweet complicity – and as she did so, Ildren's fingers closed very lightly around that fleshy hood between Anya's thighs.

'Push further, my precious, that I may tell your depth of wanting ... Mmm, yes ... Let that tip of lust poke up.' Anya closed her eyes and pushed her tongue out very far indeed, whereupon Ildren's lips closed gently around the tip and sucked it, while her fingers tightened the hood about that other tongue, in a long slow pull which elicited a tiny stifled cry of pleasure of the kind which Ildren – whose lips sucked tighter, so they held that shivering tasting tip of flesh a prisoner – found so very endearing in a woman she had earmarked as a special lover.

Anya was oiling at this woman's touch, this woman that she hated, this woman that gave her so much pain, and fear, and shame, and such exquisite peasure – this woman to whom she would give herself against her hate, this woman that she wanted now to take her, to show her all those secret luscious fleshly ways of love of which she was the mistress.

Ildren spread those liquid leaves of Anya's flesh more widely while, still sucking on that tongue, she let her fingers trace the tight embedded thong which pressed against and into Anya, as if she wished to feel the young slave's tension in that strip of tautened leather. The fingers touched the sensitive skin of Anya's groin and, pushing harder, forced themselves below the leather. Then Ildren took it like a bowstring – her fingers took the strain and lifted it away from Anya.

Ildren now released Anya's captive tongue, so she could ask of her a wickedly delicious favour. 'Your Taskmistress

'. . .' her breathing was shallow, as if Ildren was almost too excited to say it. 'Your Taskmistress,' she began again, 'would wish to fit . . . to fit this bowstring now precisely to your parting.' Anya gasped. 'She would do this very gently, so the –' her breath caught, 'so its cutting pressure would be brought to bear very slowly, yet of necessity very fully, on your tight and pleasure-polished nubbin.' Anya shook her head; she knew she could not bear it. 'It shall be so brief a pain that it shall be . . . a pleasure.' Anya shook her head again. 'Yes – your Taskmistress shall do it to you – for a count of ten. Now brace yourself against this sweet cutting ache of pleasure.' Anya knew that now she could not escape it; she tensed and closed her eyes tight shut and bit her lip and waited.

The tightness of the leather touched her very firmly, but Ildren did not release it yet. She stroked it from side to side across the stiff, projecting pip, sending seductive resonations up through Anya; far from making her shrink away from this tickling tautness, it made her want to press herself against it and have it rub more rapidly across her nubbin. 'Is this pleasure sweet, my dear, like honey dripping in your throat? Hmmm? Your Taskmistress will fix this bowstring squarely to your dart of lust . . . Yes, and thereby push the point inside you. I shall fire your tiny dart of love into your flesh and thus I will transfix you. Tell me that you wish it so, that you will bear this pain to demonstrate your love and your submission to my pleasure.'

'I . . .' Anya felt her heart had jumped to block her throat, at what her voice was saying. 'I submit my . . . my body to your pleasure, ma'am,' and a delicious churning feeling followed, deep in Anya's belly.

'My sweet and precious pet,' the Taskmistress whispered huskily. 'Let me count out the aching of your pleasure very slowly . . .'

Ildren released the bowstring gently against Anya, but still the tension bit – the surge of cutting pain was much too much to bear, as if a red hot needle had been pushed into the centre of her nub and, cauterising the incision, had heated up the blood inside to stretch the skin to bursting.

'One,' the Taskmistress announced with crystal clarity, as Anya's mouth opened in a scream, a scream suffocated by Ildren's kiss, which sealed her lips quite tightly, so the muffled sounds emerged subdued through Anya's nose, and appeared to Ildren's ears to be those sweet and stifled gasps that lovers make at the zenith of their pleasure. Ildren delved long and deep inside that mouth until at last her pulse was beating with such excitement that she had to gasp for breath herself. 'Two,' she managed, then inhaled very deeply while she used her palm to muffle Anya's moans until they had subsided sufficiently, as Anya readjusted slowly to accommodate this pain, for Ildren to remove her hand, now marked by Anya's teeth, and run it, tickling downwards, to the small of Anya's back, while the fingers of her other hand very gently closed those soft warm oily nether lips about that strip of leather, thereby sealing it, in some degree at least, inside Anya's willing body. 'Three,' she said, and Anya moaned once more with that stinging pressure, though this time certainly less strongly, and with very mixed feelings. Ildren kissed those soft and luscious lips once more, then said, 'Four. I hope your ache is sweet enough to bear; is your pleasure quite exquisite?' And, brushing her fingertips very lightly along the length of Anya's tight-sealed fleshy leaves, she touched her tongue to Anya's and she shed her spittle into Anya's mouth; like a bird of love, she dripped her droplets of desire into her fledgling, whose mouth was spread so wide in need and supplication.

'Five,' she whispered, squeezing those leaves like soft damp pastry, and moulding them against the taut-stretched leather wire inside her slave. Then, using both her hands between those legs, she teased those leaves apart, to look upon the place where the strip divided Anya and pressed against her bud. Six.' Anya felt that pressure burn against her. It seemed that Ildren would cut her flesh in two. 'Look down, my love, upon your parting. Watch your Taskmistress in her working of your flesh about your cord of pleasure.'

Anya watched, amid that concentrated aching, as Ildren's fingers pulled her leaves ever outwards from her body, until at last she could not bear the burning, and cried out: 'Seven.' Ildren was delighted to allow her slave this little transgression; she sealed those leaves and, kneeling down in front of her, she spread her own lips about them and bathed their heat in liquid from her mouth, to soothe her lover's burning. She sank her tongue in – split that fruit – and traced the line of leather upwards till she could feel her lover's pulsing at her tongue-tip. Then she released that precious fleshy fruit, that taste of salted honey, and she counted, 'Eight,' though to her it seemed a pity that the time was drawing nigh.

She stood and slipped two fingers into Anya, one to each side of the cord, and kissing her, she pushed until that cord cut into the web of Ildren's fingers, so she could thereby sense, in some mitigated way, that sharper cutting pleasure experienced by her slave, as the fingers worked into her more deeply and generated once again that delicious stifled moan. 'Nine, my sweet. Your time of pleasuring is almost up.' Her fingers, wrapping now around the cord, worked it from side to side, and in that aching working pressure on her nub, Anya gasped and moaned and threw back her head, for she knew not what she wanted now – to have it stop or go on and to burst that tormenting ache and spill her fire of lust.

'Ten!' The pressure was released and Anya then began to sting as if a thousand tiny needles were pricking in her nubbin. 'There, my darling . . .' Ildren kissed and sucked her nipples and tickled Anya's belly. 'You did so very well, for one so new. Your Taskmistress is pleased, and you may kiss my hand and thank me.' Anya's lips were shaking, though she knew not why, as she kissed those very fingers which had penetrated her. And though her body lacked release, though her pleasure was unsatisfied, yet still she felt a strange and pleasant warmth which swelled and pulsed within her. She felt her senses were in some way heightened, so that not only could she smell Ildren's musk above her own, she could almost sense this woman's beating heart within her own breast, she could feel Ildren's smouldering sensuality which she wanted now to taste; she wanted to give this woman pleasure – not in this way, in pain and domination – but by pleasuring her body softly, in tenderness and love, if Ildren would allow it. The tingling had now subsided; Anya's sex felt warm and numb.

'And now, your Taskmistress shall massage you, very tenderly, in your aching.' Ildren produced a phial of aromatic oil and knelt once more between Anya's outspread thighs and, having checked her bonds, she dripped the oil upon her outstretched fingers. She began to work it into each crease of Anya's thighs and then, using just her fingertips around the fleshy leaves of Anya's sex, very softly palpitated them until Anya found her body welcoming that very gentle touch; her leaves went very soft indeed, under Ildren's tender ministrations. And Anya knew her warmth was seeping, slowly, and yet she did not mind at all that the Taskmistress might be aware of this signal that her body made – in fact she wanted her to witness that this gentleness was what her body now required. Ildren dripped the oil upon her nubbin, which pulsed in its appreciation as the feeling seeped back in. Ildren placed her fingertip against it, underneath the hood, and very lightly pressed against it in its oiling, then released it. Anya found that lightness now so very sweet, so very agreeable in its difference from that painful pleasure which Ildren seemed to relish.

'Do you like this touch, my darling?' the Taskmistress whispered. Anya swallowed and she nodded, but she did not want to speak. 'I can feel your tiny ball of pleasure swelling up against my finger. It feels so firm and sweet. Your Taskmistress loves to feel your pleasure in this way.' Anya found the Taskmistress's words and touch were stirring her. Tiny rivulets of warmth and lusciousness were trickling down inside her to focus in that spot that Ildren now caressed. 'And now you must assist me, Anya. Your pleasuring shall bring the two of us together in a common purpose.' Anya now was slightly apprehensive. 'Do not fear, my darling. A woman should never be afraid to explore her bodily needs. Let me untie your hands . . .' Anya was frightened now at what she thought the Taskmistress might make her do. 'There now – how these poor arms must be aching.' Ildren massaged her arms and shoulders, and then her wrists and fingers, so the blood came draining back again and prickled down her arms. 'A woman's fingers are so intriguing, I always think,' Ildren looked at them and mused. 'I love to watch them working . . .' she looked straight at Anya, 'in between a woman's legs.' Anya gasped, although she had half expected something of the kind. 'Oh . . . my dear, I've shocked you now,' Ildren pouted. 'Never mind . . . your Taskmistress will help you; would you like that? Hmmm?'

Then Anya was filled with shame at what the Taskmistress bade her do. 'Place your fingers there, my love. Your little bud of pleasure should not be made to hide its head. It must be made to stand out proudly in its pinkness. Do it now for me, that I may look upon its lewdness and its longing.' Ildren made her squeeze her fingers in behind it, whilst Ildren stroked her breasts at first, then pulled her nipples until they stood out very firmly. 'I like those cherries nice and hard,' she said. 'Now squeeze your pip out; hold it very still for me. Mmm . . . It looks so sweet like that. Hold still . . .' Very carefully she reached her fingertip and scratched the nail across the surface of Anya's pushed-out, polished button, very slowly, hardly touching the skin at all, and back again, repeatedly, which set Anya's teeth on edge and sent torturing tickles to the very core of Anya's wanting. 'There, you like this don't you, my darling . . . this very gentle scratching at your pip.' The tickling felt to Anya like a burning itch which was crying out for succour. She wanted Ildren to scratch harder and more deeply at that itch, to assuage the unbearable unremitting cascading tickling which each little stroke of nail on tautened skin bestowed in sweet delicious torture. She wanted to close her thighs against this cruel and honeyed pleasuring, yet she could not. Ildren's other hand had trapped her fingers tightly against herself, forcing her to squeeze her pip out even harder, keeping its surface drumtight, so the tickling might thereby resonate more deeply, more gnawingly into Anya's body.

And yet, for all its pleasuring, that tickling was not a tickling which could bring release, for Ildren was too calculating for this to happen to her slave. She controlled the stroking, making the tickles lighter whenever Anya's breathing shallowed and her eyelids closed that little bit too languorously. She would at this stage slow Anya's pleasure, balancing her on a knife edge, which it seemed the Taskmistress would hone ever finer, but would never tip her over, and when eventually that breathing became a little more controlled, then Ildren would edge her very gently once more in the direction of her pleasure, using words of encouragement. 'Would you like me next to lick my tongue around your tip, and flick it very quickly?'

Anya's oil dripped slowly from her and trickled down the groove towards her bottom; its heavy droplets stirred and pulled her skin hairs, adding to her torment. Ildren's fingertip would pause at intervals, to gather up a liquid drop of Anya's nectar and smear it round her stiffened nub, or merely touch it to the end and pull away again, so the weighted droplet would, in its pulling, kiss and suck upon her point and kiss and pull again, repeatedly, until that droplet was dissipated and the skin of Ildren's finger, softened by Anya's oil, would touch and stroke against the skin of Anya's fleshy nub in shimmers of delight. And then the fingernail would scratch again, and start that train of tickling sharpness, making Anya drip again, until she was sitting in a cool evaporating pool of oily wetness which was spreading on the table.

'My delicious beauty – make your honeydew for me,' Ildren whispered. Taking hold of Anya's fingers, she dipped them in the pool and sucked them one by one, then taking Anya's forefinger, she dripped it once again and smeared the liquid back and forth and up and down across her pink and pulsing button, until Anya did not care that it was she who touched it, that the Taskmistress was no longer guiding Anya's hand against her body, that she was pleasuring *herself* quite wantonly before this woman, and that her body began to shake in rolling waves of pleasure in that precursor to her sweet relentless surge of wild abandonment.

A hand closed tightly round her own and held it fixed, suspended above her pulsing pip, whilst Anya tried to push her hips towards it and she moaned. The Taskmistress had caught her at the very point, and in that split second had denied her that deliverance to desire.

'Enter!' Ildren shouted, though Anya had not heard any knock.

Anya felt so exhausted and so let down – so used – by this woman's cruel denial, that she really did not care any more. She saw the figure through weary, half-closed misted eyes, yet even so, the bulky form was quite unmistakable. Her heart leapt, and then Anya was filled instead with shame and sadness at her present state – her bondage and her lustful degradation.

8

The Pearl of Love

'Marella – I take it you have come to collect your charge?'
The Taskmistress stood and placed Anya's hands very deliberately behind her back. 'You are early. We had not
quite . . . completed our little exercise, had we my darling?'
She tickled Anya underneath the chin. 'Well, never mind,
my pet,' she kissed her on the forehead, 'we shall continue
perhaps on another occasion. Would you like that?'

Anya could only glance down and be glad that, for the
present, she was escaping from this woman's cruel embrace. Ildren carefully unwound the thong from Anya's
breasts, saying, 'Oh, my darling – it has marked you. Was
it then too tight? You should have told me . . .' And she
pressed and kneaded Anya's breasts until the furrows,
though clearly visible still, were rather more subdued. Then
she untied Anya's feet and, making her stretch out on the
table, she massaged her thighs and limbs, which treatment
Anya found welcome though she was well aware by now
that she must never fully trust this woman. Ildren opened
Anya's thighs once more, but this time to bathe her sticki-
ness and heat with a coolly moistened cloth, and then to
dab her dry with a touch so tenderly deceptive that Anya
was, by virtue of experience, mildly apprehensive about the
purpose of this careful preparation – about what might
happen next.

'She is to be taken to Lord Aldrid's chambers . . .'
Anya's heart felt as if an icy hand had closed around it,
'where she will spend the night.'

'Yes, ma'am,' Marella said very dutifully, as if this were
an everyday assignment, as if she had forgotten her prom-

ise to Anya that she would recount to the Taskmistress the cruel abuse which Anya had been made to suffer at Lord Aldrid's hands.

'He wishes to continue her training – which I have, on his advice, begun. Training in the art of self control . . .' the Taskmistress added. Anya shivered. '. . . In which he found her to be lacking, though in this respect I have extracted some small improvement . . .' Ildren stroked Anya's forehead. 'Have I not, my sweet?' Anya merely swallowed. 'Now, up and be off with you before his lordship gets impatient,' said Ildren, pulling Anya to her feet.

Marella smiled at Anya, and Anya's heart surged. It seemed that she drew strength from the warmth of this woman's simple smile. Marella reached and took her hand, and Anya felt happy, as if all the fear and pain and cruelty were somehow washed away.

'One moment . . .' The Taskmistress held something between her finger and her thumb. 'She shall require this – the pearl.'

Even Marella did not care to watch the fitting of this jewel. She turned her head aside whilst the Taskmistress had Anya lie upon the table once again and hold her knees apart.

'Do not be afraid, my pet,' Ildren tried to cheer her, for Anya was very anxious now, in this very outspread state, with the Taskmistress poised above her with an unknown though small, device which Anya knew was destined to be applied in some way to her private self, or possibly – and she shuddered at this thought – inserted into her body. Ildren's eyes had narrowed, confirming Anya's worst fear, that this device was cruel. 'Be still, my precious one, though your shivers appear to me so sweet and so delicious.' Ildren closed her eyes and inhaled deeply, and it seemed that she too had almost shivered. 'Yet there is nought to fear. Spread yourself more widely. Open out to me. Submit your delectable self to my intimate attentions, and look upon my face, my darling, whilst I apply this precious jewel to your droplet.' Anya was very frightened now. How would the jewel be secured to her in so tiny and

115

sensitive a place? It was sure to be excruciatingly painful, Anya felt certain.

'Keep still, my pet, and do not raise your legs.' The Taskmistress had touched her hood to ease it back and yet this simple act had, fired by Anya's fearful state, felt more piercing than a knife-cut into Anya's flesh. 'This will not hurt – I do assure you – it will be at most a little tiny sting.' Then Ildren's voice was sterner. 'Now stop your twitching, for you must co-operate.' She decided next to make Anya use her fingertips to pull back and hold her fleshy hood so Ildren's hands were unencumbered and could administer the pearl more easily. It touched Anya and she jumped. The Taskmistress became impatient. She placed the jewel very carefully upon the table and, taking hold of Anya's nipples, she pinched them very cruelly, making Anya cry out with the searing pain of it. 'Now this time, you shall hold still, shall you not?' The Taskmistress now looked very evil, and Anya did not dare refuse her.

'Yes, ma'am,' Anya replied, but her eyes were filming over with her tears; she felt utterly defenceless against her present degradation.

And still her body twitched when Ildren touched her there – she could not help herself. The Taskmistress frowned and waited. Anya's tears welled up to blind her, and overflowed in hot and trailing droplets which splashed down across her earlobes and soaked into her hair. Ildren bent across her. The metal touched her and she shivered; Ildren very slowly tightened the miniature clamp around her pink and pulsing bud until Anya cried out at the sudden stinging bite, for she was sure the clamp had pierced her through. 'There . . . that should serve to hold it.' Ildren sounded satisfied and, wiping Anya's tears away, she helped her up. 'There we are – all ready now, as his lordship has requested.'

Anya found herself face to face with Marella; her pale appearance only served to make Anya's throat tighten and her tears well again.

'You may take her now, Marella.'

And with that, Marella advanced towards Anya and

buried her in those huge arms; she pressed her to her soft warm breast while Anya could only cling to her and sob salt tears in misery and pain. Marella's hands stroked Anya's satin locks and curled them round her fingers. 'My soft sweet child, my doe,' she said and lifted up that face to kiss away those tears. Anya, gazing upon those small bright eyes felt, not happy, yet bathed somehow in this woman's warmth, and calmed by her kindness.

Marella lifted up the hand that wore the turquoise ring and pressed it to her lips, making Anya smile amidst her newly welling tears. 'There – you shall cry if that is what you want, my honey. Does it hurt so very much?' She kissed the ring again. 'The jewel is not in truth so terrible as you, in your innocence, may fear, my darling – it is but an adornment to your beauty – as are your golden chains and as indeed this ring is. And in the same way in which your chains remind you of their presence as you move, so too this pearl betokens, though in a more precise and intimate way, so that in the loving swell of pleasure you may feel its firm restraint against you at your focus of delight. Now, tell Marella . . . Does it really cause you pain?'

Marella was correct, Anya realised, for once she had overcome the shock and fear of the unknown – that cruel fitting of the jewel to which the Taskmistress had subjected her – the pain had ebbed away and was replaced instead by a gentle throbbing pulsing of her nub against the unyielding, tight, yet not at present overbearing pressure of the clamp. 'Would you like to look at it, to see how harmless and insignificant this bauble really is?' Anya did not want to look at herself at all, and most certainly not with such a thing as this in place, and yet she did not stop Marella, who then had Anya ease her legs apart, whilst she positioned a mirror in such a way that Anya now beheld her blackness and the milk-rose pearl, half the size of Anya's little fingernail; it projected from the joining of her inky leaves of flesh and was mounted on a tiny clamp of gold, attached to Anya's nubbin. And when Anya's black fleshy hood was sleeved fully down again, the mounting was unseen, so it appeared that a pink and pearly opalescent droplet swelled from underneath to catch the light.

The pearl was in reality an adornment which served a dual purpose, for in its gripping it would seduce the wearer with its constant pleasurable stimulation in that critical place and, at the same time, it would excite desire in the beholder, who would see in it an exaggeration of that pearl-pink fleshy droplet which was hooded underneath, and would know that each tiny touch or tongue-tip licked upon this jewelled bud would transmit to tantalize the fleshy pearl beneath.

Anya's anxiety was stilled by what she saw reflected in the mirror, and yet in this she was quite definitely misguided, for this jewel, however pleasing to the eye, was in no way the innocent adornment that Marella had suggested it to be. The Taskmistress had applied to it a salve, a potent stimulus to pleasure, which would in due course incite in its unfortunate victim the most lascivious wanton desire, which the pleasure-trapping pearl would magnify, whilst Lord Aldrid would certainly require that the young slave's release be held in abeyance, for tonight at least, as part of her training in the intricate interplay of love, desire and satisfaction.

Ildren was smiling very sweetly as Marella led Anya out. She was standing beside the bondslave, who was still fastened to the wall, her body arched and her legs outspread, exactly as Ildren had earlier left her, and Anya noticed, as the door was closing, that Ildren's hand had reached to grip the wooden stem still bedded in the woman. A little shiver ran down through her and out between her legs at the thought of what the Taskmistress might do to the slave, secure behind closed doors, with no one there to witness, or to hear the poor girl's cries of degradation. And a tiny stirring came, in between Anya's legs, exactly at the node wherein the pearl was bedded, a feeling quite delicious, a feeling which Anya did not fully understand.

Once outside the Taskmistress's apartments, when the two of them were at a sufficiently safe distance for Anya to feel they were out of earshot, she stopped and took Marella's hand in both of hers.

'Marella, why have you not brought my cloak?' she asked, for despite the chains, Anya was still concerned about her nudity. What if they should encounter someone – perhaps one of the guards again?

'Anya dear, you shall not need your cloak this night, for you must have heard the Taskmistress – Lord Aldrid shall require your services and, like the Taskmistress, he prefers his bondslaves nude.'

Anya was really very worried to have Marella reiterate her destination in so detached a manner. 'But his lordship forced himself upon me – you said as much yourself. You said you would inform the Taskmistress, and – and have him chastised,' Anya ventured hopefully.

Marella could only chuckle at these words, and then, realising how upset her charge was, she took her hands quite tightly in her own and shook them warmly. 'My darling ... you have misunderstood. The Taskmistress cannot chastise their lordships – such treatment, should it prove necessary, lies only in the Prince's gift. The Taskmistress may certainly advise their lordships, and she does so very frequently, but she cannot in truth instruct them, any more than you or I could.' Marella looked concerned that Anya had somehow misconstrued her words.

'But you said ...' Anya was unhappy with this explanation.

'I told the Taskmistress, and she agreed that Lord Aldrid was ill-advised in taking such ...' Marella pursed her lips in recollection, 'such precipitate action with a novice. This was why the Taskmistress took time and effort with you this evening – to help prepare you for your ord–' she corrected herself. 'For your assignment to his lordship.'

Anya was neither convinced nor reassured by this. She felt that Marella, out of kindness, would always pretend to her that things were better than in reality was the case, to try to soften the hurtful blows that fate might hold in store. 'Marella,' she said, 'I am frightened ... Do not leave me alone with his lordship.'

'My dear, you will be quite safe with Lord Aldrid. He wishes only to advance your training.' This was what was

119

making Anya frightened. Would he . . .? Should she ask Marella? Would she get the truth?

'Will he want to . . . Will he torture me, Marella?' Anya closed her eyes. A little shiver, stronger now, had rippled through her sex, and her flesh had pulsed against the pearl which kissed her nubbin.

'No . . . no, my honeypot. His lordship would never do such a thing. He will teach you certain things, and test that you have learnt them, exactly like the Taskmistress would, that is all, though the methods certainly will differ.' Anya did not care to ask Marella to elaborate. 'And besides,' she went on, 'you will not be alone with him. Axine will be there with you.' Anya was relieved at first, but then began to wonder why Axine's presence should be required as part of her training; she was on the point of asking Marella about this when she was interrupted by the sound of many footsteps at the far end of the corridor.

'Oh, my word!' Marella sounded flustered and began straightening her hair. 'The Prince!' Now it was Anya's turn to get excited. She felt hot, then cold, then hot again as the cortège approached. Marella backed against the wall and Anya did the same, but tried to hide herself beside Marella's bulk whilst simultaneously peeping around her. The Prince stood out from the rest – he was taller, and more confident in his stride; the others hung back at a distance from him. His tunic was of red and gold; his deep red cloak was fringed with blue, that intense blueness of lightning in a storm-dark sky; his hair was short and brown, or golden – Anya could not now be sure. His gaze was piercing in its strength – she was sure of that, because that was what she remembered most vividly, even though she could not see those eyes, not yet at least. He seemed to wear – so *that* was what she had seen, there at the banquet – a gold ring through the lobe of his ear, but through only one ear, the left one. This puzzled Anya very much indeed. She had never previously seen a man with jewellery in his ears; it seemed very strange to Anya, so much so that she completely forgot to bow down as the Prince drew nigh.

The Prince did not speak at all at first, and for a long

and timeless moment, the Prince and the slave stared once again at each other, the Prince looking handsome and determined, and set apart from his entourage, the slave, standing in simple torch-lit innocence and beauty above the partly doubled over form of her governess, and framed against the rough-hewn stonework. It was almost as if, by some impossible freezing of time and wrenching of the wheel of fate, the Prince and the slave were equals, as if, in the locking of their gaze, that secret kissing of their eyes, their fortunes had now intertwined, as if those twin threads of guilelessness and admiration had wound together to form a bond between their lives in that special moment.

Anya loved the strength of character in that face – she loved those deep green eyes, that soft brown hair, and powerful chin, that nose – but most of all, those eyes. And that single earring – she liked that now – she wanted to kiss that ear lobe with the ring in place. She closed her eyes; the thought of kissing him like that had caused a tingle so delicious in that secret place, which was throbbing very gently now with the after-tingle. When she lifted her eyelids again, those beautiful green eyes still gazed at her. The Prince's lips – those soft lips – moved; she heard the sounds, but Anya was not listening to the words.

Marella stood up, wheezing. 'Yes Sire, it is the same,' Marella said. But what had been the question?

Then Anya realised that the Prince was looking at her breasts. She straightened automatically; her shoulders went back; her breathing changed; it seemed she could not control that shallowness of panting. Her stomach muscles tightened. The Prince appeared to gaze at Anya for a long time. Then Anya realised with horror that her breasts must still bear the welts of the leather thong which the Taskmistress had wrapped so tightly round her. What would the Prince think, to see her so disfigured? He seemed almost to be looking through her body, though, as if very deep in thought. Then he looked Anya in the face and those eyes which had appeared so strong and gentle now seemed troubled. His gaze worked down her body and Anya sensed he was staring at her belly, and yet

121

she doubted if the pearl could be seen. The Prince then bent over to Marella and whispered something in her ear. Marella only nodded very gravely, and the Prince again surveyed Anya, and then, lifting up her chin, he turned her head to one side, then the other. His fingertips felt soft, yet strong. Anya, looking down, beheld the Prince's fingers reach as if to touch her brown-black nipples, then hesitate and withdraw – as though, in the end, he was afraid.

'Is Ildren in her chambers still?' the Prince asked Marella. His voice was deep and soft, and yet Anya thought his voice had wavered. He looked at her again.

'Yes, Sire.' Then Anya wondered if she had heard aright:

'And yet ... How could such a thing be possible?' he whispered, almost to himself.

With that, the Prince turned and led his retinue in the direction of the Taskmistress's apartments, leaving Marella and Anya looking at each other with very nonplussed expressions.

Anya would have much time, that night, to ponder the Prince's words. She wished that she had asked Marella, directly, what it was the Prince had whispered, though she thought that, possibly, she could guess. And that knowledge would help Anya through that night which would seem to her unending, and that cruel yearning need which would swell repeatedly in waves of torment and of unfulfilled desire.

9

The Longest Night

The North Tower made Anya feel afraid. It was so forbidding. That walk had seemed so long, down the echoing corridor, which had got darker and colder, so that Marella's wheezing had forced them to keep stopping, while the dampness seeped deeper and deeper into Anya's shivering body. But she could have borne the coldness; it was the sombre emptiness of that part of the castle that had frightened her. And now they stood at the foot of the spiral staircase, and she could hear the night wind whistling against the tower walls.

Anya was too afraid to mount the stairs alone. 'You come with me, Marella – you take me up there,' she pleaded. The stairs looked very dark, and wound upwards, out of sight, around the corner.

'You will be quite safe, Anya, for there is nought up there except his lordship's chambers. You need only knock and wait until he bids you enter.' Marella sounded very patient; she had explained these things to Anya several times already.

'But why will you not come with me? There might be something up there, hiding round the corner, in the darkness.'

Marella only chuckled till her body shook. 'Now what on earth would be hiding there, my dear?'

'Some creature – I don't know . . .' Anya's cheeks were turning red. 'Perhaps a guard,' she suggested, for she was well aware how dangerous these creatures could be.

'But the guards are there for our protection,' Marella said, surprised. 'A guard would never harm you.'

'But . . .' This was not Anya's perception of the guards; she was recalling Marella's words about the guardroom and the fate of slaves who had misbehaved. Perhaps Marella too remembered, for now she interrupted Anya very quickly.

'And besides, there are no guards up there,' she said.

'Then come with me. I am frightened – of Lord Aldrid too,' Anya finally admitted.

'My dear, you must be strong.' Marella held Anya by the shoulders and squeezed her lovingly. 'All of this is part of your training. Marella should not need to take you everywhere, for you must learn to show you can be trusted; as trust develops, a slave may gain her little freedoms, and small privileges. She may win favour with their lordships – even with His Highness.'

'The Prince?' Anya's eyes looked brighter now.

Marella nodded. 'Yes – but a raw, untrustworthy slave could never be allowed within the Prince's quarters, now could she?'

Anya's heart was beating wildly as she rounded the corner of the stairway, but it was not so dark as she had feared, and there was no one to be seen. She stepped back again to check whether Marella had kept her word. The woman, rolling slowly, raised her arm and pointed, to indicate that Anya should press on upwards. A dim light flickered above a door at the end of the passageway. The walls and floor felt cold against Anya's hands and feet, and raised a shiver. The silence was so profound it seemed to weigh down on Anya, making her feel very frightened and alone. And having reached the door, she stood, then turned around as if to run, then forced herself to turn back again. Her breath misted the air and then dissolved. She raised her hand but could not strike the door. Her arm felt very heavy and her fingers would not curl into a fist. Her palm came to rest against the woodwork, her fingertips against the grain, and she remembered very clearly what this man had done to her outside the Great Hall, how she had been so degraded by his words and by his actions. Anya closed her eyes and, for a moment, she found herself reliving that swelling pulsing pleasure at the point at which the pearl now gripped her. That pulsing had almost made her want to spread herself once more against the door – the pleasure there between her thighs had felt so intense and urgent, as if a tiny mouth was round her, slowly sucking.

Anya swayed and suddenly it seemed the door had moved away as if she were falling backwards, which made her open her eyes and reach to steady herself. There, in the open doorway, stood Axine. Anya was so relieved to see a friend; she opened her mouth to speak, but Axine whispered to her first. 'Enter. You are expected, Anya.' And having closed the door behind the two of them, Axine led Anya into his lordship's chambers.

On this occasion however, Axine did not take Anya's hand, as she had done when she had rescued her in that wild chase from the kitchen; instead Axine walked ahead of her, and Anya noticed once again the self-assurance in this woman's stride and disposition. She found herself admiring the slim smooth form of Axine's body – not muscular, yet economically sculpted – those almost boyish hips, those shoulders which supported Axine's small firm breasts, that short black bush of hair, shaved and shaped in such a way as to set off Axine's delectable ears, as if exposing them in readiness for the tentative explorations of soft warm lips which might seek solace in the cool precision of those delicate fleshy folds.

Axine halted before a second, inner doorway and pointed to the stone-flagged floor, or rather, to a bowl and jug which rested there. At first, Anya did not understand what was required, so Axine demonstrated. She stepped into the bowl and, bending, poured in some water, then proceeded to wash her feet, after which she deftly stepped across the threshold and used a linen cloth to dry herself. Anya had to do the same, after she had emptied the bowl into a gutter cut into the stone floor. This ritual seemed very strange to Anya – she did not see its purpose until Axine pulled aside the heavy curtain that had filled the doorway and Anya was admitted to Lord Aldrid's bedchamber.

This inner sanctum was quite different from the picture that Anya had formed within her mind, for she had never seen a room so sumptuously appointed as the one that lay before her now. The floor was entirely covered with thick-piled carpeting and furs, which pressed between and tickled Anya's toes; underfoot, no flagstone could be seen, or even sensed – the floor felt softer than any bed that Anya had ever slept upon. But the walls – Anya was spellbound by what she beheld – they were covered with exotic drapes and tapestries which pictured imaginary lands, with unfamiliar trees and fruits and beasts, the like of which the slave had never heard told, not even in fable. There were armoured beasts with a single horn, and a beast of gold, with a neck so long it stretched above the trees; then there were curiously painted horses, with brands like jagged thunderbolts, and a giant cat, and a bare-necked chicken, ten feet tall. The ceiling was domed and set out like the night sky, with all the stars upon it, and though these stars were figured larger than they would appear outdoors, still Anya recognised the scene to be a faithful image of the winter sky, with all the familiar star patterns – the Mouse, the Wheatsheaf, the Great Deershead, and in the background, the River of Snow. There were also shooting stars which looked very real, but the painter had depicted *two* opposing moons, a pink one and a blue one. This puzzled Anya very much indeed.

The room was warmed by flames of firelight licking in the grate; the air smelled sweetly scented, and in the centre of the room, in simple splendour, was a very large low bed – a bed almost as large as the huge one in the Bondslaves' House – which appeared to be upholstered in velvet of the deepest blue. The coverlet was cast back so it draped across the floor, and in the middle of the bed, clad in a robe of golden-yellow, was his lordship, propped up on one arm. With those cold and penetrating eyes he watched the bondslaves, and waited till Axine had reached the side of the bed.

'The slaves await your lordship's pleasure,' Axine announced and bowed. Anya, standing there beside her, not knowing what to do, merely copied Axine's actions.

'So, my lickerish one – you deign to flatter us with your presence,' his lordship said quite coldly, and Anya knew then that all her fears were very well founded. Lord Aldrid had that look – his craggy eyebrows, frowning, overhung those cold blue eyes, which stared at Anya fixedly, like an eagle poised to strike. 'I trust you have learnt something since we last met? Some self control perhaps?' His voice was very stern; it made her very frightened. 'Speak up, wench. Tell me – have you learnt your lesson?'

'I . . .' Anya almost felt like crying. Axine had moved away to a safer distance, leaving Anya on her own to suffer his lordship's vicious onslaught. Her shoulders hunched; her head hung down in bleak despair. What could she say to him that would not make him turn her words against her? 'My lord . . .' Anya's arms were tense; her fingernails were digging in her palms. 'I have – I have tried . . .' Her voice just trailed away.

'Hmmph. Well, we shall see.' He sounded slightly mollified by this. 'Has the Taskmistress prepared you in the way that I instructed?'

Anya felt a coldness seeping through her belly, for she felt sure his lordship was referring to the pearl. This time, she could not answer; her shame was too intense.

'If you choose to stand in sullen silence, that is your affair . . .' Lord Aldrid's eyes narrowed and he pressed his lips together, then when he spoke again, it was very quietly, through tightly clenched teeth. 'But I warn you – you shall certainly come to regret such mulishness . . .'

Anya was now terrified, and she started trembling. Lord Aldrid suddenly reached towards her and she nearly jumped away from him.

'And insolence too,' he said, and yet it seemed his lordship was relishing the anguish that his threats caused the slave. 'Then perhaps, my dear, you would prefer instead to cool your heels in the guardroom?' His smile was very evil.

Anya began to panic at the mention of that place. 'No. Please no . . .' she wrung her hands in supplication and fell to her knees to beg him not to send her there. Those ice-cold eyes, now perched above her, sparkled as his lordship turned his head to one side to look at her, in her pleading. Anya could not help but visualise him as a bird of prey about to stab her and then to tear her body open.

'Stand up,' he ordered, very quietly.

Lord Aldrid reached again and Anya had to shut her eyes to prevent herself from squirming back away from him. His long thin fingertips touched her there – precisely in that spot. He was assessing the pearl, measuring it with his fingertips, by feel alone. His lordship's palpitations of the jewel were so delicately placed that neither Anya's leaves nor hood were brushed – he only touched the pearl – so the tiny movements were transmitted through, directly to her point of flesh. That gentle pulling stirred her, seemed to fire her lust, as if the pearl were somehow coupled through her body, as if a thread of tautness, passing up through Anya's belly, connected to the backs of Anya's nipples and stretched up into her throat then bedded in at last beneath her tongue. Each pull his lordship gave the pearl caused Anya's belly to thrust out, and then her head to fall back limply, almost like a doll's, and finally her tongue to lift and push in stirring stiffness against the back of Anya's teeth.

'I see your training has enhanced that lickerishness of spirit.' Lord Aldrid flicked the pearl; a stinging pleasure flashed up into Anya. 'Perhaps I might have been too harsh on you. Now spread, that I might look upon your blackness and your beauty.' And Anya heard his lordship's sharply indrawn breath, which made her open her eyes to see those blue-grey eyes of his – still cold, perhaps, but much less threatening – caress her burning with that cool calm gaze which stemmed her fear, yet at the same time heightened her palpitating in that spot between her thighs. Her nub had swelled to make the pearl grip, in tightness and in pleasure. 'This pearl has never looked so exquisite upon any slave's person,' his lordship whispered, and reached again, but this time did not touch, as if now he were afraid to do so. Yet it seemed that Anya felt that touch although it did not happen; her sex contracted at that pull that did not come; that feeling was, to Anya, quite delicious.

Lord Aldrid's gaze had shifted; he had noticed this little ripple of delight. 'It seems the pleasuring has begun,' he murmured, though Anya was unsure quite what his lordship meant by this. But she was sure that she wanted him to touch her once again, to take the pearl and very gently twist it in his fingers. The thought of that made Anya's pip pulsate again.

His lordship sat back on the bed, and his expression now appeared much sterner. 'I now propose to advance your training one step further – with your consent, that is,' he added, scrutinising Anya very carefully. He held up his hand, as if to demonstrate; his long thin fingers bunched together in such a way that all four fingertips were touching. That ominous gesture made Anya apprehensive once again. 'And are you in agreement with this ... rather forthright specification?' He turned his hand to examine it from the back. 'Hmmm? Or would you prefer it if, firstly, I were to remove my ring? ... There now, is that more appealing to your person, would you think?' This action only served to confirm Anya's fears. That coldness in her belly came again. It seemed to drain away those feelings that had earlier felt so sweet. 'Shall this be sufficient counterpoise to that lusting in your belly?' The coldness turned to ice inside her. 'So – no reply. Well then, we shall see your stubbornness tested to its limit.'

Anya felt like turning to run but she knew there was no escape. In this castle, their lordships and the Taskmistress would surely mould her to their will, for her body now belonged to them. But even the certainty of that knowledge did nothing to lessen the weight of it – the burden of what she knew would happen to her now – that cruel means by which his lordship would wish to penetrate her; that degrading way in which he would in time procure Anya's pleasure.

'Axine, bring a cushion to support this wench, and have *her ladyship* spread face down on the bed,' he turned Anya's chin so that she faced him and could see his wickedly sneering smile, 'that we may examine her in a more intimate manner, and thereby determine the root cause of her waywardness . . . and, who knows, sharpen up her wanting.'

Anya was drawn, face down, into the centre of Lord Aldrid's very great bed. She neither co-operated, nor did she resist; she allowed her body to go very limp in her submission to his lordship's very perverse designs, for she wanted to detach herself completely from any treatment to which his lordship might try to subject her body merely to stimulate her longing, simply to satisfy his whim.

The cushion was positioned with very great precision, so it pressed into Anya's belly and raised her hips but did not brush against her tenderness.

'The pearl must remain suspended and free from all distracting touches,' Lord Aldrid announced, and took great care that the pearl touched neither the cushion nor indeed the surface of the bed 'It will be necessary for her to be spread as wide as it is possible so to do – and then a little more, I fear, and held, open and accessible, in that position.' His lordship then explained to Axine exactly how he wished such spreading to be brought into effect.

Anya's cheek was pressed against the velvet; her fingers, stretching out above her, took comfort from its thick plush pile by clawing deeply into it. Axine's thighs trapped Anya's ribcage; her bottom pressed into Anya's back, between her shoulders; the soles of Axine's feet were softly moulded up against Anya's armpits; Anya's breasts, pushed outwards by the weight of Axine's body, moved with every breath against the soft fine hairs of Axine's calves, which brushed and tickled Anya's nipples. And Axine's hands, by locking in the crook of Anya's knees, held them high up on the bed, keeping Anya very open, so that, with Anya's belly supported by the cushions, her sex was left projecting out above the bed for Aldrid's carefully calculated attentions. The pearl, though free and unrestricted by any possible irritating touches from the bed, the cushion, or even Anya's squeezing thighs, still pulsed very gently at intervals, as Anya's mood would swell the living pearl beneath it against the nipping pleasure of the mounting, and trip those sweet yet cruel unstoppable cascades of honeyed palpitations which, even in their ebbing, would slowly well again to trip once more.

Her sex was burning to be penetrated; her body boiled with lust, and yet, pinned and held like this, she was quite powerless to help her body onwards or to prevent his lordship from doing precisely as he pleased. And now, it seemed, his lordship was pleased to take his time. Anya could not know quite when or where or even how that touch might come. All that she could do was to lie and wait and breathe and heave and thereby brush her breasts, and claw the bed and pulse and spread, until his lordship cared to touch her – where he liked.

Axine's bottom had pressed and spread on Anya's back, to the point where Axine's dense black bush curls captured Anya's downy hairs and tickled Anya's skin. His lordship's finger touched her and she almost passed out with delight – that soft and gentle brushing fingertip had stroked around that tightened inturned skin around the very mouth of Anya's bottom. That touch was feather-light against her black-brown velvet. His lordship's fingerpad now stroked her in a scarcely touching circle; it sensitised those very secret innocent nerves which should not be awakened, making Anya want to push up against that fingertip, and close that nervous pulsing mouth around it, and to kiss and suck it with her body. The finger kept on circling. The slow insistent delicious spiralling of pleasure penetrated Anya; its filaments of delectation twisted down through her bottom; its reaching tendrils rooted in her flesh and, searching, seemed to curl around and squeeze and draw and tickle Anya's nubbin from behind.

'Your jewel of pleasure is pulsing very lewdly,' his lordship observed, and Anya's face was burning, though with Axine restraining her in so firmly open a position, she could not prevent her body from responding to this meticulous fingertip seduction. And in truth, she did not want the tickling to stop. She wanted his lordship to keep tickling her in such delicious circles, until Anya cried out for his lordship to show mercy, and to strip the pearl right from her body and squeeze and draw that living fleshy pearl beneath, then split and penetrate her tortured sex with his cool hard stem, until her body heaved and burst in pleasurable relief and Aldrid squirted liquid coolness deep within her.

The circling stopped, yet Anya's pearl kept pulsing slowly. His lordship's fingers touched her soot-black leaves of flesh and teased apart their liquid gripping surfaces, then spread them back against her curls. Anya's leaves remained open, of their own accord, in soft and pliant obedience to his lordship's unspoken yet very clearly indicated requirement. And then his tongue-tip touched the inner surface of those open leaves, incising fine cool lines of liquid pleasure into Anya's warm compliant out-turned innerness.

Axine split – her leaves unfurled and spread her heat across the skin of Anya's back, as Axine's thighs, driven by the vision that unfolded now before her, had widened, and her pressing had intensified. Lord Aldrid's tongue, not pointed now, but flattened out to encompass Anya's leaves, broad-brushed her in a single upstroke which deposited a film of Aldrid's thickened spittle across Anya's openness and slowly up into the groove of her bottom.

Then Aldrid spoke to Axine. 'Hold her very firmly; keep her legs spread very wide.' Axine's sex contracted, suckering down upon the bumps of Anya's spine, so Anya felt that burning heat was boring down inside her. Her legs were tensed by Axine's hands, her sex projected out above the cushion; the throbbing there below the pearl was more insistent. Then Anya felt her already outspread leaves being held back flat against her curls, and the bunched-up fingers pressing up against her, then slipping through the mouth of her sex, which gripped and in its gripping measured out the girth of all four fingertips. Anya closed her eyes and opened out her body to that cool insistent cone of finger-flesh which pushed up into her. The knowledge that Axine would be witnessing her penetration made Anya ashamed; she wondered how she would ever bring herself to look upon Axine's face again, for she would see forever mirrored in that face her own connivance at this debauching of her person. Because, despite her shame, she wanted this fleshy cone to press on up inside her; her body yearned to be filled, to take another's flesh like this and squeeze it. That long cool searching middle finger found the mouth of Anya's womb, and Anya wanted that fingertip to push against her – to have that probing fingerpad keep kissing at her womb. Each time it touched her there it gave her such deep, voluptuous pleasure.

Lord Aldrid's other hand now spread her buttocks. 'Perfect blackness ... Let me fill your ink-black beauty,' he said; his thumb stroked across, then pushed into her bottom; the shock of penetration there made Anya's eyes spread wide. Her head went back; her heart beat fast; her breathing came in gasps – the thumb slid slowly in against the tightness of her closure. The slower it moved against her flesh, the tighter she became, until very soon it stopped.

'Your body would deny me access?' Lord Aldrid sounded grave. His frightening words only made her tighten harder, until the end of his thumb felt like a bone. 'It seems some training is required in this department, too. Perhaps your Taskmistress will be able to suggest some corrective measure ...' Anya shivered. 'But that is for the future. In the meantime, I shall overlook this one transgression. Now, you shall relax and submit yourself to this particular delight.'

His lordship then had Anya say the following words, although she was so ashamed to do so. Yet on this point his lordship proved very firm indeed – the slave must state precisely what she wanted him to do.

'I beg your lordship ... penetrate me,' she began. Lord Aldrid coughed, and she corrected herself. 'Penetrate my bottom ... please.' His fingers moved within her sex.

'Just?' his lordship prompted her. Anya was close to tears at this further degradation.

'Just as deeply as your lordship pleases.' Her cheeks were flaming. Her fingers dug into the surface of the bed, scratching out those stripes of pain and humiliation deep into the velvet.

'Good. It shall be my pleasure to penetrate you deeply.'

But Lord Aldrid's other hand slipped underneath her first, to nurture her desire. His finger tapped and flicked the pearl, whose weighted tingle shook against her in delicious stimulation. The vibrating flicks continued at a calculated rate until she felt as if her fleshy bud had dipped itself in honey, its thickness bathing her in sweetness, and then had lifted up again so the pearl was now a dangling sweet and sticky droplet, poised to drip, and in its dripping it would pull its clinging film of heavy thickness tightly round her nubbin. That feeling made her want to lift her hips and shake them very lewdly, to shake that cruelly delicious wavering droplet off that point of contact and to have his lordship's tapping fingertip instead press up against her bud and rotate against it, grinding very firmly, without respite, if needs be turning till that rigid pip of flesh was pushed inside her body – but at any rate, not stopping till her womb had liquefied and she had died of pleasure.

'That is much more comfortable – your body feels more open now – my thumb fits in you neatly.'

Anya had found that now she wanted to accommodate his lordship's hand – his fingers and his thumb. She wanted to form herself into a living glove about him and have him feel her heat; she wanted him to stroke her deep inside. His lordship's hand was moving very gently in her sea of spongy softness; the bridge between his thumb and fingers pressed into her saddle – she liked that line of pressure there; it brought a deep and diffuse pleasure. And she liked it when his fingers closed towards his thumb and, pad to pad, they trapped her wall of flesh and squeezed it very definitely. She felt that squeezing in her throat.

'You feel so soft and warm and liquid in there,' Lord Aldrid mused. 'I love you in your outspread state. I love you in your openness. I love to feel such pent-up passion in a woman.'

And now, Lord Aldrid very carefully withdrew his hand from Anya, although her body seemed reluctant to release it; the sliding of his fingers up against her inner flesh generated such deep-drawing sensations in her that her sex and bottom mouth contracted round him, and then, as she forced herself to open ('Good,' he said), the renewed pulling simply made her contract again, so the withdrawal had to be effected against these intermittent nervous pulses of her sex about his slowly drawing fingers. Then Anya felt a drip upon her lower back – a drip of liquid from within her. Lord Aldrid traced those fingers, dripping wet with Anya's oily juices, in tickling liquid smears down Anya's back, around her hips and down to Anya's thighs.

'Your body heat shall distil your musk, so I may drink it deeply – and with each delightful breath of you, I shall thereby know your need.'

Anya pressed her cheek hard into the velvet; her point of flesh was burning with desire – burning for those finger-tips to oil it too. The liquid weals of inner lust evaporated slowly, coolly, from her back, whilst Axine gently rocked above her, and Aldrid stroked a fingertip up and down her spine.

'Now sit up, my child,' Lord Aldrid said, 'and let me dandle you on my knee. Axine – bring some wine.'

Lord Aldrid's arm was cradling Anya's head, as if she were a baby; the silken smoothness of his gown was brushing on her skin. She stared, with a degree of trepidation, into that cool, lined face, and found herself examining those thick and bush eyebrows, those wispy hairs which projected from within his ears and downwards from his nostrils, and wondering what it might be like to run her fingertips up behind his head and through that grey-white hair, and to have to press her soft young lips up to that thick and wrinkled skin of Aldrid's face and kiss it. She also won-dered how his lordship might appear beneath his yellow robe – would his skin be moulded to his bones, and would her tongue-tip be required to trace each line of rib across his chest, and tickle in amongst those old grey curls? And would she find such dalliance a duty or a pleasure? She watched him raise the golden jewel-encrusted goblet to his lips, and drink; she watched the tongue that had so exquis-itely tickled and brushed her peep and draw within that mouth the blood-red drop of wine that rested on his lower lip. She watched him turn and look at her and wash her body with those ice-blue eyes, before at last he spoke.

'Some wine, my dear – to warm you in your belly?' The wine upon his breath smelled rich and aromatic.

'If it please you, my lord,' Anya found herself replying.

His lordship quaffed again and, bending over Anya, he pressed his cool firm lips to hers. She did not resist him – she opened her lips and spread, then closed them softly around his lips, sucking at them gently, like a drowsing baby, as he dripped delicious heady droplets deep into her mouth. And Anya drank that wine – each mouthful that his lordship gave her – and breathed its heavy vapour as it evaporated on her tongue, until a warm intoxication seeped right through her body and glowed within her core.

'And how do you like this style of pleasuring, my child?' Lord Aldrid asked her, whilst he tickled idly underneath her nipples, which to Anya felt heavy with the weighted warmth of wine.

'My lord – these ways to me seem most unfamiliar and –' Anya hesitated.

'Go on, my child – do not be afraid to speak your mind to me.' His lordship's fingertips caressed her nipples, each by turn, until they had hardened to his satisfaction.

'Difficult to bear . . .' she whispered, for she was apprehensive about how welcome such frankness might prove to be.

'Mmm . . . Yes, I see that,' he said. 'Yet have I caused you pain? Thus far, I have only brought you pleasure – yes?' His eyebrows raised. Anya nodded in agreement. 'Is pleasure then to be classed with pain? Is pleasure then a burden, to be cast aside as used, after very short acquaintance?'

'No, my lord . . . not quite.' Anya felt his lordship did not fully understand.

'Is it not appropriate, then, that pleasure be prolonged? If not indefinitely, then for as long as one is able?'

'My lord, I . . . It is so hard to bear, this . . . this very drawn-out pleasuring.'

'But my darling child, this is why your training encompasses these skills – to help you learn to carry your burden of desire with strength and confidence – in the way Axine does.' Axine was standing by the bedside; she smiled at Anya. It was true that Axine had confidence, Anya thought, but Axine was not being subjected to such remorseless torture as Anya. The wine had not assuaged the burning need that the pearl induced between her legs. The waves of lust would recede for several minutes, only to return with redoubled vigour, making Anya's eyelids feel heavy and her whole sex throb with unallayed desire.

'And now, assuming you are suitably refreshed, I propose to take you to that point – that delirium of pleasure – and have you balance there, as part of this, your training and also, I trust, your enjoyment.'

Anya's heart was thumping as his lordship commenced this treatment, for she felt this situation, with her sitting on his lap and cradled in his arms, was too intimate, too close, too personal for this particular style of cruel stimulation. She felt that it would have been easier if she had been restrained in some way – as the Taskmistress preferred to have her – if her body had been controlled externally, and pleasured in subjugation. She was afraid that, left free to move, she would refuse his lordship and rebel against his touch.

The wine was dripped upon her breasts, then worked around the nipples. His fingers curled around and drew upon them like a small wet mouth, until they stood out very firmly, after which he sucked them with his tongue, trapping each nipple against the roof of his mouth and pressing his tongue-tip underneath it, milking down in a slowly sucking pull. This action enlarged her nipples further, as the sucking drew fluid to the teats; this pleased his lordship. He tapped against their firmness with his fingertips, from below, then sucked again and satisfied himself about the permanence of their erection – he wanted to ensure that their black-brown rigidity contrasted suitably with Anya's soft and heavy freckle-dapped milk-white mounds – before proceeding downwards.

Anya's breasts throbbed and her nipples prickled as the

wine evaporated around them; then chilling droplets splashed across her belly as his lordship sprinkled her again, but lower down this time. His lordship made her band her knees and press her feet together, sole to sole, which opened her thighs quite fully to his caress. And now he leant her back and, moving the chain about her waist upwards, he dripped the wine in the well of Anya's navel, saying 'Do not allow this thimbleful to spill.' Anya had to keep very still whilst Aldrid opened out her leaves and traced repeatedly around their very edge with the tip of his little finger, which he had previously dipped in wine. Each time, he waited until the wine had evaporated, causing Anya's leaf edges to tighten with the sticky film of sugar from the wine, then he traced again that fine liquid line of tickling pleasure and waited patiently as Anya twitched against the itchy tightness which knitted across her skin. 'Steadily, my child,' he would say if Anya jerked too strongly, 'do not spill your cup, or we must start afresh.' And Anya then would stay exceedingly still against the tantalising ticklishness crawling over her flesh. 'Good – your training is progressing well.'

Next, his lordship was pleased to work around the pearl. He very carefully teased back Anya's hood and, dipping his finger in the goblet which Axine held close by, he suspended the fingertip above her. Anya's eyes were fixed upon the ruby droplet swelling at the end. She tried to brace herself against the splashing shock of it.

'Remember – do not move, my child,' Lord Aldrid whispered without shifting his gaze from the fingertip. Anya seemed to see the droplet, in slow motion, pull and snap away from him and drift down, wobbling drunkenly, a tiny bag of blood which hit the pearl and burst into a thousand particles which shimmered on her belly and misted in her curls. A little pleasure-shock had tapped through to her nubbin. The finger dipped and dripped again, and this time the droplet splashed into the well of Anya's drawn-back hood and seeped beneath the mounting of the pearl, filling her flesh tip with a slightly stinging warmth. The droplets dipped and splashed repeatedly, above the pearl, below it

and around it, until Anya's flesh was drenched and her
curls had netted countless misty droplets – and Anya's heat
had mixed with wine in a heavy scented vapour.

Lord Aldrid's nostrils flared; he drank that sweet musk
in and teased the pearl and stroked below it, then drawing
Anya's hood around it, he trapped the pearl in Anya's skin
and very gently pulled it. That manner of pulling felt to her
so deliciously exquisitely forbidden; it made her press the
sole of her feet together – hard – to lift her hips and push
her sex out further.

'There, enjoy, my dear. Move your hips; push out your
precious pearl – but do it very gently.'

Aldrid stretched back the skin again to expose the pearl
more fully, then used his fingertip to vibrate back and forth
across the jewel, very, very quickly. Anya felt the reson-
ance drilling up inside her. She closed her eyes and
twitched and gasped and tried to close her legs, but Aldrid
caught her thighs and held them firmly open. 'My child,'
he chided her, 'you almost spilled your wine.' And then he
had to smile, for those olive eyes of hers, set in that gently
freckled complexion, were deep wide pools of wanton sensuality; those lips upon her face were soft yet swollen,
moistened, filled with blood, and he had to pause to kiss
them. He had to purse his lips upon each red soft fruit in
turn, to lick that liquid gloss and slowly taste it with his
tongue. And then he had to resume his lesson – to draw
back the hood more firmly than before, and vibrate the
pearl of love very steadily, whilst he watched the mounting
wave of pleasure and of tension in his charge – the tightness in that belly, the misting of the eyes, the eyelids closing
in heavy weighted languor, and then those lips, those soft
sweet lips, beginning to move in silent murmurings of love
and lustful protestation, and then that focusing, that
build-up towards that exquisite pleasure, whereupon the
murmurings would melt into a moan of sweet desire – and
at that point to stop, and very gently, very carefully, to
bring her down again. He had to execute this treatment
three times in succession, but in fact he did it four times,
because he realised this slave was very special, and special

139

slaves require special treatment. And with the completion of this tickling training, he dipped his tongue and sipped the fleshy thimble of wine, then carefully licked the cup quite clean.

'My dear, I am so very pleased with you,' he said, but Anya barely heard the words. She felt drugged with heady sensuality; that constant dripping of desire within her bloodstream had made her feel so drowsy. Her sex felt enveloped in a sticky warmth and a deep and drowning longing. 'Now you shall rest awhile. Regain your strength and cool your heat.' Lord Aldrid lifted her tenderly from his lap and laid her, face down, on the bed, her arms outstretched, her thighs apart, her breasts pressed to the velvet. He had Axine prepare a folded squeezed-out cloth, previously soaked in cold, lavender-scented water, and reaching underneath Anya, he lifted her hips and spread her hot sticky leaves, then lowered her onto the cloth. The coolness bathed her burning openness; it drained her heat and seeped into her person. Then Aldrid very softly tickled Anya's back. The gentle tickling and the coolness brought such blissful relief to Anya that she fell asleep.

She did not dream – her sleep was pure deep blackness in which she was unaware of place or time – she was as a child, stretched out in peaceful, innocent, total relaxation.

Movements on the bed beside her gradually made her stir. At length, her eyelids flickered and opened to the swath of deep blue velvet surface, and Anya then recalled – the pressing cheek, the clawing fingers, the burning heat down there, replaced now by a warm clammy moistness and a distant echo of that need which had not gone away. The bed had moved again, in a slow uneven undulation. Anya turned her head the other way to see a pale and bony arm stretched down alongside her, with pale brown blotchy freckles, and coarse, yet wispy, pure white hairs. Lord Aldrid had disrobed. As carefully and quietly as she could do so, Anya turned on her side to face him. She found herself looking up above his supine form and directly into Axine's eyes. Axine simply smiled at her and Anya did not know what to do now, for she had been trying to remain unobserved for as long as possible. Axine smiled again at Anya's frown and, leaning forwards, pressed her outspread hands on Aldrid's grey-white chest then, looking now at him instead, she moved. The bed undulated. Axine's thighs were gripping Aldrid about his hips and Anya understood so very clearly what Axine was doing to his lordship. It made Anya's heart beat uncontrollably to witness such a scene, for this vision and this style of mating had broken Anya's dream – that dream, constantly refined by measured wishful thinking, in which she would take her lover in this very same position – a position which Anya had thought was known only to *her* mind – and milk his stem so very precisely, at a pace which she decided. Then, poised above him, squeezing just the end within her soft moist gently pulsing glove of flesh, she would watch his eyes expand with pure desire, and he would cry out loud her name at the spurting of his pleasure.

Axine's hips rose; Lord Aldrid's long thin stem glistened between her thighs, then sank again inside her body as Axine closed her eyes. Axine's hand slipped down his torso and in between her legs. Anya felt the inside of her belly overturn, for Axine's fingers were probing, quite deliberately, within her dense black fur. Axine was stretching back, to make her sex project and to render the touching that much more effective – Anya was sure of this, and yet his lordship did not move to stop this clear and lustful trespass. Axine's fleshliness had fanned the glowing spark of Anya's bitter-sweet denial, to make a burning fire within her. Lord Aldrid's arm was lifted, reaching out towards Axine, then it wavered, and fell instead on Anya, making her jump with sudden fright.

'So – you are with us once again, my child,' said his lordship, now propped up on one elbow. 'Come – you shall join us in this gentle relaxation. I wish to feel your lavender softness pressed against my person.'

Anya was very anxious about what he meant to do to her, as he lifted her across his old and tightened pale-skinned body. He had her sit upon his belly, and spread herself across his bony hips, after the manner in which Axine had

141

spread, but facing towards his feet. Lord Aldrid insisted upon some minor readjustments to Anya's pose, the more precisely to accommodate his purpose and his whim. He preferred, he said, that Anya bend her knees as tightly as she could, whilst keeping her feet quite flat to the bed, then she should arch her back and push her belly forwards. It was quite permissible for her to retain her balance, in this tight-arched pushed-out pose, by leaning back upon her hands, placed to either side of Aldrid's ribcage.

Anya's sex projected forwards, towards his long, upstanding stem. Her buttocks spread, and Aldrid's wiry curls sprang to tickle up inside there, against the tender ticklishness of Anya's bottom groove.

'Edge your body, arch your back, so I may feel your living flesh. Yes, that is so much better – to feel your luscious self against me.' The tightened skin of Aldrid's stem felt cool against her, but also satin smooth; she had not expected that. The smoothness stroked against Anya's soft, pursed fleshy lips. That feeling was almost pleasant – that silken smoothness brushing softly upon her intimate person.

'Axine – mould this young and beautiful thing about this old dry bone, that I may sense and taste her youthful vibrant longing,' Aldrid sighed. 'But beware, Axine – you shall require the utmost care in the handling of this sweetmeat, this fruit so ripe for bursting . . .'

His lordship's words had caused a sinking feeling deep in Anya's belly, for he meant her ordeal to continue, and worse yet, at Axine's hands.

Axine knelt and spread his lordship's legs, forcing Anya's feet apart. Her mound projected up against his long firm stem. Then Axine took each of Anya's leaves of flesh quite carefully in her fingers and pulled those leaves apart. Lord Aldrid's stem sprang back and slotted to her openness. His lordship groaned. 'So warm, so moist . . .' His flesh felt very cool against her heat, yet this contact did not cool her longing. Axine's fingers took those leaves and very cruelly, so deliciously, moulded them to that stem, pressing firmly, thinning them around it, drawing out that compliant flesh, so Anya's sticky oil was squeezed out at the feather edge, to make the seal complete, to transform her flesh into a living glove, a second skin about him. Anya could feel, against her own much quicker palpitations, the slow insistent pulse of blood which pumped into his sex. The pearl pressed against his stem and sank into his flesh; it seemed each tiny movement was transmitted to her body. Axine's fingers, trapping her against him, worked up and down in short and nervous strokes, so Aldrid's inner stem, with raised and knotted bumps and veins, moved against her peal in gentle stimulation. Now Axine drew back Anya's hooded flesh. She squeezed until the pearl was pushed out sharply, and after licking her fingertip at first, she blew it dry then very slowly rasped it across the surface of the pearl. Anya nearly died of pleasure at that point; her nubbin palpitated; like a tiny gasping tongue, it pushed the jewel in and out. Axine looked at Anya very carefully, then raised her finger once again and licked it. Anya felt delicious honeyed feelings deep within her womb as Axine held her finger out to Anya, and Anya, quaking in anticipation, tried to blow it dry. This time she held her breath whilst Axine seduced her with that rasping pleasure. Anya's knees spread wide; her hips had lifted, to offer herself more freely to that rasping tickle.

Axine bent her head and took his lordship in her mouth; her lips slid down his stem until they almost reached to Anya's leaves, and Anya could feel the gentle brush of Axine's breath within her drawn-back hood. Axine sucked and drew upon his stem until Anya felt a rolling lift within his lordship's hips – uneasy heaves – then murmurs underneath his breath. Then she watched as Axine's sucking lips drew back along his length and, at the very last second, released him, after clinging to the tip. His lordship seemed to catch his breath and Anya felt a throbbing pulsing surging in his stem. Aldrid's dense and pure white milk then bubbled out and trickled down the stem, in a slow advancing tube of thickness which enveloped Anya's jewelled bud and welled beneath the hood, which Axine had held firmly back and open, ready to receive it. Axine worked the curd-paste tenderly into Anya's leaves until Aldrid, satiated now, lifted Anya burning body off his person and back onto the bed.

His lordship now requested that Axine spread the cover across himself and his overtired slave. 'Thank you, Axine,' he said. 'You may leave us now. This girl requires rest. I fear that, in our assiduous attentions, we may have fatigued the child.'

Lord Aldrid turned his sweet young slave upon her side, so that he could smooth his hands upon that perfect back, admire those deeply freckled shoulders, and wrap those shining, curling deep red locks about his long thin fingers. Then, pushing one arm around and underneath her shoulders, he gathered up those soft warm breasts within a single hand, and nuzzled them together. His other hand was free to dangle down across those smooth-curved hips; his fingertips could run and prance within that delectably sculpted hollow, which swept so steeply downward to that outcurve of her belly that his old tired breath was sucked away and his lungs were filled with joy. His fingertips were young again and were fired with love's first dawn of sweet adventure, as they tentatively probed and parted those gentle curls – that soft underbrush of the forbidden – to release that delicious musk of nubile slave, overlain by Aldrid's passion, and then to stroke and squeeze that moist and tender girlishness within.

Anya had been made to lift one knee, so his lordship could the more easily gain access to her private self, and touch her there, between her legs. The hand that squeezed her breasts together rocked her very gently, whilst the fingers there upon her sex pressed and pulled her sticky leaves and sealed them tight together, then opened them out quite fully, and tested each of them in turn, then tightly sealed them up again, and carefully probed around the pearl. She was beside herself under the spell of so intimate a petting, yet Lord Aldrid worked her heated flesh until his paste had dried and filmed her skin in tightness, and matted in her curls. And even then, his fingers would not rest, but rolled the curls to break and crumble up those dried and crispy bindings, and pulled and teased apart each stuck-together curl, then shook away the dusted, desiccated miltings, until Anya's skin was crawling with that incessant tickling around her rootlets.

Anya was so hot and tired, and yet within that special place, it seemed her sense was so alert – and Aldrid would not leave his slave alone, would never give her peace, with those obsessive fervid touchings.

'Rest, my darling – go to sleep.' Lord Aldrid's voice was soft and deep. 'Turn over on your belly, and I will watch over you, and stroke you till slumber folds its soft black arms around you . . .'

Aldrid stroked Anya's back so softly that she almost went to sleep. And gently then, Aldrid helped Anya into a more comfortable position, still on her front, with one leg stretched out to its full extent, but the other now crooked and drawn up on the bed beside her, so Aldrid's strokings could, at Aldrid's whim – and for Anya's relaxation – extend downwards very lightly to the join between her thighs, and his lordship could softly open out and penetrate her sex, and could thereby progress that relaxing, stroking pleasure into Anya's body. Anya found that penetration stirred her animal heat.

'Shh . . . Calm your body's nervous jumping tightness. Relax and open to my stroking touch. Your body needs its sleep . . .'

Yet Anya found it hard, so very hard, to keep her body open, to adapt in pliant relaxation to that stroking of those fingers, to that constant depth of pleasure in her person. So Anya's sleep came fitfully, as if she were in fever, and Anya's dreams came, so intense, and so confused – dreams in which it seemed she was lifted, and carried bodily through the air – and, to her shame, dreams so charged with wantonness and lustful sensuality, in which she would take her lover and use him as she liked, and she would penetrate him, then bathe his body in her liquidness and heat, and make her lover kiss her in that forbidden way, and draw out his pleasure on and on, till he gasped and cried and begged for mercy. And then her body would bestow upon him that most extreme delight, whilst he murmured, over and over again, one word – her name – and she would kiss and lick and suck upon that ear – that earlobe with the ring.

And as at last the morning lift of bright grey dawn filtered through to Anya's dreaming state, she stirred. Her fingers brushed against the smooth white sheet; she breathed that familiar but as yet unrecognised faintly spicy scented air, and dozed once more, and heard but did not understand the weighted meaning of those footfalls, those sounds of busying about, those precise and careful preparations being undertaken – for her benefit alone, and for her education, the education of so very beautiful a slave – here, within the Taskmistress's apartments.

10

The Lover and the Loved

The Taskmistress of Lidir was nervous. And, what was stranger yet, she was nervous in the presence of a slave – a slave who slumbered now in Ildren's bed, a slave so very beautiful, a slave who had been dubbed a living legend, a slave who had somehow, through a very brief acquaintance, captivated the Prince's impressionable and superstitious heart, a slave deemed by Lord Aldrid to be matchless in delectability and lickerishness of spirit – in short, a slave whom Ildren would take the most exquisite, belly-liquifying delight in subjecting to the rigours of the Horse, and certainly, if Ildren herself did not pass out with suppressed desire before they reached that supreme stage of pleasurable edification, that much deeper intimacy of the Rod. And it was this – if Ildren were to take the time to analyse the situation – that was making Ildren nervous, and sending those tumbling butterflies through her belly and those delicious unannounced contractions through her sex – the thought of watching as that succulent, exotic fruit was slowly and very fully moulded to that instrument of pleasure, for Ildren's sole delight. Ildren shivered at the vision now conjured up before her – that moment of exquisite anticipation, giving way so slowly yet so definitely to that very deep and very honeyed pleasuring of her slave.

Ildren looked upon that sweet and dreaming freckled face, those locks of fire outspread on Ildren's pillow, and she wished – oh, how she wished – that she could kiss those lips now, and press them to her body. But she dared not reach to touch those lips to hers; she would not break that sleep – for this was Ildren's rule. The slave must never be disturbed, but must be allowed her rest, to awake refreshed and in her own good time, for Ildren then to take her in the manner she saw fit. Yet merely looking upon this slave, in Ildren's present state of nervousness, had fired her lust until that luscious feeling there in Ildren's belly was almost too heavenly to bear. The Taskmistress, not to satisfy that passion, but rather to feed it in its yearning, had to draw that wanting to a focus, and to parallel the slave's protracted need, and her denial.

And so, retiring to her storeroom, Ildren sought out a simple aid to pleasure, then placed a knee-high stool before the full-length mirror, and in her fully disrobed state, she placed one foot upon the stool. The golden chain, attached to the golden pear inside her, dangled down her leg. Then Ildren, throwing back her head, lowered that simple, knotted leather cord inside her mouth, to wet it with her spittle, and slowly drew it out again, then wrapped the end for two turns round her index finger. She very carefully split herself and closed the lips around the cord, and drew it slowly through them. The feeling there – as each spittle-covered knot, in sliding upwards, drew along the inner surface of her lips and then slipped across her knob – that feeling almost made her whimper. She wet the cord again and this time pushed her belly out and watched, in reflection, the drawing of her lustfulness – the gripping fingers, round her flesh, the slipping cord of pleasure, with its knotted bumps erupting through the tight-sealed tube of Ildren's lips – and she imagined a lover doing this to her body, forcing ecstasy upon her in this very special way. Ildren nearly passed out with the surging in her veins. She allowed herself that drawing pleasure three times, after which she felt her body could not take one more slippery bump of stimulation without her dying on the spot from pure delight.

Anya's dream had been so beautiful. She had lain within the Prince's strong and tender arms, her back curved against his body warmth – two love-spoons nested up together – and slept, whilst the Prince's hands extended round and very gently spread across her belly. His strength supported her, enfolded and protected her; his hand pressed reassuringly against her with each breath she took.

Anya awakened; she slowly stretched her limbs and turned upon her back. She opened her eyes to find the Prince was gone, and then to hear a soft cry, almost like the whimper of a small cowering creature. The sound seemed to have come from beyond the open door. Then Anya's mind was thrown into very great confusion at the realisation of where she was – or rather, at the recollection of where she ought to have been, but most definitely was not. For this was not Lord Aldrid's chamber, and this was not Lord Aldrid's bed. And that whimper – it had come again – what was that? Those exotic draps and fineries were gone. Anya sat up to look around. The walls were bare. Then Anya saw, with a slowly creeping chill, that the walls were not as bare as she had thought, but had inset rings in various places and at various heights. Anya turned, with mounting fear, to look upon the wall behind her, and that was Anya's very sad mistake. For on that wall, adorned as it was with rings and chains and manacles and straps, was a large framed portrait of the Taskmistress, nude and stretched upon a bed like this one.

Her arms were fastened above her head, her legs were spread very wide in the air, and her toes were pointing out and upwards. But what made Anya's belly turn to ice was the fact that Ildren's hips were drawn up – lifted from the bed. A golden chain was figured, extending like an arrow from a point beyond the frame, directly to the joining of Ildren's thighs, where it seemed to disappear, to impale itself within her body. Anya realised, with shock and shaking horror, that the chain was somehow fastened up inside this woman's body, that in some horrific way, her sex, her inner self, her very womanhood, was tethered to the ceiling of the room. Anya forced herself to look away from this image of cruel degradation, but she could not stop her eyes from drifting upwards, towards the thing which she knew would be there; that hook secured to the ceiling, above the foot of the bed, had drawn her frightened gaze against her better judgment. And then she knew that this picture was no work of vile imagination, but a record of a scene which had surely been enacted upon this very bed. Anya shivered: her breasts and belly shook beneath that awe-inspiring vision of baseness and complicity, and to her everlasting shame, the sleeping pearl of love awakened, pulsed to life again, a tiny throbbing beacon of Anya's unsatisfied desire.

Another whimper had drifted in; it had seemed much more drawn-out and anguished than the last one had, as if someone were being subjected to some very controlled torture. Then Anya heard the sound of footsteps, quickly, she lay down again, pulled the covers up about her, closed her eyes and tried hard to breathe slowly and evenly, as if she were asleep. But her heart was thumping in her throat. That spicy fragrance billowed down around her; she froze and held her breath, for now she was filled with terror. Ildren's scent receded and Anya dared to breathe again, but she was too afraid to open her eyes. She fought against the black despair that sheathed its sadness round her, and hoped and prayed that all of this might be a dream, and that she might wake up – not in *his* bed, for that was much too much to dare to wish for – but anywhere away from this place, even in Lord Aldrid's bed. Although she had hated that endless torturing of her body with delight, she had, even there, sensed some hint of gentleness behind that grey, lined face. But in these apartments, there dwelt nothing but evil, calculating cruelty.

The bedroom had fallen silent. Anya could hear nothing but the whispering of her own breathing, and the brushing of the coverlet across her ear with each and every heartbeat. She opened her eyes, and panicked. Those deep brown searching eyes stared back at her from a distance of a hands-breadth; they froze her gasp within her throat, and locked her as certainly as if her neck were broken – more surely, in fact, for Anya could not even move her eyes; she dared not even blink. The tautness ebbed right out of her. She felt her throat was severed, and now the last dregs of her life blood were seeping weakly out of her, pumped by a slow, tired, unloved heart.

'My dearest darling bird of love, your song shall greet

the dawn . . .' The Taskmistress's voice was velvet soft – so
deep and so seductive. She pressed her luscious lips to
Anya's; Anya could not move away. Ildren then knelt back
from her, beside the bed, and Anya drank her in. Her
black-brown hair, no longer tied, reached straight down to
her shoulders; it framed her face – those high cheekbones,
those matt-dark eyebrows, so precisely drawn, and those
very large deep eyes, which seemed so soft and tender, so
deceptive, like those very full warm lips. To Anya, this
woman's face seemed full of sensuality; it did not appear
cruel, and yet she knew so well what she saw was but a
mask to Ildren's nature. Anya's eyes were permitted to
move downwards. The Taskmistress was bare to the waist,
at least – Anya could see no further. Her breasts were full,
yet firm, with long and violet nipples, which were also very
pointed, almost as if they had been drawn out forcibly
from her breasts and sharpened to that shape, and perhaps
thereby had gained that colour. Anya noticed, near to their
base, small, darker blemishes – pits or tiny scars – as if the
flesh had been cut or damaged and had not knitted over.

'Perhaps you would care to test them . . . with your lips?'

Anya was so abashed at this, but Ildren only smiled and
bent towards her once again. The point of Ildren's tongue
licked slowly and precisely across Anya's upper lip, and
then up the ridge of flesh between her nostrils. Ildren then
stayed very close and whispered to Anya.

'It is time,' she said. Anya did not understand at first. 'It
is time for your captive flesh to be released – for your
flower bud to open; for you to make over your body to
pleasure, my sweet . . . to pleasure in its fullness.' Anya felt
her belly turning over. 'We two shall make the most delicious love you can imagine . . .' That churning now was
mixed with fear. 'I shall penetrate your body' . . . and now,
with consternation. Ildren held up something white. 'Turn
over . . . now, my darling . . . that I may join you in your
bed.'

The sensation, as the Taskmistress slid her body in beside Anya, was as if a poisonous snake had slipped beneath
the covers and was rippling up to bed itself against her

warmth. The downy hairs of Anya's body bristled as Ildren snuggled up behind her. 'Mmm . . . you feel so warm, my precious pet,' the snake announced, and bit her in the neck. That poison venom dripped its fiery droplets of forbidden lust into Anya's bloodstream, as Ildren's cool and very pointed nipples pressed mercilessly into her back, and Ildren's hand came round, exactly as the Prince's had, and moulded to her belly, Ildren's fingertips investigated first the well of Anya's navel, then brushing upwards, lightly tested each of Anya's acorns. 'So very firm,' she whispered in her ear, and licked her neck beneath the lobe. 'The way I like them . . . to begin with . . .' She rolled her palm across them in a slow seductive circle. 'Before I work them to the fullness of their compliancy . . .' Ildren softly laughed. 'Do not have your body stiffen at my words, not yet, that is, for your pleasure is my purpose, and you shall submit your body fully to delight.' And with that, the Taskmistress slipped down below the covers and Anya felt the woman's breath, low down upon her back. Ildren's tongue lapped, flatly, in very slow upstrokes, like a cat's tongue, against the soft pile of baby hair in the small of Anya's back. Anya somehow felt that slow delicious pulling tickling underneath her nipples. It made her arch her back away from it, whilst wishing that the tongue would follow, which it did, until Anya's body was bowed and tight, and trapped between the stirring, sticky stroking of that flat tongue in her back, and Ildren's fingertips, brushing leisurely back and forth against her tight round pushed-out belly. Then Ildren licked upwards, for the length of Anya's back.

'And now,' she said, 'your Taskmistress shall remove your pearl of love.' Anya stirred uneasily. She feared that this would hurt, for she remembered all too vividly the cruel way in which the pearl had first been fitted. But Ildren did not turn her slave upon her back for this unyoking, she had her lie upon her front. 'This way shall be more . . . *interesting* for you,' she said, causing consternation in her bondslave, who was wondering if Ildren might be referring to that item she had glimpsed before

Ildren had slipped into the bed. Ildren insisted that her slave should now move up the bed and, taking a very firm trip with both hands around the top bar of the headframe, should allow herself to hang, so her body formed a smooth and downward sweeping curve of the kind which Ildren found so deliciously inviting, and of such a flexure that the slave's first point of contact with the matress was taken low down on her belly, whilst the slave's breasts hung free, and available at any time for Ildren to render to a suitably compliant state.

Anya felt the covers moving back and sliding down her body, 'the better to look upon your beauty and your lewdness,' Ildren stated very clearly. 'Now keep your legs very straight.' The Taskmistress first adjusted the position of the bondslave's chain of gold, moving it up her back a little until it hung down from her belly, and then took hold of each of Anya's feet and lifted them across, to point towards each bottom corner of the bed. Anya's legs were angled outwards from her body. 'Point your toes – keep reaching; your legs must be as straight and pointed as the truest arrow.' The stretching and the tension in her muscles moulded each of Anya's buttocks into a smooth tight hard round mound, which was surely Ildren's purpose in this matter. And with the bunching tension reaching down from Anya's shoulders, her body seemed divided into two very clear halves, with a deep dark shadowed furrow extending from between her shoulderblades, down that sharply incised and very flexible downcurved spine, to that deeper, darker recess which cut those globes so deeply that it curved down underneath.

Anya hung; the tongue-tip struck its soft wet rounded smoothness first at Anya's nape. It dabbed and tickled liquid pleasure down that shadow-line; it moulded to that crease; it crossed the line of gold; it tasted smoothness in her skin and then it tasted velvet. Ildren's tongue now formed into a brush-like point, which whispered round the velvet back of Anya's bottom. The sweet forbidden tickle in so lewd a spot made Anya's body shake with pleasurable delight. 'Be still, my wanton darling, and I shall let your blackness kiss and suck my tongue-tip.' Anya's heart was thumping, at her lickerishness and lust, at the way she angled her legs more widely and reached out with her toes, and tried to lift and spread her bottom, to separate her mounds of flesh and pout her tight black knot of tenderness, to meet at last that tantalizingly held-back hard wet tongue, and push her secret mouth around it. She gasped and cried; her bottom pulsed repeatedly as it sucked upon the tip. And then she tried to grind her belly against the surface of the bed. She wanted that tongue to penetrate her to completion, whilst she took her pleasure in this way, with the smoothness of the cover sliding back and forth beneath her moving sex and polishing her nubbin.

Ildren's hand pressed in her back to slow her in her wanting. 'You delicious, lustful thing,' she said, 'you have earned your pleasure by virtue of your lewdness.' Anya felt no shame at this; her cheeks were red with the lust that boiled inside her. 'And now I shall remove the pearl and spring your little pip of love from bondage. You shall feel a tiny pinprick; that is all.' Anya did not care if it should cause a stab of pain, for she knew that nothing now could take away that weighted swell of pleasure deep inside her. In fact, her body would turn that little pain into a pleasure. Anya tried to lift her hips for Ildren then to reach her.

'Ah ... But there is just one thing,' said Ildren with suppressed delight. 'You shall beg me first to do it.' Anya begged her there and then; she now felt quite shameless about it. But Ildren was not fully satisfied with such ready acquiescence in a slave. She made Anya memorise, and then recite, this unequivocal declaration of the status of her slavery:

'I beg of you, ma'am, please satisfy my ...'

'Go on,' the Taskmistress encouraged her, as she stroked within the groove spread before her.

'My lickerish desires. For I am – I am nothing but a slave to love ...' Anya hesitated. The Taskmistress waited. 'And I will submit ... I will freely submit myself to any pleasurable abasement,' Anya whispered, and then she coughed; she had difficulty in going on with this degrading affirmation, 'to which my Taskmistress shall, in her wisdom, choose to commit my body. For my body belongs only to Lidir, to use . . .' she faltered. Ildren pushed the tip of her finger into Anya's bottom. 'To use as Lidir thinks fit.'

Now Anya's belly felt so tight and queasy at what her voice had said; her tongue had swelled; her spittle had thickened so she could not even swallow; her heart was racing, as if she were a frightened captured doe, and yet those deliciously uncontrollable ripples kept on shaking through her body. And then she felt Ildren's fingers slipping underneath her and gripping the pearl, opening the tiny clamp, and then the sudden burning pain, as her liberated point of flesh distended. Her nubbin seemed to swell and sting, until she was sure that it was larger than the pearl had been. Ildren took Anya's leaves and separated them very fully, and holding back the flesh that hooded round her swollen nub, she made Anya lower her belly – with her legs still outspread, and in their tense and pointed state – until Anya's open sex lay against the silken sheet. The brushing smoothness felt so good to Anya.

'There – and you may moisten my bedsheet with your seepings, that even in my dreaming, I may smell your heat upon it.'

Anya was filled with lewd and lustful feelings at these words; she pressed her openness more firmly to the sheet. Now Ildren's hands were against her buttocks, spreading them more widely. Anya felt something cool and heavy weigh against her groove, and then she heard a clink as Ildren's body brushed against her. She understood then, with a frightened sinking pleasure which contracted her sex and weighted in her bottom, what this chilling sound must be – a chain, attached to Ildren, in between her legs. A chain – Anya shivered at the tought – which passed up inside her and was rooted deep in Ildren's body. Anya raised her eyes to look upon the portrait on the wall, with that image of the chain; the vision of that intimate attachment made another, deeper shiver ripple through her womb.

Ildren's curly bush was tickling up against her; the metal links collapsed and shifted as they heaped, in moving pads of pressure and illicit pleasure against that tautened skin within her groove and then back and forth against that inner mouth. Ildren lowered her full weight upon Anya, and seemed to concentrate it in that place, then moved her hips and pressed Anya's unfurled sex into the bed, so Anya's flesh nub slid in pressured circles up against the silk. And Ildren worked Anya's nipples, exactly as she'd promised. She pulled them – tugged them down as if she were milking a cow, then twisted them and pinched the flesh below them whilst she flicked them with her finger, then she wet them and massaged them, stretched them, even tried to curl them – until she had them soft and pliant, like very well-worked dough. All this time, her hips were circling, or sometimes even thrusting, as if she wished to push, and force the heaped-up chain links into Anya's body. Anya was beside herself with the strong, insistent pleasuring of her nubbin, over which she had no control at all for Ildren's hips, and Ildren's hips alone, dictated pressure, pace and movement. Ildren would stop, and lift herself, if she thought that pleasure welled too freely, and dangle the tantalising chain against that bottom groove, and then would press again, and roll those nipples in her fingers with a hesitant, nervous action, until Anya gasped and gulped the air, and stiffened at the very brink of pleasure, whereupon Ildren acted very quickly, but with consideration for her slave.

Gently, she broke Anya's contact with the silk, amidst her soft sweet moans of protest, and turned her bondslave over on her back – with Ildren underneath. She twined her legs about Anya's and locked them wide apart, so Anya's hips were at her mercy; they could not move at all. Anya felt Ildren's heart burning up against her backbone, and then the cool smoothness of that thing – that white thing – which Ildren pushed inside her, so very, very slowly. Anya's sex pulsated as she took the cockstem in, that perfect white and polished marble cockstem.

'Pulse, my sweet and watch; draw this pleasure fully to

your body.' Anya looked down between her legs, held far apart, by Ildren's legs, and watched helplessly, defencelessly, as her pulsing body swallowed. The cool thickness of the stem distended her, seduced her and made that pleasure so much sweeter. Her body drew it to herself, right up to its marbled bumps, and held it, whilst she squeezed against it tightly. Then Ildren's lips pressed to her neck and gently sucked upon her trembling vein, and two of Ildren's fingers stretched her hood and held it back whilst, with a third, she tapped her. The fingerpad kept tapping at her nubbin, not altering the pressure or timing of that tapping one iota, regardless of the moans and murmurs, the jerks and shaking tremors, or the tightness in that pushed out bursting belly, as Anya, in trying to focus pressure in that place, arched her back and bucked against that constant delicious palpitating pleasure-ache of tapping, until she spasmed tight against that cock, and screamed and bit her lip, and blacked out with delight.

11

The Trap

From her vantage point, Anya looked out across the sunlit snow-clad countryside of Lidir – the black-latticed, blue white forests and the pure white distant hills, the pale blue skyline and the weak November sun, which softly struck through Ildren's window and bathed Anya's skin in a gentle warmth and turned her flesh to gold. A golden woman, mounted on a horse, a wooden horse with a padded back – a solid horse that did not move.

The bondslave had found this view to be preferable to the one which would have confronted her if she had chosen to turn her head the other way and look again into the room, Ildren's sitting-room, which, although of quite innocent aspect in most respects – with that fur-strewn, comfortable-looking couch by the fire, for example – now had one or two additional features which were a cause for mild concern. There were a number of items on the table – a bowl and jug, some fruit, rope, pieces of material, lengths of polished wood of a type which had looked suspiciously familiar to the slave, and several other implements which Anya did not even recognise. But it was an object sitting over in the corner which had caused by far the greatest consternation in the slave. It had seemed to be a small square-based tapering tower built of wood, and it was about half as tall as Anya; it sat solidly on the floor; at the top, crowning this strange device, was a smooth and very thick vertical wooden cylinder with a rounded crest and a flared-out base. Worse yet, from one of the hooks in the sitting-room ceiling, a length of rope was dangling down towards the thing. Anya had found herself imagining too many frightening possibilities; her gaze had been drawn back, time after time, to this sinister device, as if its presence had cast a very evil spell, so she preferred instead to stare the other way, out of Ildren's window. Her plight was quite worrying enough, without her thinking about that thing.

Ildren had kept her slave in bed from early dawn till late into the morning, bestowing long and loving womanly pleasure upon this very special creature. And then at last she had allowed her slave to break her fast at Ildren's table, with bread, a mug of milk, dried apple and nuts, of which the slave had partaken under Ildren's constant, loving attentions, sampling morsels of sustenance which Ildren had fed to her in strange and intricate ways. And when at last the slave had suffered adequate refreshment, then Ildren had taken time to stem her unwarranted fears about the wooden beast, and now was taking more time yet to mount the slave in exactly the right position. She had taken care to position first the Horse, and then the slave, in such a way that the slave could admire the view, so Ildren would not be distracted during these protracted and precise – yet necessary – adjustments by constant fidgeting from a slave who might not fully appreciate the virtues of precision, and might perhaps be anxious now for action.

'My dearest, I am almost finished,' Ildren reassured the bondslave. 'Just one more tiny wee adjustment.' Ildren pinched Anya's cheek in a very playful manner, and pouted. 'You see ... this has not been so bad as you expected.'

Anya lay on her front, along the padded beam; her wrists were fastened underneath, but Ildren had carefully drawn them forwards along the underside of the bar before finally securing them, so that Anya's breasts, now unencumbered by proximity of her elbows, were pressed very firmly to the sides, and Anya's acorns pointed up and outwards; Ildren therefore merely had to squat beside her – at whichever side she happened to be – to take her suck, without, for example, first having to reach underneath to collect the nipple on her tongue in an unduly complex manoeuvre. Anya's legs at present dangled downwards from the end of the beam; her head was almost in the centre of the Horse, and her body formed a right-angle, as if, having walked up to the end of the beam, she had simply bent over and along it – except for the facts that her hands were tied, and her feet did not touch the floor. And this was where Ildren's little adjustment was required.

The Taskmistress produced a long band of pure green silk, about a handsbreadth wide, and laid it across Anya's back, above her golden chain, so the ends hung down to either side. Then she lifted each of Anya's legs in turn and bent it, feeding the band down the inside of the thigh and underneath the crook of the knee, then around the outside and up again across her back. Finally, Ildren fastened the ends by means of a slip knot. As she pulled it tight, Anya's knees were lifted till they nearly touched her breasts, and her thighs moved upwards towards the horizontal. Anya's bottom, with that black-lipped pouch slung so invitingly below it, projected out beyond the beam. And with each tightening of the knot, the pouch pushed out more prominently, large a large and succulent ripe black plum. Ildren could scarcely dare to look upon that sweet round juicy fruit – the sight of it sent licking shivers up her body.

Anya was apprehensive about the tightness of this trussing, which left her feeling very exposed indeed.

The Taskmistress held in front of Anya a wooden bowl of water; in her other hand she held a cloth. 'Your Taskmistress will wash you now ... refresh you after your sweet exertions.' The water smelled of cloves. Ildren placed the bowl on Anya's back, immersed the cloth, then squeezed it. Anya felt the weighted bowl of liquid sway against her; the tinkling droplets, falling back, sent a shiver down her spine. The freezing wetness of the cloth touched her in her armpit; the water felt like melted ice and made her jerk; the bowl heaved, the liquid swelled, and Anya knew – in that cruelly endless second before it finally happened – that the water would well over. She had to gasp for breath; it cut her like a freezing knife across her back, then trickled into the furrow of her spine.

'I see you find its coolness suitably uplifting. But my dear, you must keep still.' Anya had to grit her teeth.

The Taskmistress washed downwards and over the first of Anya's breasts, then moving round, she attended to the other, but this time only squeezed the cloth out lightly before moulding it around the breast, exactly to its swollen form, so the acorn pointed through it. The icy coldness there took Anya's breath away, but the Taskmistress held it still in place until the dripping had subsided. Ildren then removed the cloth and pressed the backs of her fingers against the frozen beast. 'Mmmm . . .' she said. 'Your bosom is so tight and hard – like a marble sculpture.' Ildren moved around and stood at Anya's bottom. Anya closed her eyes so very tight and tensed up every muscle, and then the bowl was lifted from her back and placed above her bottom, at the tail of Anya's spine. It balanced very uncertainly.

'Do not jerk, my darling, for if it should tip, I fear it might fully overturn.' Ildren's tone suggested that she wanted this to happen, so Anya kept as still as she was able, against her shaking and her shivers. She heard the Taskmistress dip and squeeze the cloth again. She bit her lip. 'Now, we shall refresh you in that very special place . . .' Anya waited for the icy touch; it did not come. At last, she opened her eyes – and jumped. Ildren was in front of her. And then she cried out with the shock of coldness, as the bowl overflowed and the splash of water dribbled down her groove. Ildren, smiling very sweetly, merely shook her finger. 'Now, don't say I didn't warn you. You must keep very still.' And then she moved up very close to Anya's face. Anya tried to pull away, for she had noticed, with anxiety, that the pupils of Ildren's eyes had shrunk to tiny points.

'Do you know, I think you moved deliberately . . . you very naughty thing!' Ildren said, and tugged at Anya's ear. Even though such a thing quite clearly was not true, still Anya's neck and cheeks were burning with embarrassment. This woman took delight in trying to degrade her. 'If you like, I can pour it down that sweet and tender parting –

if that would bring you pleasure. No? But my dear, you should never be ashamed to take pleasure, if you wish it, in these perverse little ways,' she gloated, making Anya even more ashamed than ever. Ildren pulled away, and held up the cloth; she stretched it to a very tight straight edge.' 'And now,' she whispered, 'we will draw this cool delight up and down your parting – but very lightly. Would you like that – that tickling in that very special, very blackened place? Hmm?' Anya looked away. 'Does your blackness like such naughtiness and tickling?'

Anya's cheeks were burning bright; she hated this woman's words, but even more than that, she hated what those suggestive words were doing to her body, against her will, forcing that delicious sinking feeling deep within her belly. The Taskmistress tightened the silken knot across Anya's back, which lifted her thighs and concentrated the pressure there between her legs, and spread her buttocks even tighter, and then Ildren's fingertip seduced the slave, by stroking gently back and forth across the very tip of Anya's spine. 'There . . . does that feel nice? Now push that bottom out . . . pout that tiny mouth . . . Mmmm, that looks so delicious.'

Now Ildren was back again at Anya's head, kissing her fully on the lips, and teasing at her acorns. The Task-mistress was shaking. 'You sweet and luscious thing,' she said. 'Now place your head like this – lie upon your cheek, and turn a little, like this – good – so I may look upon your face whilst I tickle you there . . .'

From the corner of her eye, Anya could see the Task-mistress standing behind her – she could see her place the cloth into the bowl to cool it once again, then wring it very deliberately, then hold it up and draw it out very tightly, and then Anya had to watch it disappear from view. 'Now you shall pout for me – turn your face and pout your lips and . . .' Ildren's very deep and husky voice had momen-tarily failed her, 'and pout that bottom . . . now.' And then a sweetly rasping line of ice was drawn across Anya's ten-der rim of pushed-out flesh; it vibrated up inside her; it made her suck her breath in sharply. The gentle rasping stopped. 'Your lips must remain at all times pouted – I wish to look upon your lewdness, as I brush you in your puckering. Now, wet your lips and do it very nicely. Good . . . and push that other little mouth out very rudely.' The bowstring pulled across again, and Anya's hips and belly quaked with pure sweet delectation; it feels as if a silken thread of pleasure, rolled up inside her body, was being drawn very slowly out of Anya's bottom. 'My dear – you naughty thing – your bottom is pulsating. I shall smack it. No, keep still, or you shall spill the bowl. I shall smack it – for its rudeness – with my finger.'

Ildren was well aware that this style of discipline was so important for a slave, for it served, not as a punishment – though certainly it could constitute an embarrassment for any slave to have to suffer such chastisement. No, it was designed by Ildren specifically to excite a slave to the ways of lustful sensuality and, in this respect, Ildren had never known this peculiarly intimate lash to fail.

Ildren dipped her middle finger in the bowl of water, saying. 'Pout that secret mouth for me . . . Do not be so shy. Your secret mouth will love it.' Anya was so ashamed at what the Taskmistress was forcing her to do, but she was also frightened that Ildren would want to hurt her there, in that very tender place. Now Ildren sounded very much more firm. 'I expect to be obeyed,' she growled. 'Do it now!' Anya hated and despised this woman for making her do these things with such abasement. 'That is better. Push out further. And now, for your stubbornness, you shall count for me the measure of your chastisement.' The Taskmistress forced Anya to count out loud her smacks. Anya had to fight back the tears of shame. The cold wet pad of Ildren's finger struck her with a sudden snap, precisely in that spot; it made her jerk; her bottom mouth contracted. Ildren waited patiently, but Anya could not bring herself to collude in this, her degradation. At length, the Taskmistress gave up waiting for her slave to speak, and simply took the tender rim of flesh between her finger and her thumb. She pinched it hard, until Anya wailed for her to stop. 'Do I take it that you wish to co-operate, my dear?' Anya bit her lip and nodded. That tender flesh within her groove was throbbing very gently.

This time, as Ildren's moistened finger smacked, and she watched that mouth pulsate, she was pleased to hear the slave count. 'One,' and to do so very promptly.

'Good,' Ildren said, and reaching underneath to cup that ripe black fruit within her palm, she smacked her once again. Ildren loved that resilient slap of finger-end against that knot of black-brown flesh, that luscious palpitation, and now, that pulsing in her palm that signalled – regardless of the sobs and murmured protestations – the first uncertain stirrings of pleasure in her slave. Ildren's fingers split that fruit and delved within its moist warm flesh, amid the little gasps – those more definite pleasurable assertions – and searched out and closed around that hard little pip of lust. So now, each time she smacked that bottom mouth, and the slave called out the count, she gave that pip a gentle squeeze, until Anya's hips were shaking, her sex had liquified inside, and the oily, pushed-out pip kept slipping back each time that Ildren pulled it downwards, and the count was twenty-three. Ildren then had Anya open her mouth very wide indeed, while she soaked her middle finger in the water till it went quite numb with coldness, and then she pushed it very slowly into Anya's bottom, which Ildren insisted, must remain throughout in that pushed-out pouted state, and must not contract, even though the bondslave found this posture so very difficult to maintain.

Anya gasped and could not help but tighten against the shocking coldness slipping up against her delicate inner warmth, and the simultaneous pleasure of that other finger circling round her nubbin.

'Open, my sweet; let your body reach to take this pleasure.' Anya felt as if an icicle had been pushed into her person. Ildren released the pip and pressed Anya's leaves together, then gently drew the finger out and dipped it back into the water. 'No . . . no, my darling,' she instructed Anya, whilst she waited for her finger to go sufficiently cold, 'keep your mouth wide open. We have not finished yet. Now this time, push your tongue out very slowly, as I

enter you ... hold still ... pout out that little mouth ...
Good ... Mmmm ... Does that feel very nice? Keep pushing out that delicious tongue until my finger is right in ...
Good!' Anya's tongue was pushed out very far indeed, and
Ildren was regretful that with the slave in this position she
could not reach that tongue to close her lips around it. She
made a mental note that she should think about some readjustment to the slave's position before she tried this
game in future. For the present, she contented herself by
spreading Anya's flesh leaves, and exposing Anya's pearly
bud, then pressing the tip of her little finger against it and
rotating very lightly, whilst she continued slowly pulling
her finger out of Anya's body, and pushing it in again. She
watched the slave's tongue mirror that penetration and re-
traction, more lewdly still with each occurrence, until her
head arched back as if her tongue were reaching out to
touch someone, and her breathing seemed to snag on
something hard. Ildren understood that signal very well;
straight away, she stopped moving her little finger, and
gently, she removed it, and – very lightly – pressed those
leaves together, which evoked a murmur of delicious protest. Then more carefully still, she removed the finger from
that gently pulsing bottom, and patted it softly on the
cheeks.

'There – was that so very bad?' she asked her coyly, then
lifted the bowl from Anya's bottom and placed it on the
floor. 'And tell me,' she insisted, 'did you like that slapping
of your person?' Ildren had moved round to the side; her
fingers brushed upwards across Anya's breast, and lifted
up the teat to stroke it. 'Answer – did it bring you pleasure?' Anya had no choice; she nodded weakly. 'Good.
Your Taskmistress next has a very interesting style of
pleasure to which she will subject your body.'

Anya now became apprehensive about what the Taskmistress was doing – she was unfastening the chain of gold
about Anya's waist. Ildren had to work the chain around
in order to reach the fastening; Anya's heart was beating
wildly at this treatment. It was as if in some way, she felt
the chain to be a part of herself which Ildren, by breaking

that symbolic loop, was trying to take away. This fingering at the fastening made her very much afraid; it seemed to her an assault upon her person, as if Ildren wished to strip her of her last shred of dignity, and to render her as nothing.

'No – please ma'am,' she tried to beg her, but to no avail. The Taskmistress had released the fastening, and now unfolded the chain so it dangled down from each side of her body and across her bunched-up thighs.

'I wish you to be totally nude,' the Taskmistress said quite coldly, though with a tremble in her voice. She removed the chains from Anya's wrist and ankle.

Anya's tears welled up inside her. She did not understand it, but she could not help herself; the shame was overpowering as the Taskmistress slowly pulled the large chain through from underneath her belly. However, Ildren did not take the chain away entirely from her slave. Anya felt her pin it with a finger or thumb to the small of Anya's back, and then drape it down the groove of her bottom; its weighted presence clung to Anya's parting, but it barely touched her sex before dangling straight down towards the floor. Anya's sobs had ebbed away under that pressured weight which seemed to fit so precisely to the split between her buttocks. She was reminded of that chain that Ildren wore and the way it had been lowered against her in that very place, while she lay on Ildren's bed, as a prelude to that pleasurable release which Anya had found to be so sweet and so delicious. Therefore, she was anxious to know what might happen next. Ildren's fingers parted Anya's leaves, which had gone so soft and so compliant that they remained open where Ildren pressed them back against her mound. 'Mmm ... just the way I like those love lips,' Ildren murmured, then gently lifted the end of the chain from Anya's parting, until it was held horizontally, level with her back, and then she let it fall. The heavy, swinging line of pressured contact travelled down Anya's groove, making her gasp in mounting pleasure, and then emit a tiny grunt, as the lick of pressure curled between her open leaves and pressed against her nubbin. Ildren caught the chain on the backward swing and sent it down again, repeatedly and at a constant rate, until that squeezing line of luscious pleasure, that pendulum of delight, made Anya want to squirm and close her legs around it and beg for Ildren to finish her, to press those links against her nub until she burst her pleasure. Ildren caught the chain again, and reaching underneath pressed the end to Anya's belly, so the links pulled tight along the divide of Anya's separated flesh. That pressure was exquisite, yet cruel; not rolling against her in the way she needed, not firm enough to bring release.

The Taskmistress sounded distant, as if she found it difficult to speak. 'Now I shall feed this chain of love . . .' she trailed away, then finally managed, 'into your body . . .' Anya opened her mouth to cry out, but no sound at all came out. The icy fear and horror had sucked her breath away.

Ildren began by tightening the silken band, so Anya's sex felt pushed out and downwards from between her thighs, impossibly far. Anya shuddered as the Taskmistress touched her there, and those precise and probing fingers opened out her proffered sex, and then she shivered as each cold, heavy metal loop touched against the smoothness of her tender inner self as the Taskmistress worked it, link by link, into that living pouch. Anya felt herself distending under the moving weight of metal pushed inside her. That sinking kind of weight which she had suffered many times in imagination, at the stirrings of her pleasure, was now transformed into reality. Her sex felt like a swollen, overripe fruit, which was weighted down with liquid; the pulling pressure concentrated there, the heaviness behind her nub was sublime; her fruit was more than ripe for picking. Ildren gathered it up and closed her fingers round it, and traced its line of split. She sealed its leaves around the dangling end of chain, then tickled Anya's spine whilst Anya basked in the weighted pleasure splung beneath her belly. Ildren gently shook the chain and swung it to and fro, and then from side to side, and carefully pulled it; each movement was transmitted up into Anya's body; the pulling felt so deep and so delicious.

167

'Your honeydew is dripping from the chain,' Ildren murmured very softly. 'Now tell me, sweetest – does this give you pleasure, as I promised that it would? A deeper pleasure than the cockstem? Tell me.' Ildren softly squeezed her sex. Anya's sigh was deep and heartfelt.

'Good. Your pleasure shall be sweeter yet.' Ildren jumped up and moved over to the table. She collected up a jar, then dipped her finger in and tasted. She closed her eyes and threw back her head. 'Mmm . . .' she said. She dipped her finger once again and offered it to Anya, who was apprehensive as Ildren forced it through her lips and smeared it on her tongue. It tasted very sweet and musky, like nectar overlain with female heat; it was the distinctive taste of honey. Anya knew it very well for she had tasted it before, on quite a few occasions. Now Ildren held up the chain which she had removed from Anya's ankle; she took a sidelong look at Anya, then she dipped it in the pot. The slave was now a little worried. A stream of honey ran down the chain and back into the jar. 'Now, this is a little messy,' Ildren smiled. 'But quite pleasant, I assure you. Open your mouth and push your tongue out very far.'

Anya felt the sticky chain, coaxed by Ildren's carefully probing fingers, being fed into her bottom. She closed her eyes against the shame of it. Ildren carefully wiped off the excess, and after she had licked her fingers, she dipped them in the bowl of water sitting on the floor. Taking hold of the end of the chain which dangled down from Anya's bottom, she said, 'Open your eyes and look at me.' With a cold, wet finger, she tickled very lightly down Anya's spine, from the level of her silken waistband, to the very tip. Anya shivered with that icy tickle, and that pulling deep inside her. It made her close her eyes in delectation. 'No . . . keep those delicious eyes open, that I may look upon their beauty whilst I pleasure you.' Ildren wet her fingers once again. 'Now, that delightful little tongue . . . push it out again, and make it as pointed as you can . . .' Anya felt that wave of pulling, drawing down and making her contract. 'Now move that tongue round and round, in a circle.' And as she did so, Ildren stroked her moistened fingertip round and round that tender pouted, pulled-out rim of bottom flesh that gripped the tautened chain. 'There, isn't that nice? No, keep that tongue moving. There . . .' Anya was almost passing out with pleasure at this treatment. 'Your little mouth is pulsing its delight. Good. Now, we shall try another very naughty kind of pleasure. Take a breath – a very deep one – and hold it . . .'

Ildren now had hold of each of Anya's chains and pulled them, alternately, very slowly but very fully, so Anya felt that pulling pleasure shift inside her, as it rocked from back to front. 'Breathe out . . . and in . . .' Ildren kept doing this to Anya until her sex could take no more and went into a deep and pulsing spasm. 'My darling . . . you really must contain that recklessness of spirit. I want you to promise me that you will stay quite relaxed for this next procedure. I do not want to witness so brazen a display of rudeness again. Is this quite clear?' Ildren forced the slave to give her word, but Anya knew that Ildren would just as surely make her break it.

'Mmm . . . your love lips are so soft and warm.' They felt so sensitized that the slightest touch was making Anya want to squirm with delight. 'Let me spread them very fully . . . Oh! What is this hard little knot in there? It feels so firm and so deliciously naughty. Let Ildren stroke this little wet tongue of pleasure.' She used one hand to hold back Anya's hood and to hold her leaves apart. Ildren's middle finger slowly and systematically tickled Anya's poked-out nubbin, whilst her thumb wrapped around the chain in Anya's sex and kept pulling at it, then releasing, at a carefully timed rate. Then Ildren's free hand took that other chain and very firmly pulled, increasing the strain until it began to move, whereupon she ordered her slave to begin to pant, whilst she very slowly, so deliciously, and with so very cruel a pleasuring, drew that chain out of Anya's person. Anya tried so hard against that drawing pleasure, and that pulling in her sex, and that finger pressure round her nubbin, which Ildren was tickling so exquisitely, and she very nearly succeeded – until that thread of dripping honey trailed upwards in her groove, and Ildren deposited that sticky weight of drawn-out chain along the base of Anya's spine, and the line of liquid pressure there was just too much to bear. Ildren was already kneeling down beside her, not touching her at all, but looking deeply and very lovingly into Anya's eyes – those deep black pools of defenceless pleasure – as Anya's trembles swelled and waned and swelled once more, against those wrenching gasps, and the honey welling slowly down her groove, and then her belly shook in wave upon wave of delicious liquefaction.

Ildren shook her finger. 'You very naughty girl, and after you had promised me so sweetly.' But even so, Ildren's voice had faltered, for she was filled with so much love for this very special slave that she was almost moved to tears. She washed her slave, so very lovingly, deep within her groove, and dabbed her dry, and then she washed her ankle chain. She closed Anya's love lips round the chain that still lay nestled within her sex, and left the end dangling. She stroked her back, while she waited patiently.

A sudden noise – a thumping sound – made Anya jump with fright.

'Oh,' cried Ildren, in obvious dismay. The banging came again. 'Oh no! – Who could it be? Who is at my door?' Ildren sounded quite surprised at this unannounced intrusion. Anya was distressed. 'Just one minute!' Ildren cried, then whispered, 'Let me get my robe ... and here, my darling, let me cover you up.' She threw a blanket over Anya's body, leaving only her head exposed. 'There – you never know who it might be,' she said, in a kindly, protective way.

The thumping came more loudly. 'Open in the Prince's name!' a voice boomed from behind the door. Anya's heart stood still; the blood drained from her face.

Ildren then admitted the Prince, and all his retinue, who arranged themselves in a half circle near the door. Anya froze, her eyelids almost closed; she held her breath and wished that she were invisible. Why hadn't Ildren placed the blanket over her head, so she could hide completely from her shame? She could not bear the thought of him, of all people, seeing the depth of her depravity.

'We thank you, Sire,' the Taskmistress began, with unction on her tongue. 'Your noble presence brings honour to our humble quarters.' Now Anya's lungs were bursting, and she had to breathe; her heart was thumping in her throat.

'Yes, yes. The slave –?' The Prince was speaking now, referring to her. 'Is she not here, Taskmistress – as your message had advised us?'

The force of meaning in these last few words pierced Anya's heart like a knife blow. It cut her to the quick, for at that point she realised just what this evil woman had done. Now she understood the wicked inner-purpose behind these cruel seductive games. Ildren had contrived that Anya's presentation to the Prince would be crowned with degradation.

'The slave is here.' Ildren stood aside and Anya could feel the weight of the Prince's gaze upon her, even though her eyes were now so very tightly shut.

For a second, he did not speak; then his voice sounded tense.

'But Taskmistress, I do not understand ... Why is she being punished? And have I not made my own feelings very clear to you on the use of that contraption?'

'Sire – the slave is not being punished.' Ildren now could barely contain her delght. 'This is the manner in which the slave prefers to take her pleasure.'

'Taskmistress,' the Prince's voice was stern, 'do not try my credulity, and do not try my patience. Release her now.'

Now Ildren sounded hurt. 'As your Highness requires ...'

Anya was powerless to prevent the blanket from sliding down her body, and then she heard the Prince's gasp. She wished she could have closed her ears against the shadow of that gasp. The pit of Anya's shame was bottomless. She kept sinking down and down, and wishing with her heart and soul that this was not really happening, that the Prince was not witnessing her humiliation in this way. If Anya had been allowed a knife, she would gladly have cut out

171

Ildren's poisoned heart and burned it, and then cut out her own, and watched it shudder and then lie still, in a mirror of that mortal blow to her hopes and her desire.

'Open your eyes, in the Prince's presence,' the venomous creature said.

'No! No. Do not oblige her so to do.' The Prince sounded shaken.

Ildren was quite undaunted. 'Shall I untie her now, or –? Her blackness is set out for your noble self to examine, at your pleasure.'

The Prince cleared his throat, but did not speak.

'Your Highness will observe, within the cleft, that knot of flesh. That is not normally so prominent as it now appears. It has been accentuated by the spanking – in which the slave took pleasure. She will confirm this if you care to ask her.' Anya died a thousand deaths. 'Oh, and the chain – that is there because the slave insisted she prefers it to a cockstem. It seems to give her fuller pleasure that a man's part ever could. Perhaps your noble self would wish to touch and test the . . .'

'No. I – No.' The Prince sounded very upset, and very uncertain and embarrassed. But Ildren did not seem to notice this.

'You will find the slave has worked herself, in preparation for this moment. The chain is moistened with her juices . . .'

'No, I must – No. Thank you, Taskmistress, I . . .' Daylight was a tiny point above Anya's pit of black despair.

And now the Prince was gone; the Taskmistress was left alone with Anya, whose leaden body slowly heaved and dropped, and heaved again, in shudders of misery. Uncontrollable thick salt drops of fire stung her eyes and wet her cheeks and dribbled in her mouth.

'My darling dearest,' Ildren put her arm about her slave and gently comforted her. 'Do not upset yourself. These men are all the same. They are quite indifferent to a woman's feelings.' Ildren stroked her brow. 'After everything the Prince had said about you, and promised for you too. And now, when you have prepared yourself, displayed your body for his pleasure, His Highness does not want to know, and – who can tell? – even now is probably in another's arms . . . some other slave who has chanced to take his fickle fancy.'

But Anya's tears would not stem, not even when the Taskmistress, with a swelling, nervous bosom, filled with love and sadness for her charge, very softly cupped Anya's weighted flesh within her palm and squeezed it, sealing those lips of love about the chain, then wrapped the suspended end of it around her fist and pulled it, link by link, from Anya's body, saying, 'There, there, my precious pet, never fear, for your Taskmistress loves you very deeply.' Anya's sobs came louder now, and Ildren's heart swelled as if to burst through her breast. Those sobs were music to her ears.

The Taskmistress wiped the tears from Anya's cheeks and smeared the tear juice round her nipples, then sucked upon these salted, blackened, fleshy droplets one by one. She untied the slave and stretched her limbs and tenderly massaged them, until Anya's tears had slowly ebbed away. Ildren pressed her soft cool lips upon those swollen burning cheeks and lifting Anya down, she replaced the chains about her wrist, her ankle, and her waist and led her to the window.

Slave and mistress looked out, across the grey stone turrets, to the rolling snow-white scene that merged to distant blue, and each, in her own way, was uplifted by the vision of that vastness of Lidir.

Anya's heart and soul could gladly have soared, out above this place, out into the air, out into the sunlight, through that cold blue air above that endless snow, and let its icy crispness wash away her fears and deliver her to freedom.

'Together, we could rule this land,' Ildren's voice had broken Anya's reverie. 'The legend could come true . . .' Anya did not understand. The voice became seductive. 'Who needs a prince – when we have a princess?' Ildren kissed Anya very fully on the lips. But Anya pulled away

173

when she realised exactly what this evil woman was saying, and she backed against the wall.

'No, no!' Anya was horrified at such viciousness and calculating malice – and treason – at the suggestion that the Prince should somehow be set aside, or done away with. She raised her arm against the thought; it had made her very angry. 'No! How could you dare to plot against his noble person?' Anya's heart was beating wildly; she was shaking – cold sweat beaded on her forehead – but somehow she had found that strength to speak out now for truth, and honesty of purpose. 'How could you be so cruel?'

'Cruel? *Cruel?*' The Taskmistress drew herself up until she seemed a tower of terror; her face was roaring thunder. She struck that slave down to the floor, for her honesty of purpose, and then kicked her, for her forthright stance. Such candour was unwelcome, as far as Ildren was concerned.

'You thankless bitch! You jumped-up little harlot! I'll show you cruelty, if that is what you wish to taste.' And with that, Ildren stormed over to the door. 'Let us see how your Prince protects you now,' she said, and flung the door wide enough for it to crash against the wall. 'Guard! Guard!' she cried. 'This silly slut desires to entertain you in the guardroom.' Anya began to wail. 'You may do with her precisely as you wish.'

Then later, in the quiet calm, when Ildren tried to work out what had gone so wrong, she wondered whether things would have turned out differently if, after Ildren had untied the girl, she had taken that exquisitely – and yes, Ildren now quite genuinely admitted it – beautiful body, that sweetly sobbing tear-stained body, which was dripping with desire, and had moulded it to the Rod, *before* she had attempted to divulge her plan? What might have happened then? Ildren was unsure. As it was, she could only hope that the grey guards could, by way of contrast, perhaps underline the virtues of a woman's touch, and thereby help this silly little bitch to see the error of her ways.

12

The Hand of Correction

'And so we meet again, my puffed up little pigeon,' the
voice echoed round the corridor. Anya was terror-stricken;
it was the guard whom Cook had reprimanded in the kitchen. 'You shall not need your airs and graces now. I fear
that you must take us as you find us.' He took hold of
Anya's hair and forced her to her knees, down upon the
coldness of the flagstones. Then he twisted her hair round
till she screamed, and the tears ran down her cheeks. 'Ha!
Your tears shall not save you. Your tears are my delight.
Your tears just make me want to kick you, you snivelling
little thing.' He twisted her hair more cruelly than before;
she had to bite her lip until it bled, to stop herself from
screaming.

'Now, bow down to your lord and master, slave.' He
forced Anya to kiss his boots before he dragged her up.
Grasping Anya's wrists behind her, he hauled them up her
back so far that she had to double forwards from the pain,
and then he marched her like that, so she was overbalancing, losing her footing, falling forwards all the time, along
the maze of corridors and passageways, on and down the
stairs, until at last they passed a pair of sentries who stood,
unmoving and indifferent to Anya's plight, before a large
oak door.

'Get up!' he hissed, 'and shut your mouth.' Anya had
tripped and cried out and lay heaped upon the floor. The
sentries glanced uneasily in their direction. 'Keep quiet.'
He placed his finger to his lips. 'The Council is in session.
You shall pay dearly if the Prince is disturbed by your
miserable whining.' Anya's heartbeat surged at this, for she

knew the Prince would save her if he heard her. She cried out even louder than before.

'Shut up!'

'Let go of me. Do not be so cruel,' she shouted back, and caught her breath in deep and powerful sobs. One of the sentries made a move towards them; Anya wailed more loudly, and then the door began to open. Anya caught a glimpse of a great table, with their lordships seated all around it, and she heard a voice – *his* voice, she was sure of it – addressing the assembly, before the guard struck her with a cruel blow, and clapped his hand around her mouth to stifle all her cries. He swore at her beneath his breath, and slapped her down again, for she tried to bite him; then he took hold of her around the waist and lifted her bodily. Her flailing form was finally dragged round the corner, just as an enquiring head was being poked round the door.

The guard did not stop, and would not take his hand away from her mouth, until they had negotiated several corners, passed through a room piled to the ceiling with dust-laden boots and shoes, and then another full of old and faded cloaks, and had dropped down a flight of stairs. They had reached a quiet, musty passageway, with an alcove in the wall. He threw her to the floor. 'Go ahead, my dear,' he said with satisfaction, 'you may shout as loudly as you like, for only guards and servants ever come this way. But your whining will not save you. It will only make things worse.'

She would have abased herself, pleaded for some respite but she knew this would have been a pointless gesture against this hardened heart. She sobbed silent inner sobs, and dripped dry tears – she tried to stem her weakness in the presence of such cruelty. Why did he want to abuse her so, when she had done him no harm, when it was the cook who had upset him?

He lifted Anya by her shoulders, then looked into her face, and Anya saw, with cold and creeping terror, the depravity in those eyes – the black desire that burned within the grey guard's soul. She shuddered, as she knelt before him from the way he touched her, from the way he rolled his sleeve, and from the way his hand pushed down her front, so deliberately and so symbolically, between her belly and her chain, which bit into Anya's back and pulled her tightly up towards him. Her body shuddered as that hand crept downwards like a cold and giant spider. Those large black spider eyes looked down and fixed her, as those feelers parted Anya's curls and – she shuddered once again – those feelers touched her there – too gently, not roughly so that she could hate it. That touch was soft, prolonged, seductive stimulation; the shudder was delight. Those feelers pulled and palpitated Anya's sex; they made her want to spread, so those mandibles could close around and puncture Anya's nubbin, and squirt a fine cool stream of paralysing venom into Anya's body. She wanted that cold deliverance to quell her fear, to suffuse her body, and to liquify her core, and then those mandibles could suck, and in that sucking could draw her liquid self right out of Anya's nubbin, to leave her as a crispy husk which then could drift downwards, like falling dust, on the still and musty air.

The guard made her stand and bow her legs whilst he fingered her; the only sounds that broke the stillness of the corridor were Anya's laboured breathing, the clink of Anya's chain, and the slow and gentle sucking sound of Anya's liquid flesh. The sucking stopped; the hand pressed against her belly, pushing her backwards into the alcove, against the cold, damp wall, and then the sucking, working sounds began again. Anya's breasts started to shake under her nervously rapid gulps of breath, which now outpaced her heartbeat. She was made to spread her arms out and up, and to reach to grip the stonework, and then he forced her legs very wide apart, so Anya's body formed a living, softly frightened, palpitating cross.

But now he pressed his body up against her and pinned her to the wall between the hard, unyielding stone and the rough cloth of his tunic, and he kissed her – if that is what it could be called. He forced his tongue into her mouth, and then he forced his calloused fingers up into her flesh, so far that she was lifted on his hand. She had to raise

177

herself on tiptoes just to ease that force of penetration, whilst his tongue probed deeper and deeper into her mouth and tried to block her throat. Her nostrils flared; she could not draw breath fast enough to cool her burning lungs, and still the kiss continued. She was pinned and penetrated, suffocated by this hateful show of lust. How could this guard imagine that her body could ever welcome such coarseness, such base abuse as this? Anya tried to cry out against this gag of flesh and to tear her head away from him.

The grey guard's hand closed round Anya's jawbone and dug into her cheeks. He held her head fixedly against the wall whilst he mocked her. 'So, the attention of an honest man are not welcome to one so proud – to one of noble blood. Ha! A wordly tongue is not to be allowed within that royal mouth.' He spat upon the floor. Anya was terrified by such hatred, directed at herself. 'We shall see how this common tongue may yet be found acceptable – in a place where your flesh cannot lie. We shall see if it can melt your ice. Now, you shall spread those thighs until you split . . .' He pinched his fingers round Anya's nostrils, so she had to gasp for breath. 'There – so this regal nose shall not be burdened with the smell of earthy, melting flesh –' then he forced her head right back, until she was looking upwards at the ceiling of the alcove. 'You shall keep it up – stuck up – in the manner to which it is accustomed.' Anya's tears were overflowing at this gross and so unjustified abuse. She had done nothing whatsoever to deserve it. She had *never* put on airs and graces; it just was not in her nature. There was nothing she could do or say to help herself, to stop this cruel tirade. It seemed the guard had cast her in a mould of his own choosing, a mould from which she could not now escape. He was forcing her to fit this picture which his mind had conjured up; he was making her act this part, and it was so very hurtful to her spirit. 'That's more like it – keep that nose up there where it belongs. Now, if this is not an imposition upon your royal self, would you kindly point your toes out to the side, and make your royal flesh expose itself more fully to this vulgar tongue which you abhor.'

Then Anya heard a gasp. 'Black flesh . . .' The guard had knelt in front of her. She began to shiver, in her shame, and fear at what this cruel creature might decide to do, now that her secret stood revealed. 'It seems my lady stands tarnished with lack of polish, in her coldness. Now let us see how that blackened taint might burnish, and how that frost might thaw.'

She tried so hard to play that part of frigidity and indifference; she did not want her body to respond to this hateful assault. Such things should happen in loving co-operation – two minds linked as one, to a common, loving purpose, the pleasuring of the one bringing pleasure to the other, and then at last, that delicious warmth and deep contentment should seep into each lover's body. But this was nothing but a wicked travesty of pleasure which could only bring anguish to one heart and cruel satisfaction to the other, who despised her. She tried to force her body to shut off from this heartless delight, this one-sided, hate-inspired, pleasuring. But that guard knew precisely how to elicit black desire from her person, and how to make her act against that part that he had chosen for her. That tongue, so clumsy in her mouth, was now feather-light, and so wickedly exciting to her ladyship, who had not known that being tasted by the tongue of a common ruffian such as this could be so delectable. Here, in the corridor, where anyone might chance to pass, Lady Anya allowed herself – nay, proffered herself to be licked between the legs by a filthy, unwashed guard while she looked up at the ceiling – no, she closed her eyes, so that, if interrupted, she could pretend that she was innocent. She could declare it was not happening at all.

The tongue licked the out-turned tender tops of Anya's thighs, alternately, in slow, wet circles of delight, until those wet patches, on so soft and ticklish a type of skin, seemed connected through the tops of Anya's legs and across her join of thighs. It felt as if a smooth silk scarf was drawing back and forth, inside her skin, and somehow up and through her sex, from one leg to the other. Those lips browsed in Anya's moistened female curls, dissolving them from Anya's leaves, slicking them back against the paleness of her flesh, so those dripping, copper-coloured curlicues formed a strand-line round the pouting of her leaves. Those lips were suckered up against that smooth pale band of nudity encircling Anya's blackness. That tongue pressed against those heavy, blood-filled leaves, to one side, then the other, and shook them – vibrated up against them – until Anya did not want this pleasuring to stop. The tongue then entered Anya's body; the lips sucked very fully round her leaves, until that sucking seemed to draw her nubbin downwards, as if the suction made it swell and force back her fleshy hood, and then that slippery warmth of tongue slid, in one smooth action, from his mouth, and in its arching, forced the liquid walls of Anya's sex apart and slipped into her person. Her sex was trapped between the curving horn of living flesh, and the suction drawing downwards. The sensation was so deep and so delicious that it made her push her head back, and back again, until she was looking at the wall. It made her arch her back and offer out her belly, and bear down so hard, there in her sex, that it almost made her want to grunt.

The grey guard forced her next to use her sex to squeeze against his tongue, repeatedly, to squeeze it till it slipped out from her body, so that each time her sex relaxed again, his tongue would slip right in once more. And then at last he used it like a knife, to stab pleasure beneath her hood. He held his pointed knife of pleasure back, and made her snap her knees, to thrust herself up against it – she was forced to stab her nubbin firmly to that point of flesh, which was slowly edged away, until she had to curve her body out so far that she overbalanced. The guard caught her in his arms. When he stood up, the roughness of his uniform scraped against her belly and her breasts. He held her arms behind her back and, with her breasts to either side, he pushed her belly up against himself and forced her knees apart, so Anya's burning sex now rubbed against the coarse cloth of his thigh.

'And is Milady icy yet, or shall Milady thaw?' He forced

his lips to Anya's mouth. She tried to gasp for breath; it seemed that he would stop her breathing altogether.

'Ugh . . . No!' She could take no more, and wrenched away.

'Still too good for a humble guardsman. Still colder than any stone,' he said, with malice in his eyes. 'If Milady found that pleasuring so distasteful, perhaps Milady would prefer to take her passion on a rougher edge . . .?'

'No!' Anya was petrified by the evil in that face, the hatred in that voice.

'Perhaps her ladyship would prefer instead to bend across my knee . . .?'

'No, please . . .' Chilling waves ran down Anya's back and forced contractions in her bottom.

'Perhaps Milady would draw warmth and pleasure from chastisement in this way? Already, Milady's cheeks are flushing very warmly. Perhaps this style of pleasure tempts her noble self?'

The grey guard performed that degradation then and there, in that corridor, without ceremony or preparation. He simply bent down on one knee and had Anya bend across the other. She tried to stop her eyelids squeezing out those tears of shame, but still she could not look upon that hard-hearted countenance; she kept her eyes averted as she was made to bend across his knee. But that only made him mock her, in his wickedness.

'Is Milady now quite comfortable? Answer!' Anya's belly shuddered, as if an ice-cold hand had pushed up into her. 'Answer now, or –'

'Yes . . .' Her voice was barely audible, yet it made that shudder come again. He steadied her between one hand, weighted upon her buttocks, and the other, pulling, squeezing, kneading at her breasts. Anya waited for that hand to strike her flat across the bottom. Her skin tingled, in that expectation; the roughness of his hand seemed magnified, so each movement seemed to tear at Anya's skin. His hand was lifted – her tiny bottom mouth pulsed – she could not bear the suspense; her body almost wanted that stinging blow to smack across her nervous, creeping goose-fleshed skin and deliver her to her shame.

181

'Turn over.' Anya wondered if she'd heard aright. 'Milady shall take her chastisement in a more appropriate place.' Anya felt a hand of fear closing round her belly. 'That place which causes us offence, by its cold indifference to pleasure. That place of raw yet soot-black meat.' The shiver ran out through the join of Anya's legs. 'Let us hope the heat of this rebuke will cook her meat to toothsomeness.'

Anya was shaking as she was now made to lie on her back, across his knee. She found that pose to be even more degrading than lying on her front. Her body formed an arch across him, supported between her shoulders, pressed against the coldness of the floor, and his knee, which pushed into the small of her back. Her feet, reaching down, could scarcely touch the flagstones. He had her spread her thighs and push her palms beneath the chain about her waist, then spread them out across her belly; her fingers had to stretch towards her sex but were not allowed to touch it. She had instead to press, to make her arched-out belly even tauter. 'Now I shall smack that part, and smack until it melts into submission.' A deep-drawing contraction came in Anya's womb, at the thought of what this man would do to her. That large, rough hand was raised – but then lowered gently, to pat, and then stroke downwards, in the open join of Anya's thighs. The hand was raised again, but this time to his mouth. He wet his thumb with spittle and, making Anya move her feet a little more apart, he fitted that thumb tip underneath in the mouth of Anya's bottom, and very slowly, yet very fully, pushed it into her. And now, he moulded the rest of that very large palm to Anya's sex, so two fingers pressed to either side of Anya's fleshy leaves, and the palm itself was close against the mouth of Anya's heat. Her legs were spread so very wide, and yet still the space between her inner thighs seemed too narrow to accommodate a hand so large as this. Those outer fingers pressed so firmly into Anya's creases that she could not have closed her legs around that hand, even had she dared to want to. Those pressure lines were so very pleasant – they were wickedly delicious. They seemed to

182

make a squeezing tickle along each line of crease; it made her feel so open and so unprotected, as if that pressure might suddenly increase to sever her flesh down to the bone, to make her open even wider.

'Your ice cold flesh is warming. It is swelling in your heat.' It was true, though she did not want it so; her body could not help it. Anya could feel the urgency focusing in that band of flesh compressed between his fingers; her leaves were slowly pumping up with blood, pulsing her strength of heartbeat up against his firm restraint. The hand was tightened round her; the thumb was pushed more definitely up into her bottom; his other hand was raised. She watched through half-closed, heavy eyelids – her fear was there, but her fear was tempered now with wanting, not a wanting for pain, but a yearning want for deep and luscious pleasure. It was this painless, full and lustful pleasure which Anya's body now required. She would willingly give her body over to such pleasure, if only this cruel guard could see it. From the upheld hand, two fingers were stretched out, side by side. She had to bite her lip while she watched them quickly drop, and smack against her leaves. That shock of smacking made her cry out and jerk her hips, even though it was not truly painful, but it made the blood pump into her burning leaves of flesh with that much more insistence.

The guard carefully and slowly rubbed those leaves from side to side, and then, looking at Anya, ensuring she was watching still, he raised his hand again. The stinging smack against her swelling made her buck her hips again, and roll her head to fight off that surging need for her fulfilment. The guard waited, gently touching Anya's ever thickening leaves, until her head had stilled, her eyes were open, and she looked at him again. His jaw was set against that pleading in her eyes. He bedded his hand more firmly to the joins above her thighs, so the pressure forced an ache of wanting into Anya's sex. The cruel hand of stinging pleasure was lifted up, and, dropping like a stone, the fingertips snapped against those tight and polished flesh leaves, sending a delicious aching shock of pleasure

183

through them. Then he finger-smacked her without mercy, very steadily, slapping down the length of Anya's bursting, blood-filled leaves, and slowly back up to the top, then concentrating on the fleshy hood, until her sex was filled with an aching welling flame of pleasure and that sharp vibration, transmitting through her rigid, puffed up leaves, right into Anya's nubbin, made her cry out: 'No – Ahh, no, please, I beg of you, not this way . . .' for her pleasure verged so very closely on release, and Anya was so ashamed that she would disgrace herself before this guard by taking wanton gratification in so debased a manner.

'Well now . . .' The guard rested his fingers against her burning flesh, and then squeezed it in a way which brought Anya very deep and cruel pleasure, as the pressure ebbed and then swelled again as if to burst her. 'And has Milady thawed?' Anya turned her face away; she licked her lip, then swallowed. 'Answer . . .' His voice sounded so unsparing. 'Has your stone cold flesh then warmed to my common touch?' The fingers kept pulling, palpitating Anya's leaves, until he had forced her to reply. 'Speak,' he demanded very softly, but squeezed those lips up tight and held them under that constant ache of pleasure.

'Yes . . .' she said, in shame and throbbing, miserable pleasure. But he would not let her be:

'And this uncouth style of discipline, this smacking of her person – does Milady's royal flesh take pleasure in that too?' Anya shut her eyes; she did not want to answer; this question was too cruelly intimate, too abasing. She could never bring herself to say it.

'Answer.' Anya sealed her lips so very tight; he could never make her say it. 'Very well.' There was satisfaction in his voice. 'Since this discipline means nothing to you, we shall take it one stage further.'

And now, each time he smacked those fingerpads against her pleasure-soaked leaves of flesh, he forced her first to hold her breath and to bear down very hard into the join between her thighs, and to contract her bottom tightly round the thumb that pushed inside her, so her belly felt as hard as iron and her sex was pushed out further, after

184

which the slaps were that much more telling. The ache of pleasure was so great that after only five such slaps – each one timed precisely to come at that point where pleasure ebbed away – Anya began to gasp and moan; she tried to close her legs about the hand that held her cruelly open, against those shameful contractions which made her nubbin pulse so hard and so very, very lewdly. The guard quite simply stopped and watched, and waited till they slowed. Then he made her squeeze very tight indeed – the first time, he was unsatisfied about her strength of squeezing, so he made her start again and hold her breath again whilst squeezing – for a count of ten – while his hand was poised above her, ready to descend. And this time Anya's sex began to spasm even though the hand had yet to drop. Her belly shook; she gulped for air, for she was ready now to deliver her body to this shameful degradation there and then – but now the guard had decided not to allow her that release. He jumped up, and dragged her to her feet. Anya was still shaking; her sex was still contracting as she was made to stand there, under his direction, with her feet placed wide apart, her hands behind her head, and the grey guard's fingers pulling at the curls of Anya's bush, pulling Anya's leaves apart, holding Anya very open as Anya's pip pulsated in her desperate wanting for release.

The guard then waited until the contractions in her sex had lessened, though they would not stop completely, and Anya, after each very short respite, would feel again a pulling sinking feeling which her body tried in vain to fight against, and then that irrepressible tumbling squeeze of pleasure focused in that spot. It made her thighs shiver in their tension, and the tiny gasping tongue between those leaves, held so wide apart, reach as if to touch against warm flesh that was not there. He flicked that pulsing tongue, waited till her shivering belly shakes had stopped, then kept wetting his fingers and milking it slowly, then pausing, keeping her legs wide apart, then repeating the milking until she gasped out, '*Please* ...' She could not bear that pleasure any more. Suddenly, he let go of her, but would not let her close her thighs; the guard stood up, and smiled a smile of evil satisfaction.

185

'And so, her ladyship's flesh had lost that edge of lofti-
ness and finery.' And then his voice was grating: 'Her
ladyship is now nothing but a bitch in heat.' Anya's neck
was burning, in her shame. 'A common wench whose
flesh,' he placed the back of his hand against her openness,
and drew it sharply away, as if it had hurt him, 'Whose
flesh is boiling up with lust. A wench who pleads for satisfaction.' Anya was mortified. Her heat was there – she
could not deny it – but she had been forced into this cruel
state of degradation by what he had done, and now the
guard was blaming her. It seemed so wickedly unfair. 'Do
not look away from me. We soldiers like a simmering pot
of flesh like this. In fact, we must not let its heat escape
before we serve you up.'

He forced Anya to march before him in a most degrading way, by standing behind her, then thrusting his hand
between her legs, cupping her swollen mound and holding
it a prisoner, whilst her wrists were pinned, high up behind
her back. That hand was so large that it almost lifted her
from her feet, and then once more, she could not even close
her thighs; she had to walk with her legs apart. And in this
shameful fashion, the shaking prisoner was marched along
the corridors, then up into the courtyard, in broad daylight, for everyone – freemen, peasants, guards and masters
– to see.

They laughed to watch her stumble in the muddied
snow, and then to see her dragged back to her feet, only to
be led with greater roughness than before – with his fingers
now thrust inside her flesh 'to keep a firmer hold' – towards that very gatehouse where she had been admitted to
the castle, then through a door and up into the guardroom.

186

13

Defenders of Lidir

The wave of sickly heat, the staleness and the smell of sweat and long-spilled beer met her, and the raucous laughter stopped. Anya looked down, at the paths cut through the congealed sawdust drifting on the floor, and then through half closed eyes she risked a look at that discordant crew – the short, the tall, the ruddy-faced and the pallid, the unkempt, the unwashed, the drunk and the downright filthy and, sitting at the table, a man clad, not in drab, but in a black leather jerkin, a man who clearly stood out from the rest. And Anya glanced around the walls, bedecked with swords, and knives, cudgels, drums, horns of bronze, and red and gold banners. Above the fireplace, stretched all the way across the wall, was a tapestry, fringed in red and gold braid, which seemed to be an image of this land, showing hills and forests, lakes, fields of corn and rivers stretching to the sea; below this picture were rows of ciphers – symbols of thoughts and words, Anya recognised them to be – which probably told a story. In the middleground, set against a storm-filled sky, was a great grey castle – the Castle of Lidir – and in the foreground, an image of a woman in white, with head held high, and long red hair that flowed around her shoulders. She seemed so strong and so defiant. How Anya wished that she could show such courage now, against her captors.

Then all those eyes were fixed upon her as the guard held her up. Her wrists were back to back above her head, and the hand was in her crotch; her feet were scarcely touching the floor. She was held up like a chicken at the market. And Anya felt as limp and lifeless as that chicken. Those eyes, scattered about the room, by the fire, lolling up against the wall, and sitting round the table, were so intent, so piercing; a dozen knives struck through her flesh and bedded in her heart. The last remaining drops of Anya's self-respect welled out of those wounds and left her drained of any spirit.

'Another pigeon for the pot,' the guard declared now, shoving Anya down the steps, he sent her sprawling across the table, overturning mugs of beer and plates of meat and game and pastry. Anya just lay there, face down amid the disarray, for she was too terrified to move.

A hand stretched out from the opposite side; it grasped her by the hair and pulled remorselessly until she cried and squirmed and thrashed her arms, but all to no avail. The pulling still continued, and now her hair was twisted, forcing her over on her back, so her feet were on the table; she had to crawl upon her back through all the food and drink; it was the only way she could stop her hair from being torn out by the roots. And in this manner, screaming, crying, fighting back, she was dragged across the table until her flailing arms were seized by strong, not large, but determined hands and she was staring upside down, at a rugged youthful face, a smooth yet incised blue-black chin, pale blue eyes and black, black, slightly wavy hair, and those lips that descended now to seal about her own, to imprison them in a powerful but sensitive and deliciously upside down embrace which, against all her fear and pique and indignation, somehow made her belly want to melt.

'Though my table is all bollixed up under your direction, your Captain likes your fire, wench. Your Captain likes your heat.' And as he bent to kiss her again, Anya felt the lukewarm beer seeping slowly underneath her shoulders and soaking down her back, like the heavy, honeyed seepings lower down, which her slowly overturning tightening belly was squeezing so deliciously from her so defenceless person. For that kiss of self-assured tenderness seemed so overwhelmingly sincere, so lusciously inviting, so welcome, that her body cried out for those strong soft lips again.

His hands cupped around her cheeks and beneath her

upturned chin, and held her very gently whilst he kissed her – a host of tiny kisses planted on her eyelids, cheeks and chin, the corners of her mouth, that furrow in her lip, below her nose, and then more definitely, moistly, on her upturned bottom lip, just sucking at its fullness. Without releasing that gently captivated swollen fruit, his hand moved down her body – it tiptoed down her length, across the swelling of her bosom, across that hardening knot of brown-black softness which was now angled to the side, as it capped the heavy weight of Anya's milk-white breast, and then the hand crossed the rounded smoothness of Anya's belly, so tight in her desire; it parted Anya's softened curls, and then – more tentatively – those softened leaves, to reveal that tiny, pearly bud of flesh, which was swimming in a tiny pool of Anya's female liquor. And Anya's need was so intense, with that kissing, oh so gentle, that nothing mattered to her now but that the kissing should continue, and progress. She did not care that she was outspread on the table, with food and drink spilled all about her, with all those other eyes upon her, ogling her. But now those whisperings and muttered gibes had all but died away. Anya felt as if her body heat – the weight of her desire – was rising from her in a column, and anyone with a heart that was not stone could surely feel that heady weight of sensuality which now descended on the room to intoxicate those erstwhile gloating eyes, to melt those hard hearts with that soft and tender distillation of Anya's loving need.

Anya opened her mouth to make her lips into a liquid, pouting 'I', to take the Captain's tongue, not to suck it, but to stroke it with the tender, ticklish, inner skin of Anya's lips. And when his little finger touched her, the shudder was transmitted to those lips about that tongue; they pressed around it in a shivering band of nervous flesh. Anya cried a tiny, muffled cry of pleasured protest, through her nose, and her tongue-tip curved to touch his, very lightly. Her tongue-tip showed his little finger how to touch her, how to elicit that depth of blackness of desire, by circling gently round and round that pulsing nub, only barely touching and tapping at that liquid coated tip, at the pace her tongue-tip now dictated. And in the way her lips pushed up around it to draw his tongue more fully into her mouth – the more clearly to expose it to that precisely licking tip – so his fingertips pressed back the hooded join of Anya's leaves, the more definitely to subject her sweet and pushed-out, defenceless nub to those tickling strokes and tiny palpitations that his finger now bestowed. Each brush of Anya's tongue evoked a brush upon her nubbin; the stifled gasps of pleasure kept sounding through her nose. The tongue withdrew, but very slowly; her lips sucked down it to the tip, until that last seductive drop of spittle was shed into her mouth. The Captain looked at Anya for a very long while, and all that while his fingertips, though unmoving, held those leaves of flesh apart. Anya was dissolving in a sea of liquid honey. He looked upon her in her desire; she offered her body to him, in her eyes. She wanted this very powerful kind of loving to transform her; she wanted to drown in this oily sensuality. The Captain seemed to fill her with such delicious, black excitement.

'Your Captain has never met a wench so hot and so inviting.' His voice was very deep and smooth. 'He wishes to take this invitation slowly, he wishes to taste this tempting heat.' Anya swallowed. The Captain took her by the waist and slid her towards him till her head and arms now overhung the table; her back was arched and her breasts pushed out. He licked in Anya's armpits; he licked into that delicious cup of soft, red curls; his tongue lapped at her body scent, that heat of Anya's fears. Then the Captain stood, and kicked the chair away and gathered her in his arms. And now the jeering started; Anya closed her eyes against the grinning faces, the nudging elbows, the knowing winks and shaking fists; she shut off her ears against all the crudity of tongue, and curled up away from those touching, pinching, probing fingers, reaching out towards her, as the Captain carried her, past the taunting line of guards, to a doorway in the corner of the room.

He opened the door and peered inside. 'Out!' he shouted.

'That wench should have been returned two days ago!' Two very dirty, very sheepish guards emerged, with a bedraggled, grimy bondslave close in tow. She looked at Anya with hollow, frightened eyes, and then was hauled away. It made Anya very fearful of what might have been in store for herself, if the Captain had not happened to be here to keep these beasts at bay.

And for how long might her ordeal last? The Taskmistress had said nothing about that. She realised for the first time that nobody else would be aware of her fate. How would they know she was here, if the Taskmistress did not choose to send for her, if the Taskmistress did not choose to tell them? She tightened her grip about his neck; what if she were to be left down here forever?

The coarseness of the taunts broke in and stopped her dwelling on this thought. 'Save some of that dainty pigeon flesh for us, Captain!' Anya was burning up with humiliation at such brutishness. 'Just whistle when you need some help!' She hated these creatures, for their savagery and baseness. 'Give her good measure, Captain. – But mind you do not burn your stopper!' These animals were disgusting. Anya clung around the Captain's neck, for protection from this ruthless vilification.

'You'll get your turn!' the Captain cried, as he carried her through the doorway.

Those words so casually expressed, were icy fingers round her heart; her body went very limp and heavy; her blood was turned to water. She looked upon that face which she had trusted, which she had thought she had understood, and then she had to look away; how could all her feelings have been so totally misplaced?

The Captain stood her on the floor, then slammed the door and bolted it against the shouting and the banging. He kicked it, and then the thumping stopped and finally, the mutterings died away.

Anya had been taken into a small, low and very humble room, which looked like a cell, except that it bolted from the inside. Daylight filtered through a long thin window in the corner. The floor was blanketed in straw. There were three small beds, also covered with straw, and two simple chairs, but no other furniture. The place had the same stale smell that the guardroom had, though this time, it was overlain with dankness.

'Choose your bed, and spread yourself upon it.' The Captain simply placed a foot upon a chair, and began to unlace his boot. He seemed so cold-blooded now, and so insensitive to her feelings. Anya was trembling. 'Did you not hear?' He had raised his voice. Anya could not move. The Captain kicked off the boot, and then untied the other. He did nothing further until this too had dropped to the floor. Then he walked over to where the petrified slave was still standing by the door. His face was very close to Anya's. Though she could neither trust nor understand them now, still his eyes seemed to hold such power over her; his eyes were melting her.

'Spread your legs.' He never took his eyes from hers whilst he touched her with his fingers. 'You shall accommodate my touch. You shall do so whenever I choose to penetrate you – do not tighten – in the fashion of my choosing.' Anya had to spread herself to take him fully in, to allow his fingers to probe so deeply up into her person. She was trapped, between that gaze and that penetration, and that turmoil deep inside her. That honeyed taste of fear, that baseness of submission, seemed to cause a churning pleasure in her womb. The Captain then withdrew his hand and wiped it in the curls of Anya's belly.

'Your moistness is very much to your Captain's liking. But you shall make more moistness yet, before the two of us are finished.' Anya was too ashamed to look at him. 'Now, you shall spread your body on the bed, as your Captain has instructed,' he whispered, and he kissed her, drawing her defenceless lips within his mouth, to suck upon their fullness. He held her chin and studied her face. 'Your Captain wishes to punish you, for your disobedience.' Anya's upper lip began to tremble. She opened her mouth; she wanted to protest, to beg him not to do it.

'No,' he placed his forefinger across her lips to seal them. 'Do not speak . . . except to offer yourself, and to thank me.' His eyebrows raised; the backs of his fingers stroked patiently up and down across the smoothness of her belly. He waited.

'I . . . I th . . .' She was shaking, but she could not say it; she could not agree to this, when she was so afraid of what he might do to her, when she had no way of knowing how severe this punishment might turn out to be. 'Please, do not . . .' her eyes were cast down and to the side, in innocence and fear. 'Do not punish me,' she begged him very weakly, for she knew it was in vain.

The Captain's gaze did not falter. 'Turn around,' he said. She was so frightened. She did not want to turn her back to him – with him in so stern a mood – not now that she had disobeyed him a second time. 'Put your hands behind your head.'

Anya felt the chain of gold about her waist being moved up her back, and then up her front, by turns. He was edging it up her body; the chain tightened against her as it encircled her ribs and moved up, until it was pushing against the underjoin of her breasts and the links were pressed into that very tender flesh. The Captain forced the chain so far up Anya's back that her breasts were lifted up, away from her body, and then she was forced up on her toes. One hand was used to hold the chain, pushed up between her shoulderblades, whilst the other hand was smoothed very firmly up her belly, up and underneath her arms, then up and down across those rubbery, lifted, pushed-out nipples, now rippled by his fingers, until that rubber flesh had hardened to his satisfaction.

'Now, tell me I may punish you, in the way that I deem fit,' he commanded, softly in her ear. And in this manner, playing with her nipples, then making her push out her belly and open her thighs again so he could touch her, play with her between the legs, and make her drip whilst her breasts were held up for his pleasure in that sling of gold, and she was kept lifted up on her toes; in this fashion, he procured that slave's abasement. Although she wanted him to throw her down upon the straw, he would not permit her that deliverance from her shame. She had to walk that length of floor unaided, in submission, and – he would not direct her – she herself had to select the bed of her own degradation, and then, worst of all, spread herself in the manner which she deemed appropriate to a punishment, the style of which remained as yet unspecified.

Anya lay on her back, along the bed, in the centre of the room; the softened daylight kissed the roundness of her breasts and belly; her arms lay palm-uppermost, limply by her side; her thighs were slightly parted. The straw prickled into the skin of her back; it scraped her legs and scored the tender flesh of Anya's buttocks. The Captain gazed upon her with a look of indecision on his face – she prayed that he had mellowed. Anya's eyelids half closed; her thighs opened slightly more.

'Lie across the bed.' His tone was cold and stern. He made her lie with her hands beneath her, underneath her hips. 'Put your feet together; point your legs straight up.' She was shaking in her defenceless and exposure to his whim. 'Your blackness is enticing . . . So delicious to my eyes,' he murmured. 'The punishment of that blackened pot shall be so sweet, my wayward little doxy.' She was frightened to the core. She could not keep her legs still, from the straining, and the fear of what was to come.

'Do not tremble – not yet at least. That pleasure shall come later.' He raised his hands as if to strike. Anya watched that hand in terror; he pulled back his sleeve to reveal a band of black leather around his wrist. It was this that the Captain meant to use upon her person; Anya knew it, even before it was unbuckled. Her belly churned as if a living snake were squirming around inside her; the Captain meant to attend to her secret self, not with his hand, but with this trap of degradation. She could not take her eyes from it, as the Captain held it by the buckle and drew the thin and supple tongue of leather out between his fingers. Then she jumped – he smiled. He had smacked it, with a crack, against his palm.

'Spread your legs, but keep them straight.' Anya's belly seemed to sink and sink, as she spread herself before him;

194

it felt as if an invisible hand had reached up into her belly to grasp the tail of that slithering snake and now that hand was drawing those reluctant flexures out from between her legs. The Captain stood between her legs and stretched his arm out above her. He draped the tongue of leather down across her skin; he stroked it back and forth across her nipples, until they had turned to hard black stones, then trailed it in a tickling line all the way down her belly, then hesitated. He brushed the cool smooth leather tongue-tip along the crease at the top of her leg, to the left side, then to the right, whilst he watched her expression. Anya swallowed against the delicious taste of tickling, which made her want to close her legs around the tongue and trap it in the crease. The Captain pressed his hand against her right thigh, to stretch that delicate skin to tickling tightness, then raised the strap and quickly smacked it down, at the very top, in that very tender, hollowed spot, just below the crease.

The sudden shock of degradation was worse to her than pain. 'Look at me, do not turn away. As you offer your body in its openness, so you shall offer your eyes, in submission to my will.' His fingertips brushed softly into that place that he had smacked. 'Now.' He raised the tongue of leather. She watched, although she did not want to. She wanted to squirm away from it; she felt so exposed and so ashamed and so very, very helpless. There was nothing she could do to make him stop. She was too afraid to plead. That leather fell a thousand times before it finally struck, and each imaginary lash, each plea for mercy that she had not uttered, had sensitized her flesh, so that when at last it happened, her hips jerked uncontrollably upwards from the bed.

'Good.' And now, the Captain smacked her left thigh in precisely the same deliciously ticklish hollow, and sent an exquisite shock of pleasure through her body. Again he stroked her with his fingertips, and when he smacked her there once more, she spread her thighs so wide that her belly muscles ached.

'I wish to punish you in your mound of sweet delight,'

he said, whilst unbuttoning his jacket. 'Remain in that position, for the present, I wish to look upon your wantonness.' Anya's neck was burning as she was forced to watch him disrobe, whilst her body remained so outspread and offered in this way. She looked upon that form – the cleanly sculpted torso with its dense black wiry hair and that tight flat belly. That heavy, thick cockstem, seen through half closed eyes, was standing very stiffly upwards.

He made her press her feet together, sole to sole. Her hands, reaching from beneath her, had to clasp around her ankles, holding her very taut and very open to his touch. And then he made her twist her hips to the left. He ran his fingers down the exposed side of Anya's mound, before he smacked that firmness twice with the leather strap. Each smack shook her; it sent a ripple of black delight through her mound and deep into her person.

'Raise your hips, squeeze and tighten – push it out. Now.' He smacked again. The shock of pleasure transmitted to her tightly squeezed nubbin. He made her twist the other way. 'This time you shall squeeze so very tight, and moan.' He pressed his fingertips against her leaves, and held them to the side, then smacked the leather tongue quite closely up against them while she squeezed. Anya felt that moan so deep within her belly. And now his fingertips reached between her leaves, exactly at their joining, and caught and rolled that liquid pip, and would not let it go. 'No. Shh . . .' he whispered. 'You shall not make a murmur. Your pleasure shall not come, unless the kissing of this strap elicits that delight . . .'

Anya's body was melting at his touch – that controlled tightness, that very gentle rolling of her tip, massaged with Anya's body oil. He smacked her very systematically around that pushed-out, bursting mound, from the crease towards her leaves, and up around the hood, keeping always too far away from it to precipitate her pleasure, then down the other side, and back again. And at each smack, his fingers were softly squeezed against her nubbin, until her hips began to roll, and Anya caught her breath and moaned. The Captain pushed his finger very hard into her flesh, above the hood, and waited till the pulsing slowed, and then he closed his fingers fully round that nub again, and now each time the strap descended round her mound, and in her tight-stretched crease, he milked that nubbin, until Anya felt she would dissolve in wetness and that tide of pleasurable abeyance would surely drown her in delight. 'Ah, please,' she cried out softly; the milking stopped. The Captain's cockstem throbbed in slow pulsation; Anya wanted to take its thickness fully to herself, to squeeze herself around its throbbing firmness.

'Tuck your knees up. Spread that soft black pussy.' The Captain pushed against her feet until she was doubled and her hips had lifted from the bed, and then he knelt upon the bed in such a way that Anya's back was supported by his upper legs. Her pushed-out mound was level with his navel; his weighted flesh rested in the groove of Anya's bottom; it felt silky smooth against her taut black velvet. 'Spread those lips apart and hold them back. I want to see your heat.'

Anys was burning to be taken. That fleshy plum was throbbing its silken smoothness up against her ticklishness. Anya wanted that silkiness to penetrate her, right up to the bumps, but the Captain would deny her that fulfilling pleasure. He took the strap and held it closer to the end, so the tongue was now rather shorter, and he used it in that way to smack the inner moistness of her opened leaves, to the left, then to the right, pausing at intervals to bathe her leaves in her own liquid heat – not to assuage that burning prickling in her stimulated flesh, but to make the slapping that much more sharp, and telling, by virtue of the wetness of that skin, until Anya's leaves felt so full and puffy that she was sure she would never be able to close her thighs against the pressure of that swelling.

She gasped; the Captain pushed two fingers up inside her melting flesh; she thrust herself against him. 'Shh . . . stay still. Keep those lips very open; expose that pipe and squeeze; squeeze it out and lift.' He made her pull her flesh hood back until her nubbin pushed out very far, and then he pressed the heel of his hand into her mound, to stretch the hood back further until the flesh about her nub was stretched to bursting. He had her hold it like that, tightly back, while he raised the strap and waited. 'No. You shall not look away,' he said, and Anya had to look through misted, liquid eyes; she jerked, and then the smack stabbed like a needle in her nubbin, and the wave of stinging rippled through her sex and up into her belly; and when the stinging lulled, the feeling was as if a hole had been pierced into her navel, and warm oil was being poured inside and was welling downwards, filling her, making her swell with warm, soft numbness. The Captain then withdrew his fingers, dripping with her heat, and worked those fingers about her rigid nubbin, until the final throes of prickling had subsided, and the feeling – that heavy ache of swollen pleasure – had fully seeped back in. And then he put his fingers into her again, this time lifting them to push her nub out harder, and smacked her once more, and then again massaged her, until her breasts now felt so heavy, and so swollen, her belly felt full to bursting point with that oily warmth, and her body slowly seeped – its thick and liquid musk of pleasure welled out, overflowing slowly down her groove to bathe his silken stem, and drip at last upon the upturned tip of Anya's spine.

He rolled his stem within her groove, oiling it with her musk. He placed his palm against the small of Anya's back; his other hand was pressed against her belly, to steady her, and he lifted her body and turned her over. Her breasts pressed into the straw, which nipped and pinched against those weighted mounds and scratched against her nipples. Her belly was now raised up on his kneeling thighs; his cockstem nudged and probed the curls of Anya's bush.

'Open your body to your Captain,' he murmured. His hands slipped underneath her from behind and pressed into the tops of her thighs, close against the creases, to spread her – he lifted up her hips and rocked them, then very gently lowered, Anya felt the swollen plum end catch against her, split her leaves, and lodge. Her sex contracted round the tip and milked it and she heard the Captain's indrawn breath; it made her squeeze again to try to burst that plum within her body. The Captain placed his hands about her waist and pulled her bodily onto his stem, like a glove of liquid flesh. He bedded very deeply in her, until Anya could feel his bag against her, dangling between her legs, almost as if it were a part of her, and his wiry curls, prickling and springing in her groove, and now that cock-tip, deep within her, kissing at the mouth of her womb. She arched her back and pushed against him, for she wanted that pleasure deeper yet – she wanted to spread that inner mouth to suck upon that tip, and squeeze it with her sex until it milted so hard that those miltings squirted through into her womb in strands of liquid pleasure. But most of all, she wanted him to touch her on the nubbin, to wet his fingers with her heat, to oil them around that pushed-out tongue of pleasure, to make it palpitate like a tiny, bursting heart, and to milk it in the way that she was milking him; she wanted him to form his fingertips into a tiny mouth and draw that pleasure down and down, until it made her thighs reach back and grip so tightly about his waist that she took his breath away; then he could hold her open, with his thumbs bedded to her creasing joins, and thrust into her, and squeeze her nubbin between two fingers till she died of that delight.

But the Captain denied her that deliverance to pleasure, and yet he made her body shake. He spread her round, tight buttocks, and made his fingertip whisper through her velvet, very gently, from the point of Anya's spine, moving round and round in a tightly tickling circle, then very softly brushing down against that stretched and tender, very ticklish skin, that soft, soft velvet blackness, in a whispered breath of brushing, gently back and forth, until Anya almost felt that softened tickling up inside her bottom, as if it were stroking very lightly at the wall below the endpoint of her spine. And then his fingertips reached round underneath her and touched her nubbin. Anya rolled her hips and tightened. The touching stopped; the hand extended and stroked her drum-tight belly. That stroking made her tighten once again, and try so very hard to burst that cock inside her; she thrust back against him and she grunted, and she squeezed and held until his tightness felt like throbbing iron. The Captain held her very still, her legs spread very wide, his hands pressed up against the sides of Anya's mound. His breathing sounded very deep and laboured. And then he groaned and gasped and lifted her – the cock slid slowly out against the tightness of her gripping, which did not want to let it go – and those shaking hands lowered Anya slowly down again. She was burning with denial as she felt, amid the half-restrained cries of the man above her, the weighted droplets splashing, very warm and very thickly, low down on her back and merging, with continued dripping, to a pool which slowly cooled and turned her skin to gooseflesh.

The Captain lay beside her with his head pillowed on her back, and while he rested, he played with Anya and toyed with her burning body. 'I like a wench in heat,' he said. He tickled his fingers down her back and up across her buttocks, then split them, by edging her already outspread thighs even more apart, so her knees were bent and her hips were lifted slightly off the bed. He dipped his fingers in the pool of milt and dripped it in the upturned well of Anya's bottom, repeatedly, until his milt had made a viscid pool of pearly-white within her blackness. Then he very carefully teased apart those globes. 'Open,' he whispered. Yet Anya found this very difficult to do. 'Open,' he repeated 'Your body shall drink this essence in, for my amusement.' Anya tried to relax her tightness, as his fingers pressed within the groove to help her. 'Good.'

Anya felt the cold wet miltings sliding down inside. The Captain dripped those thick and milky droplets yet again, and made her drink them with her bottom, then making her raise her hips a little more, he slid his finger in. Anya opened her mouth and pushed her tongue out – she had not even realised what she was doing, and now it was too late. She felt so ashamed at this. The finger inside her tapped and tickled against the outer wall of Anya's bottom, then traced a line of forbidden pleasure up, and down again; the feeling was so sweet that Anya felt as if a strand of pleasure was being pulled right through her, down along her spine. And while this illicit pleasuring continued, his other hand massaged those remaining miltings into the skin of Anya's back, and down, using just two fingers, into the tender flesh of Anya's bottom groove, and around Anya's sensitive, finger-gripping, pushed-out bottom rim.

And now, he turned the woman over on to her back and, with her knees tucked tightly up to her chin and her thighs pressed hard together, he forced his cockstem through the tightly stretched lips of Anya's sex and worked it in and out, not touching her at all to give her pleasure, until finally he gasped again, withdrew his cock and spread her thighs and milted on her belly. Anya watched, in her denial, those melting slugs of whiteness, lowered on their stems of slime to fill the well of her navel and then she felt them spread across her belly and seep into her hairs. She felt so cheated. She had given her body and he had taken pleasure entirely at her expense, with no regard at all for her needs.

The Captain rested with his head at Anya's breast, sucking at her nipples, sucking underneath them, each of them in turn, so they felt alternately very warm and wet and soft, then cool and tight again, as he blew against them till the spittle had evaporated. And when this sucking had progressed sufficiently, his fingertips dipped into the pool of milt upon her belly, and he had her bend her knees – suspend them in the air – and place her hands about his head and cradle him, running her finger through his hair – whilst he dripped the milt into the join of Anya's leaves, and worked it round her nubbin, easing only when her breathing turned to heartfelt little gasps, then dipping once again and working – lightly touching, or very gently pulling – till the gasping rose again, then opened her out, spreading her with his fingers, and keeping her stretched like that, with the walls of her sex apart, yet very still in tension, not allowing her to move against him, not letting her contract, until her breathing softened, whereupon the dripping and the lightly pressured squeezing of her nubbin would progress, with her held very definitely open during this very prolonged and cruel pleasuring, until the milt was all used up. Then he laid her on her side, with her knees tucked up quite tightly and her arms folded across her breasts, and covered her with straw and bade her rest.

The Captain dressed, buckled on his wristband, now scented with her heat, and looked with a kind of love upon that slave – that sweet complexion, with those heavy lidded eyes, that gentle softened breathing, and those full and luscious lips, which he was tempted now to kiss, yet he refused himself that pleasure. And then he unbolted the door, and stepping through the doorway, announced in a voice of crystal clarity: 'Men – the wench is ready for you now. Regrettably, I cannot stay. I entrust her to your care.'

Anya heard the animal cries, the yelping of that stampeding pack, and then the scuffles, grunts and shouted curses as they tumbled through the doorway. They tripped and clawed each other as they fell upon the bed, in the fight to be the first to get to her. She was almost suffocated in the heap of bodies.

'Wait, lads. Wait! Don't let's fall out over the wench.'

'And let us get a look-in too!' someone shouted from the doorway.

Anya's body was being mauled by fingers pinching at her breasts and bottom, and trying to force themselves between her tight-shut thighs. She was so afraid, but could not even raise her arms against them without leaving herself even less protected against the vicious probing. The voice of reason then continued:

'Let's get her where there's room to move – let's get her on the table.'

'Aye,' a voice behind her said. 'Then all shall have a piece.' This raised a lively cheer; it made Anya feel sick to her stomach.

'I know which piece *I* want,' a fourth voice croaked.

'We all know that, you dirty bugger!' The assembly broke into howls of laughter. 'But you'll have to wait till last. I'm not going anywhere that you've been first.'

'Oh no?' the croak rejoined. 'But I've noticed you're not averse to licking up the Captain's spurtles and his droolings.'

'Lads, just calm down,' said the restraining hand. 'Look – them as wants can have her; them as don't can keep their peace. Right?' Another cheer went up.

Anya's feet were gripped by rough and eager hands, and she was pulled to the floor.

'Stop! Leave me alone!' she cried, as the fear now threatened to overwhelm her. She tried bravado. 'You are less than human – you are beasts!' she screamed at them, which only served to make their laughter louder and more hearty.

'You're right, my dear, in one respect, as you shall shortly see . . .'

Anya was dragged through the straw and up the step, and out into the guardroom. Then she was lifted by her hands and feet and swung up, until she landed with a crash upon the table. Strong hands held her arms, and others spread her legs. She shut her eyes and cried, 'No! You shall not touch me!' then found the strength to open her eyes again to glare at those evil, filthy creatures.

'Pigs!' she spat at them.

'Ha! Pigs, she calls us. Look at the state of *her*!' The speaker grabbed her by the hair. 'Mistress Tangleweed regards us all as swine.' The derisive laughter made her grit her teeth against the taunts, and worse, against the redness which was filling out her cheeks, for she knew just how bedraggled she must seem. 'Mistress Mophead, covered in beer and bits of straw and,' he squashed a pie between his palms and smeared it across her belly, 'pigswill from our table –' The room was now in uproar. 'Not to mention our Captain's fevered dribblings! This wench with private parts so black, she must frig herself with charcoal sticks – she tells us *we* are pigs!'

Now Anya was fighting back the tears; she would not allow her spirit to be broken by these vile, despicable worms. The speaker held her by her hair, and underneath the chin, so she could not move whilst he glared down into her face and lashed her with his tongue.

'So – may we take it that so perfect a person as yourself will not refuse a wash?' Anya tried to struggle, but she

203

could not move. He turned to the man beside him. 'Get the bucket.'

They doused her down with water, amid all her screams and kicks, and scrubbed her from head to foot with a vicious bristle brush, until the tender skin of her breasts, her belly and in between her thighs, was raw and scratched. And then they turned her over, scrubbing her shoulders and down her back. They parted Anya's buttocks and used the brush very roughly up and down her groove until she cried out loud, but they would not stop until she was red raw, right down to her toes. She was turned on her back again. 'And now perhaps Mistress Perfect is clean enough to have her black pot filled to bursting by a pig-sized cockstem?' The guard approached and began to kneel upon the table, between her thighs. Anya's leg was free. She did not hesitate. She bent her knee, and with all the strength that she could muster, she kicked out – and caught him very low down, in the ballocks of the swine. The grey guard groaned, then toppled backwards and landed with a crash upon the floor.

'Devil take her! She's made him wet himself.' The murmurs sounded awed. 'I'll swear she's kicked the ballocks off him altogether!'

'Who's next?' Anya shouted, for now she did not care. She was really very angry and, if they had dared to step within her range, she would have bestowed that corrective treatment on each and every one of them, with equal satisfaction. Yet odds of seven to one – even when the one was spitting fire and brimstone in the faces of those obnoxious, spineless fools – were in truth quite overwhelming, and Anya knew this well, though this would never stop her when she had the bit between her teeth.

'Defenders of Lidir?' she mocked them. 'Ha! You are nought but worthless, spineless scum!' She added, 'Come near me and I'll have your pig-like ballocks for mincemeat, and feed them to the ducks,' – a turn of phrase she owed largely to Marella.

Their expressions suggested that it was doubtful that the guards had been addressed with such forthright vehemence

– ever – by a slave. For a second, no one spoke, nor even moved a muscle. If Anya had been fast enough, in that stunned, immobile silence, she might even have escaped, except that, even if she had managed to do so, there was nowhere she could run to, and nowhere she could hope to hide.

'Right lads!' They pinned her by her arms and legs, then gagged her, so she could not bite them, or humiliate them with the truth. 'This foul-mouthed hussy can cool off on the battlements. We'll see if that tempers her fiery edge to the warmth that we require.'

Anya was half dragged, half carried up the winding staircase and out into the sunlight of that thin cold afternoon. They dragged her through the snow. Its freezing coldness cut her bare flesh; it made her cry into her gag and try to gasp for breath against the shock of tightness in her chest. 'Take these ropes and tie one round each ankle. We'll dangle her over the side.'

Anya's blood turned to ice; her backbone turned to water. 'Half an hour, head down, like that, should be enough to bring her to her senses.' There was nothing she could do to save herself, and gagged, she could not even plead. She tried to kick out, but they held her down while they looked the ropes around each ankle and quickly knotted them. Then Anya nearly passed out with the shocking coldness of the snow against her belly and her brèasts, as they calmly turned her on her front while her hands were tied behind her back. 'She shall hang with her legs kept wide apart; let the chill wind drain that heat.' Already numb with the coldness seeping through her body, and now paralysed with fear, she was made to stand, with feet apart, and her calves against a gap in the parapet which did not even reach her knees, whilst the coils of rope were anchored firmly to iron staples in the stonework, several feet apart. Anya felt dizzy; her body was unsupported against that wall of nothingness, the vast and empty space which hung out there behind her back – those open arms of endless falling, just waiting there to greet her. The wind sucked at her in icy gusts, first pushing against her, then suddenly drawing back again, threatening to pull her backwards over the wall. Her calf muscles ached from the constant strain of trying to keep her balance. The loops of rope felt slack against her ankles. She was terrified that her muscles would become too tired, and she would sway too far, and then, with her hands tied, unable to save herself, and the guards in front pushing her feet back to the wall in sudden jerks, she would topple over backwards. And there would be nothing to stop her falling whilst the ropes uncoiled, and falling still, when perhaps they broke or came undone or slipped off her feet completely, until she plunged head-first to the rocks a hundred feet below.

Waves of giddy sickness overturned her belly; she could not breathe; the gag, wet with condensation, had blocked her mouth completely. Her fear was trying to block her throat. She was suffocating slowly. Her field of vision was shrinking, then expanding, as the waves of terror struck, and the numbness gave way to a prickly feeling down her spine and up her thighs and out across the surface of her belly. Strong, insistent hands were gripped around her shoulders, pressing, forcing her backwards, though she was resisting, though she would not bend her knees; they forced her back and back until those strong hands took her weight, so she was helpless, and she was looking upwards at the sky; the guard began to lower her; she closed her eyes and heard, against the singing in her ears, a soft and distant murmur, like the bubblings of a mountain stream, and a faint cry – the cry of anguish that she could not utter. And then the cry was louder and more urgent, and suddenly her heart leapt, for she knew that cry was real, and that voice was unmistakable.

'The Prince!' the shout went up.

Now there was consternation all around.

The guard who held her turned and, in that moment, eased his grip. Too late, he grabbed for her again and missed, and Anya slipped away from him, unable to save herself, and then she felt that she was falling, slowly, endlessly sliding backwards into that pit of terror, down that vertical wall.

Then with a sudden jerk, she stopped – and she could see the Prince above her, leaning over, reaching down impossibly far, his face a mirror of her terror, for his fingers stretched in vain to reach her – and then she felt the loop of rope round her left foot move – it slipped against her, over her anklebone; the knot was creeping down her heel. She twisted her foot to try to stop it, but her skin, through cold, was smooth as glass. The loop had passed the point of no return. She screamed into her gag. The Prince cried out: 'No!' She swung sideways, like a pendulum, dangling by her right foot, hit the wall and bounced, out across the precipice, and then swayed back again. A wave of nausea hit her, for she was looking straight down at the slowly twisting rockscape far below. Her foot was aching from the strain of keeping it crooked about the rope, the rope that was looped too loosely round her foot; her muscles were crying out to stretch to ease the searing pain, but she knew that if she did, the rope would surely slip and she would plummet to her death upon the rocks.

And now it was the Prince's turn to overbalance, almost, and Anywa wanted to cry out 'No! You must not!' as he hung so precariously over the parapet, as he edged his fingers further down the wall. But still he could not reach her; the despair was in his eyes.

'Brace yourself. Keep your foot bent tight,' he shouted. 'You must not let it slip.'

The Prince took the strain of the rope and pulled, and prayed the knot would hold, and that he could keep the pulling very smooth and even.

The wind was rising, cold and cutting, turning Anya very numb, so the burning ache in her calf and foot was dulled but now her muscles would not respond, did not belong to her, and she felt so very, very tired. The Prince was straining every muscle, shaking, pulling, inching the dead weight of her body slowly, painfully up the wall, until at last her foot was but an inch or two away from him. And then his heart sank.

Her heel had jammed against a tiny overhang in the stonework, so that now, each time he pulled, she did not move; instead her foot began to straighten, and the rope began to slip, and Anya's eyes grew wider in her terror. So he had to lower her carefully, and leaning out, to try to edge her body away from the wall while he lifted, but now he did not have the strength to do it. He fought against the rising fear, the tears of black futility, but it was no good; he could not do it; he had to admit defeat and ease her all the way down again, knowing all too surely that time was running out for Anya. The rope kept sliding slowly up her foot, edging over that smooth and delicate heel and she was powerless to prevent it. Her wrists were bound, her fingers scrabbled at the wall, but she was slipping – she knew it – and now her fear was quelled, almost, by the inevitability of her fate, and the sureness of that love – that soft cocoon of love – which swathed itself around her even in that blighting of her hope.

'No!' he cried. But Anya's heavy eyelids wanted so much to close. 'You must not give in! I shall not let it happen!' And suddenly she was struck with an even greater panic – at what he meant to do – for he was lowering himself too far now, lunging wildly so that he would surely overbalance altogether. They would plummet together down into that chasm. She screamed inside. This was not what she wanted; she wanted him to live – for the two of them – not to give himself unto death because he could not save her.

And then her heart stopped as the Prince seemed to fall; her eyes were wide with terror; yet even as he fell, his arms were reaching – not towards her, but outwards to the side. And then she saw it – that rope which had already failed her still dangled next to her almost to the level of her feet. His hands flew out and, scraping down the stonework, snatched and knocked the rope away at first then somehow wrapped around and caught it, and he swung round, through the air, then, as the rope took up the strain and bit into his forearm, his body jerked and he landed with his feet against the wall. Suddenly, impossibly, the Prince was there beside her, the rope wound tight about one arm, and his body angled outwards, so he stood against the great stone wall. Now Anya felt her weight being taken. A powerful arm closed about her waist and in that instant, she was suddenly transformed, secure. It did not matter that she still dangled, upside down, a hundred feet above the ground, for she knew, that whatever happened now, that arm would never, ever let her go.

'Don't stand there gawking, pull us up!' she heard him cry. She closed her eyes and felt all the pain and fear and tension seep right out of her.

And now she was standing upright on the battlements, her body was not spattered on the rocks, and she was looking up into the very eyes that she had thought were lost to her forever. Those eyes were not gentle now, but burned like fiery coals.

He cut her bonds and pulled away the gag and kissed her with that melting heat of love which can never be contained by chains of slavery, or chains of caste, or chains of creed or station – that overpowering love which overturns all ills and salves all wounds and bathes away all tears.

'You have saved me,' she whispered very softly. 'I knew it. In my heart I *knew* that you would not forsake me.' He did not speak; his eyes were filled with tears. He kissed her very fully once again before he picked her up and held her, cradled effortlessly on one arm – that arm that had swung around to save her – with her face buried against that warm strong neck, and that golden earring dangling down against her cheek, whilst he unsheathed his sword against those guards.

'That my own men should do this thing, and to a treasure without price!' His anger knew no bounds. 'Protectors of Lidir?' he cried. 'You disgrace that name. You are worse than creatures in the gutter. You are lower than slime. Get out of my sight, you despicable crew.' And as they hung their heads, the Prince ploughed through them, beating them with the flat edge of his sword, and as she passed, the slave upon his arm was pleased to kick those cowering guttersnipes to speed them on their way.

14

The Legend

Anya mused upon the Prince's words. She repeated them under her breath, time upon time, as she dwelt upon the story of her rescue. *A treasure without price*, he had said. *My heart bows down before your beauty.* His words had been so beautifully romantic; they had made her melt.

He had looked upon her tear-stained, shivering, scratched and battered, yet still bedraggled as it was, so delicious body, and he had kissed warmth into those ice-cold, purple lips, again and again. His eyes had been still, dark bottomless pools of yearning. She knew he really cared. He had set her down and wrapped his cloak of red and blue about her, and had kissed her yet again, then carried her from that place and down across the courtyard, through the snow, up the great staircase – without any effort, as if her body and limbs were feather-light – past the Great Hall, past all the servants and the guards, who stood aghast to see their Prince, the Prince of all Lidir, a beast of burden to a slave – a slave adorned with the Prince's cloak – and on and through the Bondslave's House, with all the shouting, as word of their arrival sped before them, through the lounge, past the females' quarters and the bathhouse, through the giggling throng of delighted faces that by now had lined their route, and then at last, between the stone-faced sentries, and into the Prince's suite.

Four of the most lovely creatures Anya had ever beheld – the Prince's slaves-in-waiting – welcomed them. The slaves were adorned with jewelled chains and necklaces, and gold rings in both ears; flecks of gold were brushed onto their cheeks and breasts, and dusted in their hair. One of them, appearing slightly older than the others, had earrings set into her nipples. The thought of having that tender part pierced right through by a needle made Anya's flesh creep. The slaves bowed down before the Prince, then smiled at Anya, and kissed her on each cheek, as if she were a sister. She was placed at the Prince's table, on a large chair, almost like a throne, upholstered in velvet of the deepest purple, while the slaves-in-waiting served her with a delicious repast – rich and savoury meat, peas and parsnips brushed with butter, and that warm and crusty, soft and very yeasty bread which Anya so enjoyed. They placed before her a large clear goblet, which bore the image of an eagle carved into the glass, and filled it with a sweet, sharp frothy drink, whose taste reminded her of nuts and honey. Then they brought a golden platter, laden with small, delicious, perfumed fruit in a pale red crispy husk.

When the meal was finished, the Prince removed her chains. Anya was not frightened – she wanted him to do it.

'Anya,' he said (he even used her name), 'you shall not need this symbol of your bondage. This night, we two shall meet as equals.' A shiver of delight rippled through her, for she had already worked out, in detail, the manner of their meeting, which was not as slave and master, neither yet as simple peers, but rather, as a man giving himself, in love, to a woman consumed by a very special fire – that burning heat of passionate need which will not be denied.

The Prince now directed his slaves-in-waiting. 'Bathe this woman,' he said. 'Salve her wounds, and dress her in nothing but the sweetest aromatic oils, then bring her to me.'

The Prince's bathhouse filled Anya with awe. Though smaller than the one located in the Bondslave's House, it was much more lavish in its decoration. The walls were pure white alabaster, its vaulted ceiling was tiled in turquoise blue, the cornices were picked out in gold leaf, and upon three of the walls were mosaics, in clear, bright colours – a red dragon, a large green tree bedecked with cream-white doves, and a great jewelled sword which sparked blue fire. The fourth wall was blank, but the fifth

211

carried a stained glass window, figuring the banner of Lidir – the castle, the hills and forests, the ciphers, and the woman dressed in white. Anya looked upon that image with wonder once again. It seemed to glow, as the evening sunlight billowed through the windows, to turn that alabaster white to soft warm pink.

'Come, now.' The slave with chestnut hair, and gold rings through her teats, led Anya down the marble steps. The two of them sent ripples out across the stillness of the water, and dancing yellow bands across the ceiling of the room. The water felt warm, not cold, as Anya had expected. She did not understand how this could be. It gently lapped against the tops of her thighs. The other slaves, bearing pots and bottles, and a thick, soft yellow wadding, full of tiny holes, then joined them in the pool, and bathed her from head to toe, immersing her fully beneath the water, time and time again – on her back, then on her front, sitting, kneeling, then on her side, and after each immersion, anointing her with creams and oils, until it was clear to Anya that this washing was some ritual whose significance remained unexplained.

At last they supported her on her back again, to spread her thighs, and open out her sex. The leading slave – the one who was older than the rest – oiled her fingers in a pot of faintly almost-smelling cream, then slipped them up inside Anya. Anya could feel the fingeres smear the ointment carefully round within her sex. She could not prevent her body from reacting to this gentle yet insistent provocation. The woman opened her more fully, to allow the water to swirl around inside her, then anointed her again, very slowly and deliberately reaching up inside her, and working her fingertips round the mouth of Anya's womb. Once more, she opened her, to let the water fill her, then made Anya contract, to squeeze it out. Then she spread out Anya's leaves, which felt thicker now, and also very warm, for they were filling up with blood. She smiled, as Anya's bud was revealed, pushing out and upwards, very hard. She touched it with the tip of her finger, lightly stroking upwards, underneath it, till it pushed out rather further. This woman seemed to know exactly how to touch her. Then the woman closed the leaves of Anya's sex round that swollen bud, and worked them, sliding them from side to side, so the bud was rolled between them, until Anya had to clench her teeth against the surge of pleasure which now threatened to engulf her. Her bud was so distended that it could not be retracted; it remained, peeping out prominently from beneath her fleshy hood.

The woman smiled again and had Anya turn over, on to her front. Those oily aromatic fingers opened out her cheeks, then gently probed and searched within the groove until they found that knot of flesh, then very smoothly slid inside her – two fingers, working systematically round inside her bottom, making her want to tighten up against them, making those sweet, forbidden feelings surge to take her breath away, making Anya's nubbin swell into a bursting button between her pushed-out leaves. She wanted the woman, with those fingers still reaching up into her as deeply as they could, to slip a hand between her thighs, and underneath and round, and to spread her leaves and nip that nubbin very sharply, whilst Anya closed her thighs against that wrist and squeezed against those fingers, till that shock of pleasure spasmed in her belly and burst between her legs. The fingers opened her bottom; the water spiralled up inside her. Her bottom tightened, but the fingers held her open; then the oiling and the rinsing was repeated.

At last Anya was led from the bath and dried; she was laid down upon a low, upholstered deep blue table, with a silken cushion beneath her head, whilst her body was searched minutely. No bruise or scratch was left untreated, no matter how small; each was carefully dabbed with a tiny pad of soft cloth moistened with a sweetly smelling salve, which did not sting at all but seemed to evaporate on contact with her skin, leaving it cool, refreshed and perfumed with the scent of honeysuckle. And then the younger slaves-in-waiting wanted once again to examine Anya's markings. Her leaves were turned to one side, then the other; her bright red curls were combed back to expose the whiteness of her mound, and to reveal the way the brown-black tincture of her skin was shaded across her leaves to perfect blackness at each edge, and then to pink within. They raised her hips and bent her knees; they spread her so they could study the swath of colour bridging across to merge into the pool of velvet blackness around the mouth of Anya's bottom. And they discussed amongst themselves what manner of body paints or dyes they might apply to simulate these unique colour brands upon their individual persons, thereby to enrich their lovemaking by bringing surprise and delight upon their lords and masters. Anya felt so happy and so proud that these markings she had thought her bane were looked upon with so much admiration by these very beautiful women, who must surely be the pick of all the slaves within Lidir. She also felt very much aroused, with all the fingertip touching and the brushing, and the opening and closing of her leaves, with that constant gentle stimulation in and around her nubbin.

Anya was made to stand up whilst the leading slave checked her, back and front, brushed her hair and then bade her lift her arms above her head. The slave then brushed the hairs beneath Anya's arms, fluffing them up and saying, 'Now your perfume will caress the air,' which made Anya's cheeks begin to colour. Then she had her spread her legs whilst her coppered bush was teased out in a similar fashion. 'There,' the slave announced, and gently pinched that pushed-out, moistened nubbin, 'your musk would force a cockstand in a dead man.' Anya's cheeks were crimson.

Then finally, she was declared fit and ready to grace the Prince's bedchamber.

She stood at the foot of the large oak bed, with its intricately carved panels adorned with eagles, a dragon, the sun and stars, and images of very many female nudes, their bodies disported in a great variety of lascivious poses. The Prince reclined upon the bed and looked at her. He too was nude, apart from that single ring through his left ear. The slaves-in-waiting had taken up their stations at his head and at his feet, upon the bed, or kneeling down beside it, touching him, stroking at his thighs, across his belly, in the

curls and up across his chest. The leading slave – the one
with rings set through her nipples – lay closely up against
the Prince. Her thighs were spread, like the women's on the
carvings. The Prince's hand lay between her thighs. His
fingers were idly toying in her bush, toying with the leaves
about her sex. The woman was spreading herself to allow
the Prince's fingers up inside her. The Prince's cock was
stirring, and the slave lay back, smiling.

Anya did not like this setting – not one bit. It was not
as she'd intended, not at all as she had planned this meeting in her mind. Her heart was beating very fast indeed, for
they were four and she was one, but still, she felt she must
assert herself and instruct them very clearly.

'Thank you,' she told the slaves in very certain terms.
'You shall not be needed. You may leave us now.'

No one spoke. The stroking stopped. The young slaves
glanced nervously at the leading slave, whose mouth had
fallen open. The Prince regarded Anya with a fixed stare,
as if he were afraid to blink. Anya steeled herself.

'Your services shall not be required,' she repeated.

The Prince withdrew his hand from between the thighs
of the leading slave. She turned to him for support, but she
did not get it. The Prince merely raised his eyebrows, and
then he nodded almost imperceptibly. The slaves-in-waiting stood up, bowed to the Prince and then to Anya, and
left without a word.

Anya was alone with the Prince and now she was in
charge; her plan was firmly back on course.

But first of all, she lay down on the bed beside him, with
her head upon his chest. She took his arm and curled it
round her and asked him to tell again, with all the details,
exactly how the Prince had come to save her from the
guards. And while this fairy tale unfolded so deliciously to
her ears, her fingertips tickled very lightly in amongst the
curls upon his chest, and softly down his belly, and at
times, she would raise her head to question him, or merely
to stroke her fingertip round behind that earlobe with the
ring, or to kiss him gently on the chin, or more warmly,
softly – moistly – fully on the lips.

'I could not get you out of my mind,' he began. Anya's eyes opened very wide. 'From that first moment, at the banquet, you filled my thoughts.' She smiled, recalling how their eyes had kissed. 'Last night, you even filled my dreams.' She brushed her lips very slowly up his chest and closed them briefly round his nipple, then rested her ear upon him while she listened to his heartbeat. 'Even in the Taskmistress's rooms, even when you . . .' he could not bring himself to say it. 'It hurt me – to see your precious beauty subjected to such degradation.' And Anya closed her eyes at the memory of that pain. 'But even then, my heart knew, although my mind still would not admit it . . .' He closed his hand round her breast, and Anya placed her hand on his. 'I think I was afraid.' She lifted up and looked into his eyes.

'Afraid?' she said.

'I could not understand those feelings.' The Prince seemed lost for words. 'Your beauty, when first we met; that look . . .' He sighed. 'Those eyes had overpowered me. No other woman has ever made me feel that way. And when we met that second time, in the passageway, it was almost like a physical blow.' Anya remembered then that he had seemed almost too afraid to touch her.

But those eyes which had smitten him now caressed his face and kissed his eyes, and drank in his desire.

At length, Anya spoke. 'Tell me the part about the Council,' she said, for she liked this part best.

'When I left the Taskmistress's apartments, I was already late. The Council was in session. Naturally, I was required to take the chair, although I did not wish to do so.' Anya snuggled up to him and hung on every word. 'However, I very soon became enmeshed in the debate, which was both prolonged and acrimonious, concerning the levels of tribute to be exacted from each province of Lidir – a difficult problem, with few easy answers, since each province varies in size and wealth and population – broken down by class and of course, acreage of tilth, and then . . .'

'Yes,' Anya steered him in the right direction. 'And then what about the vision?'

The Prince coughed, and took up the tale at a more appropriate point. 'Then suddenly, the hubbub died. To me, the room seemed to go very quiet, yet the assembly was still in the midst of a very fierce discussion – I could clearly see their lordships' mouths moving in speech, and several of their lordships banging on the table – but it was as if I had been struck deaf. I could not hear a word. And then the assembled persons almost seemed to glow; the colours of their robes seemed so strong and vibrant . . . and it was then that I heard the voice.'

'Where did it come from?' Anya could not contain herself. The Prince looked through her; his eyes seemed glazed.

'It seemed to come from . . . not from anywhere. And yet it seemed to surround me. It was the only thing I could hear.' He looked troubled. He sounded as if he himself still could not believe it.

'And the door of the Council Chamber?' she prompted. 'Was it open when you heard this cry?' She knew that this wonder must have happened as the grey guard dragged her past.

'No. I don't know – it could have been.' He looked straight at her. 'But it was not a cry.' Her eyes were very wide indeed. 'The voice was soft – very soft – yet somehow all around me.'

'You did not recognise that voice?'

'No . . .' He looked very distant. 'But it was such a beautiful voice, very soft . . . yet very sure.'

And Anya felt quite certain about that voice – she could picture the owner very clearly – and she knew that it was magic.

'And that voice – that beautiful, magic voice – what did it say to you?' asked Anya, with rapture in her face, which made the Prince smile, for she already knew quite well what the voice had said, from the previous telling of the story. And yet she had to hear him say it once again.

'It said: *Be true unto your heart.*'

Anya's eyes were filled with tears; she could not speak. She fell upon him, kissing him very softly and repeatedly,

217

till those living tears dripped from her trembling upper lip to splash her sweetness down upon his cheeks, across his lips and into his open mouth – and he tasted those warm and softly falling tears of Anya's joy.

This time, she did not force him to complete that tale – of how he had rushed out of the Chamber, to the consternation of all around, then tried, and failed, to find the Taskmistress, and then had embarked on a single-handed, headlong chase through the castle, through the Bondslave's House, the kitchens, the stables and the dungeons, looking for her, and finally had, by chance, stumbled upon a young slave, just returned from guardroom duty, who had remembered seeing a slave answering to Anya's description being brought in by the captain – since all of that must now await another telling. For now, Anya wanted to give her Prince that special kind of love, that strong, insistent, very physical love. She wanted to render him a slave of love – her love – and to brand him with the white-hot iron of Anya's own desire.

She knelt astride the Prince's belly, facing him, so she could watch in his expression the burgeoning of his pleasure. Her hair hung down across her shoulders; her back was arched, which pushed her breasts out strongly, as she wanted them to be, and made her nipples point upwards. The Prince raised his hand to touch those inviting, precariously balanced, black-brown berries, but Anya very gently pushed him down again. She pressed her palms to either side of his face and held him like that, for a second or so, to indicate to him that he should keep very still, and then she placed her finger across his lips to seal them. She wanted no distractions. Finally, she closed his eyelids, which flickered open after a moment, then closed again obediently under the weight of Anya's frown. She was really quite insistent that this requirements be upheld.

Anya used her palms to trace the form of the Prince's chest, in such a way that, simultaneously, they moved up and outwards, a fraction of an inch above the surface, so her fingertips just brushed the hairs and sensitized the skin. That feather-light touching progressed upwards, across his shoulders, down his upper arms and back again, then very tenderly round his neck and up behind his ears. Her little finger very lightly, very nervously, tapped upon that earlobe, the one that bore the ring. She bent forward until her face was poised above him, and her breathing whispered out across his cheeks. His eyelids flickered, but they did not open. Anya smiled. Her breasts hung down and, with her breathing, swayed above his chest and dabbed those soft brown fleshy buttons against his skin until his chest curls tickled those pliant knots of flesh to tightness. Anya's fingertips worked upwards from the Prince's ears, softly up into the roots of his hair, lifting, teasing, sending crawling tickles up across his scalp, almost making him want to move his head away. And then he felt the soft, precise, wet tip of Anya's tongue stroking over his eyelid, then pressing in the corner, tracing a fine line of liquid down one side of his nose, across his upper lip, then back across the lower, then very slowly, very finely round the opening of his nostrils – making him want to jerk away – first one, and then the other, then moving upwards to the other side of his nose, dabbing moistly in the corner of his eye and out across the eyelid, causing him to see dancing, coloured stars of light.

He felt his nostrils pinched – quite lightly – and he had to open his mouth to breathe, whereupon his nostrils were released, and then that small warm tongue was slipped between his lips, where it seemed to rest, making tiny, nervous, deliciously sweet vibrations against that sensitive skin, until he had to reach his tongue to touch hers, tip to tip. The feeling was as if a stream of liquid fire had passed from her to him; in that brief touch, the Prince could sense the trembling heat of passion in the slave. His cockstem throbbed and pumped up harder, till it ached.

Anya sat back; her sex felt swollen with her heat. She used her hands to spread herself, to open out her thighs more fully, and to spread apart her leaves, for she wanted her liquid heat to trickle out and to seep right through his skin; she wanted to drug him with her passion and to burn him with her fever. She wanted to plant that seed of inner need within him – that craving need, which no one else would satisfy, and that seed which would root and grow until nobody – not even she – would ever have the power to kill it.

She held her body fully open whilst she kissed herself against his skin – across his belly, round his nipples, on his arms and shoulders, and up on to his neck, depositing loving, liquid circles of her musk upon him, marking his body with her scent, marking him for her own.

Anya reached back and curled her fingers round his stem, not tightly but very lightly so her fingers enveloped him but barely touched the skin; each movement of her hand was a whispered brush of aching delight against that pulsing plum of flesh. She tightened her gloving finger once, and then released them again. The Prince sighed very softly. Anya pressed two fingers of her other hand up to the knuckle in her liquid pot of flesh, then, while she slowly pushed them in his mouth, she worked the outer skin of his cockstem firmly, yet with intermittent nervous jerks, up and down. The Prince's moan was stifled by her fingers. In a smearing trail of honeydew, she slid her openness down his belly, past his navel, until she could feel his curls prickle up against her out-turned leaves, and his rigid cockstem curving closely up to her from behind. She spread her thighs as widely as she could, and then she spread her buttocks, until she felt as if her thighs were hung upon a hook of living flesh; his taut and throbbing cockstem lay along her groove and touched her, flesh to tender flesh. She wet her fingers in his mouth and reached back to massage the plum end of his cock, whilst she squeezed it rhythmically between her buttocks. She watched his face intently, but she did not change the pace of squeezing, nor the sliding pleasure of finger pressure upon that upturned plum. And when at last his head began to move from side to side in strong, insistent jerks, she knew to stop that intimate massage, and instead she lapped her tongue back and forth across his nipples, whilst she placed her closed fist low down against his belly and pressed it into him, until such time as she judged the massaging and the squeezing might

220

resume. For she wanted to fill him up to bursting point with unallayed desire before permitting that final, devastating transport of delight. In fact, she hoped to make him pass out beneath the burden of that pleasure, when it came.

Then, having wet his nipples so they glistened with her spittle, and having sucked them, and nipped them with her teeth, to bring them up to hard and wrinkled stiffness, she moved her hips back up over his belly and spread her slipperiness about the firmer, harder nipple of the two, which happened to be the left one, then closed her eyes and very gently rocked until that flesh point snuggled up against the tiny pushed-out pip of flesh between her outspread leaves. She worked her nubbin; like a hungry tongue, it licked across the nipple, and slid around, in slow, delicious circles of thick and oily pleasure, kissing him with her flesh, until the pleasure surged so strongly in-between her legs that it made her double forwards, tightly in a circle, against that impending threat of premature delight. Her face was buried in his hair; her misted curls, beneath her arms, suffused the air with languor; his lips reached to touch and suck upon those soft and dangling shaking mounds of black-tipped flesh, that with each and every movement of her hips, kept brushing over his face.

Anya caught her breath, but managed to wrench herself away, and knelt up, outspread above him, to let her musk roll down to fill his nostrils, to fill his mouth, and to drive him to distraction. She took his head and turned it to the side; she brushed the hair back away from that ear which so intrigued her, to expose that smooth and bare surround, then curled that rubberiness into a cone of flesh and spread herself over it, sealing her liquid leaves down upon the smooth, bare skin around it. The ear sprang back against the walls of Anya's inner flesh, and then she moved, very gently, very slightly, for she wanted him to hear those soft and liquid sounds inside her, that distant echo of her heartbeat, and that very earthy, slow drip of her heat. She wanted him to understand her body very fully, and in a way he understood no other. And while she moved, she stroked his hair, and smiled upon him, though he could not see her smile.

Anya wanted next to kiss him with her sex – not to kiss him on the body, but to kiss him on the lips. But first, she lifted him and kissed that ear which had been inside her; she licked the earlobe that carried the ring, and turned him so he looked at her. She did not want his eyes closed now; she wanted him to see, and to kiss her whilst she kissed him with her soft and delicate female self. Her black leaves spread like lips about his lips; they sucked upon them, drawing them inside her as she kissed them in that very special way. Her eyelids were weighed down with a soft, voluptuous pleasure as his tongue reached up inside to spread her and to taste her in her openness, to drink that dripping musk. And whilst she tightened and relaxed, and sucked upon and squeezed that gently probing, softly slipping tongue, Anya pressed her fingers to her leaves, pulling back the hood, and urged on by the inner pressure of that tongue, she drew wet circles of pleasure, very slowly round and round her poked-out nubbin, pausing, when the pleasure swelled too strongly, to smear that honeydew across his eyebrows, and to take his head within her hands and hold him tightly to her. Then when the pleasure, even with those loving pauses, became too sweet to bear, Anya lifted from him, kissed him with her mouth and, checking that his cockstem was still hot and swollen unto bursting, she turned her Prince over onto his front.

She spread his thighs and arranged him so his cockstem lay beneath his belly and his bag lay on the bed, between his outspread thighs. She traced her fingers down his backbone until she had found, within his groove, the tip of the Prince's spine. She wet her finger, stretched the skin, and drew the finger slowly round that very ticklish tip, and then she brushed further downwards into the groove, making him contract. She spread his buttocks even wider and tickled in the gap, stroking just the fingerpad back and forth across that sensitive skin. Anya pursed her swollen leaves together and fitted them to that groove, then lay down upon him, moving, pressing against him, spreading him

222

and working herself more closely up against him until the Prince could feel that hot and weighted velvet droplet brush against his bottom mouth, tickling the skin. Then Anya moved her flesh leaves upwards in his groove until her nubbin found that hard, rounded tip of spine, and she worked herself against it whilst she kissed his shoulders, licked his back and – when her pleasure rose too sharply – bit him in the neck. The Prince could feel her seepings trickling, in intermittent, hesitant droplets, down into his groove. That constant pressure, through his back, was transmitted to his plum – the circling of her hips was rolling him from side to side, turning a gentle stimulation into an overpowering need for pleasurable release.

Anya now would work him, slowly, ever onward to that release. She turned the Prince onto his side and had him bend his knees quite tightly to his chest. She wanted him this way so that she could have very free and easy access to his person, whilst she pleasured him in the manner of her choosing. She wanted his parts completely at her mercy. She would control his pleasuring very closely, and would in fact postpone his pleasure several times in order to sweeten his deliverance.

The Prince's cockstem was already very stiff indeed, and was pulsing with his heartbeat. Anya very carefully wrapped her hand round his silken skin, to feel that heartbeat and to ease that upcurve slightly outwards, away from the Prince's belly. She wanted that fleshy part to be, in a sense, abstracted from his person, so that any touch or brush which brought pleasure to it would be a touch or brush, or suck perhaps, which she herself bestowed directly. She pressed two fingers into the topside of his cockstem, at the point at which it fed into his body, which pressure served to keep it held away from him; it also kept it both rigid and balanced in its tension, so each tiny adjustment of her fingertips was magnified into a wavering dance of that very swollen plum. Anya now traced, with the forefinger of her other hand, a slow line down the undersurface of his stem, starting at the tip and pressing definitely, yet not too firmly, working downwards, down that centre line, that thick tube slung just below his skin, down to the base, where she pressed her finger firmly in, trapping his stem between those fingers on the upper side and the forefinger, pushing into him from below, and in the process evoking a soft moan. She used that grip to keep him firm whilst she pressed and stretched the skin in a slow and rhythmic motion, so his plum skin appeared to her alternately very tight and polished, then softer and more silky, and a clear fluid droplet welled in the tiny mouth at the tip of his cock. She worked him in that way, pausing only to stroke his brow or to bend, and to dab moist kisses along the tight curvature of his back, down one side, then up the other, yet even in these pauses not releasing him, but encircling the base of his stem with a finger and thumb and pressing back against his body, keeping his cock a prisoner in its taut-stretched skin, keeping him aware, keeping that deep and swelling ache of pressure tight – enough to make him want to burst, yet not quite enough to trigger him.

Throughout this pleasuring, Anya watched him very carefully. She would make that cockstem seep. She kept him closely collared with her finger round the base, and jerked the collar very quickly, until she saw him tense and hold his breath. Then she held him tight but very still while, with the other hand, she rubbed her fingertips back and forth along the strongly curving tube-filled bridge between his cockstem and his bottom. And under this very close attention, this rapid working till he gasped, and then the pressured stroking, she was pleased to watch his body seep, as the droplet swelled to dripping point and lowered on its thread to rest upon the bedsheet, then welled again, until his cocktip was connected by a continuous tube of liquid to a heaped up droplet down below. Anya dipped her finger in the liquid he had made and, kneeling up, so that the Prince could clearly see, she spread her thighs and pulled back her hood and worked its liquid slickness round her nubbin until her knees began to buckle – until she could not bear the pleasure any more.

And this time, before she began to touch the Prince again, she had him – still lying on his side – lift one leg from the bed so his stem rose up at an angle. Bending down, she closed her lips about that pushed-out bridge beneath the root zone of his cock, and sucked him very hard. And while she sucked, she licked him there, probing her tongue against his tubes, until the sucking and the probing made his cockstem sway. She formed her fingers into an open ring and slid this tightly down and up over his plum, smoothed now with his seepage, whilst she sucked upon and softly pressed her teeth into his bridge. His groan was now more heartfelt, so she desisted, but took his cockstem fully in her hand and, making him keep his leg upraised – as a sign of his submission – she kissed him on the lips. Whilst she kissed and sucked upon his lips and gently probed her tongue into his mouth, she was reassured to feel that hot and swollen cockstem pulse in random, nervous spasms like the flutterings of a wounded bird against her hand, which held it not too tightly, not too softly, not varying the pressure at all, yet keeping that bird of love at all times aware that it was her captive and that she would release it only when she chose to. And yet she did not think this treatment cruel; she thought it necessary to her purpose, and though she herself was burning up with unallayed desire, she would never take her pleasure until her Prince had been delivered first to that fullness of release.

Anya now desired to penetrate the Prince. She told him she would do this thing to him. And she made him lift that leg up even higher.

'You shall make yourself very open to my touch,' she said, for she had learnt her lessons well. She wet her fingers with her honeydew, by pushing them inside herself, then she held his cockstem tightly whilst she pushed them into him. The Prince groaned and tried to close his legs; his cockstem nearly spasmed. 'No, Sire, you must wait,' she whispered very firmly. 'The time is not yet nigh. I must be allowed this tender touch without any interruption.' And against his tightness and his softened murmurs, Anya pushed her fingers in, right up to the knuckle. Now, whilst she used the fingers of her other hand to massage his plum

225

with nectar, she stroked him with a slow seductive pressure, in that very intimate way, her fingers deep inside his
body, until he cried out. 'Please . . .'

'But, Sire.' she said, with wicked innocence, 'I have yet
to taste you . . .'

Then Anya spread her lips about that plum and very
gently sucked it, as she moved her fingers in and out of
him, and on the instroke, curled them round to push
against his root zone from within, until she felt him go so
very tight against the constant probing, and those salt-seep
tremors of forepleasure went upon her tongue. The Prince
shuddered and emitted a wrenching groan. Anya calmly
released that plum and drew her fingers carefully out, then
turned him on to his back. His stem was shaking with
strong, contracting throbs. 'Wait,' she commanded. 'Do
not let your pleasure spill. Tighten. Hold your breath.
There . . .' The Prince gritted his teeth. Very slowly, very
leisurely, Anya knelt astride him. 'Now,' she said, 'beg of
me to burst your pleasure,' and she lodged his cockhead
between her tight and burning leaves of flesh. 'You may
beg me. Go ahead,' she said, and with very great assurance.

He had no choice. 'I . . . I beg of you . . . to do it,' gasped
the Prince of all Lidir, and to a slave, at that.

Anya's face lit up with pure delight.

'It shall be my pleasure to chastise you in this way,' she
said, and the Prince was forced to laugh at this, even in his
present state of torment.

And as her body took him fully to itself, she lay down
upon him and kissed him in a wave of true and burning
passion, pushing her breasts against his chest, gripping him
with her thighs, urging his pleasure with her hips, holding
him down, hand to outstretched hand, pushing her tongue
into his mouth, bedding it beneath her own. And when he
thrust and bucked until his cocktip kissed the mouth of
Anya's womb, she squeezed so tight she burst him; she
covered his lips with hers to suffocate his moan, to render
him powerless while that force of pleasure seemed to suck
and spit and draw and draw, right through him to his
backbone.

To Anya, even though she had not taken full release, that feeling of deep, suffused warmth was delicious. Before this night was through, there would be time – much time, she knew – for that pleasurable release to take her breath away, before this night was through.

And afterwards, when the Prince was curled around her, fast asleep, her back pressed up against him, his hand about her belly and his hand about her breast, and delicious thoughts were kissing her mind – pictures of the ways in which she might take him next – she heard him murmur softly in his sleep:

'My Princess . . .'

Anya smiled a smile of very deep contentment.

'My slave,' she whispered in reply. It was indeed a cheeky thing to say, but was in fact quite true.

NEW BOOKS

Coming up from Nexus and Black Lace

Nexus

Displays of Experience by Lucy Golden

June 2000   Price £5.99   ISBN 0 352 33505 X

Twelve new stories from the masterful Lucy Golden. The twelve stories in this collection reveal the experiences of those who dare to step outside the bounds of everyday life. Sometimes a woman just needs to risk the unknown. For some, it widens their horizons; for others it is an agony never to be repeated. For all twelve, it is a tale of intense erotic power.

Skin Slave by Yolanda Celbridge

June 2000   Price £5.99   ISBN 0 352 33507 6

Nudist genetics student Belle Puget remains an uncaned submissive, until Geisha, slave of dominatrix Dr Jolita Cunliffe, introduces her to Japanese bare-bottom chastisement. Belle joins the Paine Institute on remote Furvert's Island where, free of western taboos, Cunliffe's sadistic rival Darwinia Paine makes naked nurses addicted to her whip, trying to unlock the secret of eternal youth. Belle must ultimately choose whether to bare her buttocks in submission, or wield the lash herself ... forever.

The Dungeons of Lidir by Aran Ashe

June 2000   Price £5.99   ISBN 0 352 33506 8

The Prince has been called away from the Castle and from Anya, his beautiful betrothed. In his absence Ildren the Taskmistress plots to regain her hold over the copper-haired, dark-eyed slave. Anya disappears into the vaults below the Castle where she is at the mercy of the Taskmaster's harsh whims. A Nexus Classic.

Brought to Heel by Arabella Knight
July 2000   Price £5.99   ISBN 0 352 33508 4
Lustful desires provoke these girls to their perverted pleasures, but such wickedness is soon exposed by that most stern mistress, the cane, and then the guilty must come under her cruel kiss to suffer sharp sorrow and sweet pain. The pest, the predator, the pilferer – each with appetites for dark delights. Tempted, they feast upon forbidden fruit, but they cannot escape paying painful penalties. All must submit to discipline as they are sternly brought to heel.

Purity by Aishling Morgan
July 2000   Price £5.99   ISBN 0 352 33510 6
Henry Truscott, dissipated hero of *The Rake*, finds himself faced with the prospect of living on his brother's charity. His efforts to create a new fortune lead him along a path of debauchery and perversion, from stripping girls in Mother Agie's brothel to indulging three ladies at once in a Belgravia drawing room. Nor are his associates idle, with his wife being pursued by the sadistic d'Aignan while the flame-haired Judith Cates becomes embroiled in Sir Joseph Snapes' bizarre sexual experiments.

Serving Time by Sarah Veitch
July 2000   Price £5.99   ISBN 0 352 33509 2
The House of Compulsion is the unofficial name of an experimental reformatory. Fern Terris, a twenty-four year old temptress, finds herself facing ten years in prison – unless she agrees to submit to Compulsion's disciplinary regime. Fern agrees to the apparently easy option, but soon discovers that the chastisements at Compulsion involve a wide variety of belts, canes and tawses, her pert bottom – and unexpected sexual pleasure.

Animal Passions by Martine Marquand
June 2000 Price £5.99 ISBN 0 352 33499 1
Nineteen-year-old Jo runs away from the strict household where she's been brought up, and is initiated into a New Age pagan cult located in a rural farming community in England. Michael, the charismatic shaman leader, invites Jo to join him in a celebration of unbridled passion. As the summer heat intensifies, preparations are made for the midsummer festival, and Jo is keen to play a central role in the cult's bizarre rites. Will she ever want to return to normal society?

In The Flesh by Emma Holly
June 2000 Price £5.99 ISBN 0 352 33498 3
Topless dancer Chloe is better at being bad than anyone David Imakita knows. To keep her, this Japanese-American businessman risks everything he owns: his career, his friends, his integrity. But will this unrepentant temptress overturn her wild ways and accept an opportunity to change her life, or will the secrets of her past resurface and destroy them both?

No Lady by Saskia Hope
June 2000 Price £5.99 ISBN 0 352 32857 6
30-year-old Kate walks out of her job, dumps her boyfriend and goes in search of adventure. And she finds it. Held captive in the Pyrenees by a bunch of outlaws involved in smuggling art treasures, she finds the lovemaking is as rough as the landscape. Only a sense of danger can satisfy her ravenous passions, but she also has some plans of her own. A Black Lace special reprint.

Primal Skin by Leona Benkt Rhys
July 2000 Price £5.99 ISBN 0 352 33500 9
Set in the mysterious northern and central Europe of the last Ice Age, *Primal Skin* is the story of a female Neanderthal shaman who is on a quest to find magical talismans for her primal rituals. Her nomadic journey, accompanied by her friends, is fraught with danger, adventure and sexual experimentation. The mood is eerie and full of symbolism, and the book is evocative of the best-selling novel *Clan of the Cave Bear*.

A Sporting Chance by Susie Raymond
July 2000   Price £5.99   ISBN 0 352 33501 7

Maggie is an avid supporter of her local ice hockey team, The Trojans, and when her manager mentions he has some spare tickets to their next away game, it doesn't take long to twist him around her little finger. Once at the match she wastes no time in getting intimately associated with the Trojans – especially Troy, their powerfully built star player. But their manager is not impressed with Maggie's antics; he's worried she's distracting them from their game. At first she finds his threats amusing, but then she realises she's being stalked.

NEXUS BACKLIST

All books are priced £5.99 unless another price is given. If a date is supplied, the book in question will not be available until that month in 2000.

CONTEMPORARY EROTICA

THE ACADEMY	Arabella Knight		
BAD PENNY	Penny Birch		
THE BLACK MASQUE	Lisette Ashton		
THE BLACK WIDOW	Lisette Ashton		
THE BOND	Lindsay Gordon		
BRAT	Penny Birch		
DANCE OF SUBMISSION	Lisette Ashton		
DARK DESIRES	Maria del Rey		
DISCIPLES OF SHAME	Stephanie Calvin		
DISCIPLINE OF THE PRIVATE HOUSE	Esme Ombreux		
DISPLAYS OF EXPERIENCE	Lucy Golden		June
EMMA'S SECRET DOMINATION	Hilary James		
FAIRGROUND ATTRACTIONS	Lisette Ashton		
GISELLE	Jean Aveline		
HEART OF DESIRE	Maria del Rey		
HOUSE RULES	G.C. Scott		
IN FOR A PENNY	Penny Birch		
ONE WEEK IN THE PRIVATE HOUSE	Esme Ombreux		
THE BOND	Nadine Somers		
THE PALACE OF EROS	Delver Maddingley	£4.99	
PLAYTHING	Penny Birch		
THE PLEASURE CHAMBER	Brigitte Markham		
POLICE LADIES	Yolanda Celbridge		
THE RELUCTANT VIRGIN	Kendal Grahame		

NEXUS CLASSICS

A new imprint dedicated to putting the finest works of erotic fiction back in print

Please send me the books I have ticked above.

Name   ....

Address   ....

            ....

            ....

            .... Post code........................

Send to: **Cash Sales, Nexus Books, Thames Wharf Studios, Rainville Road, London W6 9HT**

US customers: for prices and details of how to order books for delivery by mail, call 1-800-805-1083.

Please enclose a cheque or postal order, made payable to **Nexus Books**, to the value of the books you have ordered plus postage and packing costs as follows:

   UK and BFPO – £1.00 for the first book, 50p for the second book and 30p for each subsequent book to a maximum of £3.00;

   Overseas (including Republic of Ireland) – £2.00 for the first book, £1.00 for the second book and 50p for each subsequent book.

We accept all major credit cards, including VISA, ACCESS/ MASTERCARD, AMEX, DINERS CLUB, SWITCH, SOLO, and DELTA. Please write your card number and expiry date here:

....

Please allow up to 28 days for delivery.

Signature ....